Interview English
Ends For Win-Win!

求職

英語
● 錄取
● 加薪

一試双贏

面試時是否聽到「Please Speak in English」就倒抽一口氣？
寫自傳你還在用 There are 5 people in my family 開頭嗎？

吳悠嘉／黃梅芳／倍斯特編輯部 ◎著

從常遇到的考題下手

本書教你準備面試會被問到的
重點試題，學習如何適切的應答。

我有疑問篇

本書引導你正確的詢問方法，表達出
你對應徵職務的關切與重視。

突破臨場反應題

本書提供周全的答題技巧，增進你
臨場應變的能力，使你有好的表現。

自傳寫作範例與寫作文法解析

示範精彩自傳範例讓你寫出令人
印象深刻的自傳。

特約編輯序

　　寫這本書時，我將自己融入到各個職業的角色。蒐集大量的資料，研究各行各業，瞭解各職位需要的知識技能，工作說明，生涯發展，與該行業比較受到關注的議題。透過這本書，讓我有機會看到每個職位的輪廓，體會各個職位角色。

　　市面上對於有關求職面試的著作，種類繁多，但大多僅是提供綜合概念，似乎少有專門探討個別職位面試的，希望對您在準備求職面試時有所幫助。

　　這本書，不僅僅是應徵者在準備求職面試的參考書，同時也是一本瀏覽各行業的入門的指南。

黃梅芳
Anlita Huang

特約編輯序

　　對於語言學習我相信來自於真實世界的教學材料相當重要。通常我會選擇與學生有切身興趣或工作需求的題材為學生上課，這樣學生不僅會更有興趣參與學習，更能把課堂學之內容直接活用在工作或課業上。

　　職場英文是現在有在上班工作的學生最有興趣也是最需充實的一部分，而求職過程中的英文自傳與面試更是讓許多學生在準備時緊張不已。

　　我幫很多學生修改過自傳，也常在課堂上幫學生練習英文面試的回答與技巧。看到許多學生在寫自傳時只想照本宣科，模仿範例，反而寫出來的文章非常死板，而且還是錯誤百出。在編寫這一本書，我使用的都是在我教學過程中所看到學生常犯的錯誤，根據不同程度放入不同行業的章節中。希望讀者在學習這些自傳時，不是只將範例拿來改編，而是可以參考別的學生常犯的錯誤而作為借鏡，以思考自己是否也有相同的寫作問題。而面試的問題更是收集針對不同行業的特定內容去做編寫，希望讀者不是只有練習到一般的面試問題，而是有針對此行業深入的應答，來幫助讀者在面試時更能有突出的表現，增加業者的印象，並成功得到應徵機會！

吳悠嘉

編者序

　　《求職英語一試双贏》是一本協助各行各業的求職者，面對應徵面試可以有一個好的求職英語學習專書。隨著國際化的趨勢，職場需要以英語來面對應徵求職的趨勢是越來越多，也越來越普遍了。如何跟上英語普及的腳步，讓你可以不要輸在英語這個應試項目上，這是本書用心編寫的初衷，也是因應許許多多求職者的需要，期盼在應徵的口試與自傳的寫作技巧上，都可以有好的自我加強與訓練，讓英語應試不再讓你頭疼。只要抓對技巧和應答的方式和內容，就可以真正在應試中加分。本書也提供了一些激勵小故事，讓讀者可以學習，以期在該領域有好的表現，希望你可以得到就業和求職上的鼓勵，這也是有心想要在職場上發揮的讀者，可以參考分享的。充分的英語題目與解答，讓你在求職領域有信心的發揮，不再怕，反倒可以勝卷在握地找到自己合意的職位和工作，請好好的使用這本應徵指南喔！

倍斯特編輯部

目　錄

CONTENTS

國外業務

1-1 常遇到的考題

Q 1

What drew you to apply for this sales position at our company?
是什麼最吸引你來應徵我們公司的這個銷售職位？

First of all, I have worked in this sector for over 5 years. I would like to have the opportunity to utilize my contacts and experience to sell the top-notch products your company has manufactured. Secondly, I would welcome the opportunity to travel internationally, and apply my English language skills in my work. In addition, I am an amateur cyclist after work. I am a loyal customer myself of your company as well. The bicycles your company produce have been the top quality products in the market for years. I believe selling something that I personally enjoy using so much makes me even more successful as a salesperson.

　　首先，我已經在這個行業工作超過五年了。我希望有這個機會去整合我的人脈與經驗來為你們公司銷售你們所生產的優良產品。其次。我很期待有這個機會到不同國家，並將我的英文技巧運用在工作裡。除此之外，我工作之餘是一位業餘的自行車手。我自己也是貴公司的忠實顧客。貴公司所生產的腳踏車一直以來都是市場上品質最好的產品。我相信銷售我個人如此喜歡的產品會讓我成為更有績效的業務人員。

Q

2 What do you think is the most important skill for a salesperson?
你認為對一個銷售員的最重要的技能是什麼？

Personally I think the quality of the product should come first. When a sales representative can provide a high quality product constantly, she is providing the customer with the most important feature of the customer service, which is an excellent product experience. In my sales experience, I always make sure that the products that I represent are high quality and have good value, so I have the confidence that I am providing my customers with the best possible products. However, I believe that offering tremendous customer services should also put in top priority. In the meantime, I also make sure I present the superior and satisfactory customer service to all my past, present, and future customers. I think no product can sell itself without having a friendly, knowledgeable, and caring service.

　　我個人認為產品品質應該是排在第一位的。當一個業務人員能夠一直提供高品質的產品，她/他提供了客戶服務中的最重要的特質，也就是一個很好的產品經驗。在我的銷售經驗中，我總是確保我所代表的產品都是高品質，並且有很好的價值，所以我有信心來提供我的客戶最好的產品。不過我相信提供卓越的客戶服務應該也要排在優先。同時，我也確保我提供了優越的和滿意的客戶服務給我所有的過去，現在和未來的客戶。我想沒有一樣產品可以自己就賣得出去如果沒有友好、知識化、貼心的服務。

Q 3 What makes you a good sales person?
你有什麼樣好的業務人員的特質？

I am a very detail-oriented person, and that helps me in sales in many ways. I always make sure that my customers are completely informed with the details so that I can provide the best possible service. I feel like I've had a great achievement when I have made a sale by using all my talents and efforts. I always put the needs and wants of the customers first. I never put too much pressure on my customers, while I let them make their decisions carefully, and ask as many questions as they wished. As trying to be as professional as possible, I make sure that I know everything about the product I'm selling, so that I can answer any questions customers may have to their satisfaction. I also like to get to know my customers personally, so I can better serve them. Actually many of my customers oftentimes have become friends of mine.

我是很注重細節的人，那在很多方面幫助我的銷售工作。我總是確保我的客戶徹底被告知細節，所以我可以提供最好的服務。當我為了一個銷售使用我所有的才能與努力，我會覺得我有了一個很棒的成就。我總是把客戶的需求與欲望放在首位。我從來不會施加太多的壓力給我的客戶，而是讓他們仔細地做出他們的決定，並儘可能地問很多他們想問的問題。由於試圖將儘可能的專業，我確保我知道一切關於我賣的產品，讓我可以回答任何客戶可能需要感到滿意的問題。我也喜歡去親自了解我的客戶，這樣我就可以更好地為他們服務。其實我的許多客戶常常成為我的朋友。

Q 4 Tell us about your most successful sale cases.
告訴我們你的一些最成功的銷售案例。

In my sales career, I have developed a systematical pattern that I have followed and made most of my successful sales. Once a customer has expressed an interest in the product, I take the initiative to make the contact with the person and answer any question he/she may have. Next, I inform them with the details of the product features and benefits they may not be familiar with. My most successful sale case was one actually a customer who was referred by the other client I had. She was a friend of my client and I was told she was thinking of buying a car but she had some awful experience with other salespeople before. I immediately contacted the person, and just let her know about me. I gave her much time to compare, study different models and patiently told her all the features of the cars. Not only was I ultimately able to close the sale, she actually brought in about ten referrals because of her satisfactory buying experience.

在我的銷售生涯中，我已經發展了一個我遵循的系統化銷售模式，並成功地完成我大部分的銷售。一旦一客戶表示對產品的興趣，我主動去聯絡，並回答任何他/她可能有的問題。接下來，我會告知他們他們可能不熟悉產品特點和優勢的細節。我最成功的銷售案例是有一個客戶她是我另外一個顧客介紹給我的。她是我的客戶的朋友，而且我被告知她在考慮買車，但她與之前其他銷售人員有一些不愉快的經驗。我立即聯繫了與她連絡，只是先讓她知道我這個人。我給了她很多的時間來比較與研究了不同車型並耐心地告訴她的汽車的所有功能。我最終不僅能夠完成銷售，因為她滿意的購車體驗，她居然帶來了大約十個轉介的客戶。

5

What do you think your former colleagues would describe you?
你覺得你的同事會如何描述你？

I think most of my colleagues would first think I have remarkable interpersonal skills. I really enjoy being a salesperson that I can meet with and learn about lots of interesting people from all walks of life. At work, I have made extra effort to build up good work relations with all my colleagues and supervisors. I believe a harmonic work atmosphere can motivate any employees to work harder and better. I also think my colleagues would describe me as me as a very organized person. I have kept detailed records of all the customers that I've served. If I weren't so organized, I wouldn't be able to service a wild variety of clients that I have.

我想我的大部分同事首先會想到我有非凡的人際交往能力。我真的很享受作為一個銷售人員，我可以遇到和了解很多來自各行各業有趣的人。在工作中，我會做額外的努力來與我所有的同事和上司建立良好的工作關係。我相信和諧的工作氛圍可以激發任何員工更加努力地工作到更好。我也認為我的同事會形容我是很有條理的人。我一直都為我所服務的客戶做很詳細的記錄。如果我不是那麼有條理，我就沒法那麼多種類的客戶提供服務。

Q 6 What do you think your former supervisor would describe you?
你的前雇主會如何描述你？

At the company where I worked before, it was an interesting environment, and I found it enjoyable but challenging. I think my former supervisor would describe me as a self-motivated person, as well as a cooperative team member at work.

Although we were responsible for our own sales, and worked independently most of the time, it was important to be able to keep up with all the team members. I was able to mostly deliver adequate and well work performance by thriving on challenges and working well under pressure. Meanwhile, I was considered being an enthusiastic and committed team member for bringing much positive energy and good work atmosphere.

在我之前工作的公司，那是一個有趣的環境，並且我覺得那很愉快但有挑戰性。我覺得我的前上司會將我描述成一個會主動自我激勵，還會在工作上與我的團隊合作良好。雖然我們負責自己的銷售工作，大部分的時間是獨立作業，不過能跟上所有的團隊成員是非常重要的。我樂於挑戰且在壓力下工作良好，並能提供足夠和良好的工作表現。同時，我被認為是一個熱情和堅定的團隊成員能帶來正面能量和良好的工作氛圍。

7 Being a salesperson, what rewards you the most?
你覺得當業務人員讓你最有成就的是什麼？

The most rewarding part of being sales person for me is the time I make contacts, and talk with my clients so I can help them make the right decision choosing a suitable product. I like to be able to provide my customers with the best service as possible as I can. I am conscientious that I make sure that a customer knows about the product they are purchasing, and how to use it to its fullest potential. Once I had a customer who was assigned to restructure the magazine department at the library where she worked, and needed to fill in a large number of magazines in this section. We had a great time making selections together, and she was really pleased with the variety I was able to help her select.

對我來說做為一個銷售人員最有成就的部分是與我的客戶進行接觸交談，所以我可以幫助他們做出正確的決定選擇一個適合的產品。我希望能夠盡可能提供我的客戶提供最好的服務。我認真地確保客戶知道他們所購買的產品，以及如何使用它來充分發揮其潛力。有一次，我有一個客戶在她所工作的圖書館被分配到要重組雜誌部門，並需要在此部門補入大量的雜誌。我們一起進行選擇時進行的很愉快，而且她是真的很高興我能幫助她選擇這麼多種類的雜誌。

Q 8 What are your long term career goals?
你的長期目標是甚麼？

I am interested in all aspects of the sales sector, and see myself in the long term spending some time working in a variety of roles. I have worked in this profession for over 6 years and I believe I have accumulated adequate contacts, connections, and experiences. I expect to remain in sales throughout my career, moving from direct sales, and eventually into a management role. Long term, I see myself as a sales manager at a large corporation. I really enjoy being in sales, and I believe that I have the ability to manage a large successful sales team. I have prominently shown leadership skills whenever my team is in need of a strong leading role. I believe I have the potential and whatever it takes to be a successful supervisor in the sales department.

我對業務工作的各個面向都很感興趣，我將會自己長期花一些時間認識這一行業的各種角色。我已經在這個行業工作超過 6 年，我相信我已經累積了足夠的客戶、人脈和經驗。我預計將我整個職業生涯都待在銷售這一行，從直接銷售最終進入管理角色。長期來看，我期待自己成為一個大型公司的業務經理。我真的很喜歡在銷售這一行工作，而我相信我有這個能力管理一個大型成功的銷售團隊。每當我的團隊需要一個強而有力的主導人物，我不斷地突出表現我的領導能力。我相信我有這個潛力與所有需要具備的能力來成為一個在銷售部門成功的上司。

1-2 臨場反應篇

Q 1

Have you always met your personal and professional sales goals?
你一直都能滿足你的個人和專業的銷售目標嗎？

I have always met or even surpassed my professional sales goals, and most often my personal ones too, especially in the last few years. In my sales experience, I have learned to set my personal goals at an achievable level, which could be very high, but not unreachable. I worked at a company where the manager set the sales goals very high, and that was his method of keeping the sales representatives motivated. Unfortunately, the result was that the entire sales staff struggled much to reach the goals and none of us in our department were able to achieve them. It just discouraged and depressed the whole team. Personally, I have always at least met my personal goals, and I work very hard to exceed them.

　　我一直都能達到或超過了我的專業的銷售目標，還有我的個人目標，尤其是在最近這幾年。在我業務經驗中，我已經學會了把我的個人目標設定在可以實現的水平，可以很高，但不是遙不可及。我曾在一家公司那裡經理將銷售目標設定的非常高，這是他保持業務人員積極的方法。不幸的是整個銷售人員感到很掙扎來達到這些業績，結果我們部門沒有人能夠實現這些目標。它只是讓整個團隊很沮喪和鬱悶。就個人而言，我一直都至少達到我個人的目標，我非常努力地工作來超越這些目標。

Q

2

Do you prefer a long sales cycle resulting in the sale of a large term, or a shorter cycle with more frequent sales?
你比較喜歡一個較長的銷售週期販賣大型商品，或者較短的週期頻繁的銷售？

I think both types of sales that have points intrigue me. My preferences to a longer sales cycle lie in that it gives me time to personally get to know the customer, and educate them about the benefits and features of the product. I can adjust the pace accordingly depending on the individual client. Some customers like to have sufficient information about their purchases, and have a lot of in-depth questions. Others are more interested in having more personal benefits like special delivery service or discounts. On the other hand, shorter cycles are more intense, since a salesperson typically doesn't have the luxury of much knowledge of the customer, or the time for extensive explanations. I like the challenge that I need to get right to the point about the product's features and benefits, and I'm confident that I have the ability to showcase the reasons why it's the best choice for the customer.

我覺得這兩種類型的銷售都有它有趣的點。我個人喜歡較長的銷售週期的點在於因為它給了我時間去了解客戶，並教育他們有關產品的好處和特徵。我可以調整過程的速度根據所各個所處理的客戶。有些客戶喜歡購買知道很多的資訊，並且有很多的深入的問題。其他比較感興趣的是有個人化的好處，譬如特別的運送服務或折扣。另一方期來說，短期的銷售較為密集，一個業務人員通常不會有太多寶貴的時間來了解客戶，或者是撥冗來解釋產品。我喜歡這個挑戰我必須馬上迅速打入重點介紹產品特徵與優勢，並且我有信心我有這個能力展示為何它是客戶的最佳選擇。

Q
3
How would you deal with a colleague you seem to be unable to maintain a good working relationship?
你會如何處理一位你似乎無法與他能夠建立好的工作關係的同事？

That would certainly be a unique situation to me. I've had no problem maintaining a good working relationship with any of my colleagues. Of course there are all types of people. There are times some people are less motivated in a work team or simply unhappy in their jobs, but people always need positive connections. That is what I find a connection with a colleague by finding something in common or simply giving some warm greetings. For example, in my second year at work, I was assigned to a team that had one member that the rest of the team disliked. I knew everyone needed to fully commit to make the project work. Even though I was not the team leader, I tried to make a connection with him and discovered we both had a passion for comic books. We did not become the best friends or anything, but through our common interest, I was able to build enough connections and engage him in the project. I believe there is always something that can bond us together.

對我來說這將會是一個很特別的情形。我一直在與同事建立良好工作關係上沒有任何問題。當然什麼樣的人都有。有些人有時會在一個工作團隊裡會比較缺乏動力或只是單純對他們的工作不開心，但是人們永遠需要正面的關係。我會藉著跟一位同事找出共同興趣或單純地很熱情地打招呼來找出建立關係的方法。之前有一個例子，是我在工作第二年的時候，我被指派到一個團隊裡有一位成員其他人都不喜歡。我知道每個人都需要全力以赴才能讓這計畫成功。雖然我不是隊長，我試著與他建立關係並且發現我們都喜歡漫畫。我們並沒有變成好朋友或怎樣，但透過我們的共同興趣，我可以跟他建立足夠的關係並讓他投入這個專案。我相信總是會有一些事可以讓人們結合在一起。

Q 4   What are your strengths and weaknesses?
你工作的優點與缺點是什麼？

I would say that my greatest strength is that I'm a goal oriented type of salesperson. I like to thoroughly plan out the sales cycle, and stick it to the end. In sales, I have found that I am most successful when I pay attention to every piece of the sales cycle, from the first contact, to the completion of the sale. I also have the ability to come up different sales approaches very fast. I am an innovative thinker and assertive communicator in my sales, and am able to work with many different kinds of customers at once. My greatest weakness is sometimes my tendency to take too much risk. I know being a salesperson must be aggressive in a good way, but my competitive nature could take me a bit too far at work.

我會說我最大的優勢就是我是那一種目標取向的業務員。我喜歡完整地規劃出銷售的計畫，並堅持到底。在銷售方面，我發現我做得最成功的是當我注意每一個銷售的細節，從第一次接觸到銷售的完成。我同時也有非常快拿出不同的銷售方法的能力。在我的銷售方法中，我是一個創新性的思想者和有信心的溝通者，而且我能夠在一次與許多不同種類客戶工作。我最大的弱點是有時我傾向於冒太大的風險。我知道作為一個銷售人員必須是用一個好的辦法去積極，但我的競爭本能可能會讓我做得太過度。

1-3 我有疑問篇

Q 1

What qualities does your company consider a successful salesperson possess?
請問貴公司認為擁有什麼樣的品質才是一個成功的銷售人員？

While there are several factors that contribute to success in the sales profession, there are a few things our company expects *a sales rep to have in order to maximize her/his potential and the results she/he achieve. First, you must have a system, that is, a process for identifying, qualifying, and developing selling opportunities. In order to obtain the greatest return on your investment of time and effort, you must be able to systematically qualify opportunities quickly using appropriate measurable criteria. Also, you must have a 100% commitment to doing the very best job you can, and to providing the best possible service to your customers, your colleagues, and others who depend on you. Your personal value is not measured by the size of your paycheck, but rather by the quality of service you provide to others. I personally consider the most important quality is to have belief in yourself, in our company, and in your product or service.

*a sales rep=a sales representative

雖然有許多因素可以有助於在銷售行業中的成功，我們公司有幾個特質是期待銷售代表擁有來以最大限度發揮她/他的潛力及實現她/他所期待的結果。首先，你必須有一個系統，也就是識別、鑑識、並發展銷售機會的過程。為了讓你的時間和精力投入獲得最大的回報，你必須能夠有系統地使用適當的衡量標準，讓你迅速地辨識到銷售機會。此外，你必須百分之百地投入，盡力將工作做到最好，並提供最好的服務給你的客戶，你的同事，及其他工作上依靠你的人。你的個人價值不是由你的薪水的多少，而是由你提供給別人的服務質量來衡量。我個人認為最重要的素質就是要信念相信自己，相信公司，相信你的產品或服務。

Q **2** **How is the commission structured in this position?**
這個職位的佣金是如何計算？

The commission structured in this position is base salary plus commissions. A salesperson receives a regular salary plus performance-based commissions under this structure. Sometimes, the company will increase the base salary and decrease commissions over time, or decrease base salary and increase commissions until the salesperson is on straight commission. However, it only works for the salespeople who are primarily money motivated, and will continually try to earn more money. At our company, you can choose to work up to an income level at which you are comfortable, and then level off at that level. We understand that earning more money is not the only factor to prompt the sales reps to work any harder or longer. The company's ultimate goal is to have a group of experienced, successful and content salespeople.

這個職位的佣金計算是底薪加佣金。在此計算方法下，銷售人員會收到固定薪資加以績效為計算的佣金。有時候公司會隨著時間增加基本薪資和減少佣金，或降低基本薪資和增加佣金，直到銷售人員是直接完全領取佣金。但是，它僅適用於主要動機是想多賺錢的銷售人員，並會不斷嘗試賺取更多。在我們公司，你可以選擇工作達一個舒適的收入水平上，然後在該水平趨於平穩。我們了解賺更多的錢並不是去激發銷售代表工作更努力或時間更長的唯一因素。公司的最終目標是擁有一批經驗豐富的，成功的和滿足的銷售人員。

Q

3

How do you motivate your sales staff?
你都如何激勵你的員工？

I'm a big believer in not just giving money as the incentive. I want to give my team memories to treasure through unique experiences. Each of the last five years, we've had motivating contests with a different theme each year. The program is announced at the annual company barbeque party. Once she/he reaches her/his goal, each sales rep can walk into my office and take the prizes she/he deserves. One year the prizes were Armani suitcases engraved with their names and $40,000 worth of coupons of the SOGƱ department store. As the whole sales department gets engaged in the competition, people from other parts of the company become part of the enthusiasm, too. Quite honestly, these are prizes that any one of our employees would love to have.

我非常相信不是只有給錢可以激勵人心。我想給我的團隊珍貴的回憶去珍惜這獨特的經驗。每一個在過去五年中，我們每年都有不同的主題的激勵比賽。該內容會在每年公司的燒烤派對公佈。一旦她/他達到她/他的目標，每個銷售代表可以走進我的辦公室，領取她/他應得的獎項。有一年的獎品是個人化訂製阿瑪尼手提箱雕刻他們的名字和價值 4 萬元的 XY 百貨的優惠券。當整個銷售部門競爭激烈時，整個公司其他部門的人也感受到一部分的熱情了。坦白地說，這些都是任何我們的僱員會喜歡的獎品。

4 What is next in the hiring process?
應徵過程的下一步是什麼?

After the interview process, the HR department will have some pre-employment assessments on the candidates. Since we started the process by establishing a clear job description for our sales reps, we can establish a specific job benchmark for this sales role. From the assessment, we can understand all candidates' performance styles and ambitions and we can see how closely these candidates map to our established job benchmark. By now we have done a very thorough job of evaluating our candidates. If they make it to the assessment, we have a high degree of confidence that they can do the job and do it well. In this step, we can confirm our findings, look for cultural fit and dig into any gaps or open concerns. Based on the results of your interview and assessments, a job offer of employment may be sent in mail. At this point we will discuss the specific details of the offer.

在面試之後,人事部門將會對應徵者做一個應聘前的評估。自從我們開始這個過程透過為我們的業務代表建立明確的職務說明,我們可以為業務角色建立一個特定的工作基準。從評估中,我們可以了解所有候選人的表現風格和野心,並且我們可以看到這些候選人可以如何密切地對應到我們既定的工作基準。在這時我們已經對候選人做了非常徹底的評估工作。如果他們通過評估,我們有信心,他們可以這個工作做的很好。在這一階段中,我們會確認我們的招聘,尋找與公司文化與氣氛相和之處和發現任何意見差異或疑慮。根據你的面試與評估結果,聘用通知可能會用郵件送出。到那時我們將會討論這份工作的細節。

自傳篇

1 範例

1-1. 自傳(1)

Since I was a child, my parents have taught my elder brother and me to be a virtuous person. Growing up in this type of family, I care much about being humble, honest, and responsible. My parents also have great influence on my interest in reading and traveling.

Although I majored in Engineering at Tamkang University, I also took some courses related to the Department of International Business. The courses made me determine to work in the profession of international sales. After I finished my undergraduate study, I applied for the graduate school in the Department of International Business and earned an MBA degree. I learned a lot from taking courses, conducting projects and writing my thesis during my two-year study. Besides, I made persistent efforts on improving my English. My highest TOEIC score is 910 taken in November 2011.

In order to have a better understanding of the industry, I applied for the summer internship in Intel Taiwan in 2011. At first, I leaned how each department operated in the company. During my work in that summer, I had a weekly meeting with my mentor to discuss my job performance and share work experiences with each other. At the end of internship, I wrote a report analyzing the current international business trends and made a presentation in my department. At Intel Taiwan, I have learned that being passionate, responsible and trying to do better at work are important to keep myself and the company progressing.

I am sincere, open-minded, and willing to learn. I consider myself as the qualified candidate for the position in your company. I would appreciate the opportunity to have an interview and look forward to hearing from you soon.

自我小時候開始，我父母就教我哥哥跟我要當有美德的人。在這樣的家庭長大，我非常在乎要能謙虛、誠實與負責。我的父母也對我對閱讀與旅遊的興趣有很大的影響。

雖然我在淡江大學主修工程學，我也在國際企業學系裡修了一些課程。這些課程讓我決心要在國際業務的領域裡工作。當我完成大學四年的學業時，我申請了國際企業研究所並取得了工商管理碩士。我在我兩年的學習裡從修課、做專題、以及寫論文中學到很多。除此之外，我持續努力在加強我的英文。我最高的多益成績是在 2011 年 11 月拿到 910 分。

為了要更清楚了解這個產業，我在 2011 年申請了台灣 Intel 公司的暑期實習工作。一開始，我去學習公司每個部門是如何運作。當我工作的那個暑假裡，我每星期與帶我工作的指導者討論我的工作表現與彼此分享工作經驗。在實習結束時，我寫了一篇分析當今國際商業潮流走向的報告並在我的部門做了一個口頭報告。在台灣 Intel，我學習到在工作中保持熱情、負責、與嘗試做得更好對我與公司的成長是很有幫助的。

我是一個誠懇、心態開放、並且願意學習的人。我認為對貴公司這份工作我是符合資格的應徵者。我將會相當感激能有面試的機會並希望很快能接到消息。

1-2. 自傳(2)

Graduated from Fu-Jen Catholic University with the degree of major of International Trade and Finance (ITF) and minor of Computer Science and Information Engineering (CSIE), there was a motivation to be a person who could play and study well during my study. （請閱 2-2）In my major of ITF, , I took some important courses like Microeconomics, Macroeconomics and Global Marketing to anticipate myself to get more profound knowledge. In the meantime, I also studied the programming language Java, and received high grades on subjects such as Calculus, Discrete Math, Data Structure, and Differential Equations. As for my extracurricular activities, I participated in the tennis club and photography club at school. I was assigned to be the club leader in my junior year and continued to be the consultant for the rest of the time at school. My interpersonal and leadership skills were well developed while I held several exhibitions and seminars as the leader.

I went to Melbourne University during my summer vacation in 2011 to take the lectures that I was interested in. After that, my English improved tremendously by changing the way I learned English before. Next April in 2012, I registered the TOEIC and the result was 850 scores. （請閱 2-2）

I finished the military service on July 30th this year. I believe my prominent trait makes me the suitable candidate is my persistence in my personality. Unlike most young adults in Taiwan, I always keep on my goals to the end and rarely give up anything I work hard on. Please take my application into consideration. Thank you.

從輔仁大學畢業，主修國際貿易與金融（ITF）副修資訊工程（CSIE），在學習期間我總是激勵自己要成為一個會念書又會玩的人。在我主修的課程中，我的一些重要的課程，比如微觀經濟學，宏觀經濟和全球營銷讓我自己在這領域中得到更深刻的認識。在此期間，我還研究了程式語言 Java，並在一些科目如微積分、離散數學、數據結構，以及微分方程獲得高分。至於我的課外活動，我參加了學校的網球社和攝影社。我在大三那年被指派成為社團的社長，之後的時間繼續成為社團顧問。在我多次舉行展覽和研討會的時，我的人際關係和領導能力都得到充分的訓練。

我在 2011 年暑假期間去墨爾本大學修了一些我很感興趣的課。在此之後，通過改變我以前學英語的方式，我的英語水平大幅提高。在隔年 2012 年四月，我參加了多益考試結果取得 850 分。

我在今年 7 月 30 日完成兵役。我相信使我成為合適人選的突出特質是我個性中的堅持性。與大多數在台灣年輕人不同的是，我始終對我的目標堅持到底，很少放棄我在努力工作的事情。請把我的工作申請列入考慮。謝謝。

2 自傳寫作教室

2-1. 自傳(1) 寫作文法解析／小評語

　　在自傳中許多人都會在第一段描述到自己的家庭背景。台灣學生最常開頭的第一句就是「There are five people in my family.」或者是「My family has five people.」這兩個句子文法上都沒有錯誤，但是在英語中當在描述哪裡有多少人或物時，比較普遍的句型還是「There is」或「There are」。另外一個常用的句子就是像以上自傳中第一個句子，要描述一段從小到大的經驗，除了像第一句開頭「Since I was a child,」也可以用「Since I was little,」或「Since childhood,」。在這一段可以多針對自己的家庭如何去培養出一些對工作有幫助的個性影響。

　　許多時候自傳的第二、三段多是敘述在學校所學的知識、學生生活、或以往工作經驗。在這幾段的重點就如自傳裡每一段都要保持的重點，不論是所學知識或是之前的工作經驗，它們是如何對現在或未來的工作有所影響或幫助。很多時候學生自傳最常發生的一個錯誤就是想講的東西太多，沒有一個有系統的整理，而且提起許多部分與所應徵的工作並沒有任何相關之處。這幾段學生常會習慣使用完成時態，不過在描述學校經驗與之前的工作時，保持使用過去時態即可。除非是要強調到目前為止到還是事實的句子，譬如第二段與第三段的最後一句。

　　最後一段通常只要在簡短地推銷自己以及希望公司能夠考慮給予面試或工作機會即可。

2-2. 自傳(2) 寫作文法解析／小評語

在英文寫作中，如有一些專有名詞的縮寫，第一次提到的時候還是要先寫出全部名稱，再將所寫放入之後的括號中，之後提到時使用縮寫即可。如第一句中的兩個主修名稱 ITE 跟 CSIE，很多學生就會直接用縮寫，要記得不是所有閱讀此文章的讀者都有相關的知識，所以一定要在第一次用全部名稱解釋。「Graduated from Fu-Jen Catholic University with the degree of major of International Trade and Finance (ITF) and minor of Computer Science and Information Engineering (CSIE), there was a motivation to be a person who could play and study well during my study.」這一句犯了一個台灣學生很典型的文法錯誤，這兩個子句中很明顯的是兩個不同的主詞，「Graduated from Fu-Jen Catholic University…」是指從這個學校畢業的人，「 ,there was a motivation…」則是只有一個動機。第一個子句中做了一個主詞的省略，原本句子應該是「When I was graduated from Fu-Jen Catholic University…」。

在英文文法中，要做這樣主詞的省略，條件是句子中的兩個主詞必須是相同。所以這個句子應該改成「Graduated from Fu-Jen Catholic University with the degree of major of International Trade and Finance (ITF) and minor of Computer Science and Information Engineering (CSIE), I always motivated myself to be a person who could play and study well during my study.」

第二段最後一句，「Next April in 2011, I registered the TOEIC and the result was 850 scores.」這是將中文直接翻譯造成台式英語的講法。報名參加考試英文動詞應該用 take，分數也不是直接講幾分，這句正確的寫法應該是「Next April in 2011, I took the TOEIC test and had well performance by scoring 850.」

激勵小故事

Office WORK

Secret of a Legendary Salesperson

Born in poverty, Joe Girard sold 13,001 cars over 15 years to individual car buyers, not fleet sales. He holds the Guinness World Record for being the world's greatest salesman. In 1973, he sold 1,425 cars, and in one month, he sold 174 cars which is a record that still stands today. Harvard Business Review (HBR) senior editor M. Ellen Peebles spoke with Girard about overcoming personal hardship and how he, one at a time, created thousands of relationships in his deals. Now he speaks to people around the world about how to sell after being out of the car business. Here's the story he tells about how he always put his customers first.

I grew up in the ghettos of Detroit. I started selling cars in 1963 at the age of 35. I had no job, no savings, and was in serious debt after failing my home construction business. My wife told me there was no food left in the house to feed our children. I begged a local car dealer to give me a desk and a phone. I promised that I would not take business away from any of the other salespeople. I wore my finger on the black dialing rotary phone trying to get leads. One night, when all the other salesmen had gone home, I saw a customer walk in the door.

When I saw he carry a bag of groceries walking toward me. I immediately got down on my hands and knees. I told him how much my family needed food and how much we would appreciate if I could bring home some bacon, and I made my first sale. The customer said that with everything he had bought over the years, insurance, houses, cars, he had never seen anyone beg like that. Then I borrowed $10 from my boss in my commission and bought food for my family. From then on, I appreciate every person who bought from me so much. I would tell them, "I thank you, and my family thanks you. I love you."

傳奇業務的祕密

出生在貧困家庭，喬·吉拉德超過 15 年，沒有銷售給車隊，但銷售給個人購車過程中出售 13,001 輛。他是金氏世界紀錄上世界最偉大的推銷員。1973 年，他出售 1,425 輛，並在一個月內，他賣掉 174，直到今天仍然創下紀錄。哈佛商業評論雜誌資深編輯 M. 艾倫皮布爾斯與吉拉德談到克服個人困難，以及他如何一次一個創造了數以千計的客戶關係。現在已退出的汽車業務業，他現在在告訴世界各地的人們怎麼銷售商品。下面是他講述了他如何總是把他的第一個客戶的故事。

我在底特律的貧民區長大。我開始在 1963 年 35 歲時銷售汽車。我那時失業，沒有積蓄，並且在從事建設業失敗後有著嚴重的債務。我的妻子告訴我，家裡沒有食物養活我們的孩子。我懇求當地的汽車經銷商給我一個書桌和電話。我承諾不會搶走任何其他銷售人員的業務。我的手指一直撥著黑色撥號旋轉手機試圖獲得機會。在一天晚上，當所有其他的業務員都回家了，我看到了一個客戶走進門口。

我看到的是一個客戶拿著一帶雜貨袋走向我。我馬上用我的手和膝蓋跪著乞求。我告訴他我的家庭是多麼需要食物還有我們會多不勝感激，如果我可以帶一些錢回家，然後我成交了第一筆生意。客戶說多年來他買保險、房子、車子，他從來沒有見過任何人乞求成這樣。然後我向我的老闆從我的佣金借了 10 美元來買食物給我的家人。從那時候開始，我感激每一個從我這裡買了這麼多的客戶。我會告訴他們，「我感謝你，我的家人也感謝你，我愛你」

行政人員

1-1 常遇到的考題

Q 1

What software programs are you proficient in?
你精通什麼樣的軟體程式呢？

I'm proficient in Microsoft programs such as Word or Works, Powerpoint, and Excel spreadsheet. I took the Microsoft office certification program and received the certificate last year. I'm also able to manage a website. I'm very comfortable using Microsoft FrontPage and taking a class of the program Adobe Dreamweaver now. I'm an eager learner who is willing to invest massive amount of time making myself as computer literal as possible to reach the job requirement. I'm confident in my ability to learn any new programs quickly. I also had some experience maintaining the database of the former company by using Microsoft Access. I had done work like adding and updating records and running predesigned reports. In addition, I participated in the process of the design phase of the database to building it, designing forms and reports, and managing security.

　　我精通 Microsoft 的程式，如 Word 或 Works，PowerPoint 和 Excel 電子表格。我已經參加了微軟 Office 的認證課程，並在去年獲得證書。我還能夠管理一個網站。我能很流暢的使用 Microsoft FrontPage 而且現在在上 Adobe Dreamweaver 的課程。我是一個熱心的學習者願意投入大量的時間讓我自己的電腦能力盡可能地達到工作要求。我有信心我有能力快速學習任何新的程式。我也有過一些通過使用 Microsoft Access 維持公司的資造庫的經驗。我有做過一些比如添加和更新記錄和運行預先設計的報告。此外，我有參與了數據庫設計到建設的階段，設計表格和報表，並做安全管理。

Q 2 Why should we hire you?
我們為什麼要聘用你？

I sincerely believe that I'm the best candidate for this job position. I have all the professional knowledge required by this position and strong interpersonal skills. I'd describe myself a dynamic team member, with the ability to thrive on new challenges, and work well under pressure. Despite the fact that there are many applicants who have the ability to be considered qualified. What really stands me out is my attitude for excellence. I always put every part of myself into achieving the best possible performance. In addition, I am always the first person in the office and the last one to leave. I am not afraid to ask questions and learn from every mistake. I have the work ethic of a champion. I work as efficiently as possible. I triple-check everything I do to ensure complete accuracy. I strongly believe that I'd make great contribution to the department, as well as the company.

　　我真誠地相信我是這個工作職位的最佳人選。我有所有這個職位所需的專業知識以及很強的人際交往能力。我會形容自己是一個充滿活力的團隊成員，擁有旺盛接受新挑戰的能力，並在壓力下工作良好。儘管有很多的申請人都被認為擁有合格的能力。真正讓我突出的特質是我的追求卓越的態度。我總是利用自己的每一個部分來取得最佳的表現。另外，我永遠是在辦公室裡第一個到，最後一個離開的人。我不害怕問問題，並從每一個錯誤中學習。我有一個像冠軍般的職業道德。我讓自己的工作效率發揮到極致。我再三檢查我所做的一切，以確保完全準確。我堅信我會為這部門以及公司帶來許多的貢獻。

Q

3

What did you like or dislike about your previous job?
對於你以前的工作你有什麼喜歡或不喜歡的地方？

I really enjoyed the people I worked with at my previous company. It was a friendly and fun atmosphere and I actually enjoyed going into work every each day. I felt the management team was great as well. They knew all of their employees well and tried to make those personal connections. One of the reasons I am leaving is that I felt I was not challenged enough at the job. After being there for many years, I felt I was not able to reach my full potential because of the lack of challenge and there was no room for advancement in the company. While I did enjoy working there and appreciate the skills I developed while with the company, I felt my skill set could be better utilized elsewhere, where my capabilities were more recognized and there was the opportunity for growth.

我真的很喜歡我以前的公司一起工作的人。那裡的氣氛很友好和有趣，事實上我每一天都很樂於在工作中。我覺得那裡的管理團隊也很棒。他們熟識所有的員工，並設法建立與大家建立個人的關係。其中一個我離開的原因是，我覺得我沒有辦法在工作上有足夠的挑戰。在那裡許多年之後，我覺得因為缺乏挑戰性我無法達到我的全部潛力，並且在公司沒有進步的空間。雖然我也喜歡在那裡工作和感激公司予我開發的潛能，我覺得我的技能可以在其他地方得到更好的整合，以及我的能力可以得到比較多的認可使用且有成長的機會。

Q

4 **Do you easily get bored doing repetitive work?**
你很容易對做重複的工作感到厭倦嗎？

No, even though I understand that the nature of performing repetitive tasks typically produces boredom, which can result in errors and mistakes. I always try to alter my routines, and challenge myself to get the job done more efficiently. This helps the time go by faster and I usually get more done. When possible, I also use technology to my advantage and automate tasks by using the tips, tools and techniques provided by the accessible software and hardware. I've learned that by doing so, I can avoid dwelling on the negative aspects of repetitive work and keep a positive attitude of mine. Not to mention that my greatest strength to well perform on any repetitive work is my tenacity. Whatever I do, I have to see it finished with making my full effort and potential.

不，即使我明白，在執行重複性質的任務時，通常會產生厭煩，這有可能會導致錯誤和失誤。我總是試圖改變我的例行行程，並挑戰自己，把工作做得更有效率。這有助於讓時間感覺過得較快而且我通常會比完成更多的事。如果可能的話，我也用科技來成為我的優勢，利用可去得的軟體和硬體所提供的技巧，工具和技術來自動化執行任務。我已經學到通過這樣做，我能避免困在重複性工作的消極面，並保持我一個積極的態度。更何況我最大的優勢就是我的執著能在任何重複的工作下保持良好的表現。無論我做什麼，我一定要用我滿滿地精力和潛能看到它完成。

5 Can you work well under pressure?
你可以在壓力下保持良好的工作表現嗎？

Yes, definitely. In fact, I find it stimulating to work in a dynamic environment where the pressure is on. In my current position, I face deadlines consistently. I find that when I'm under the pressure of a deadline, I can do some of my work most successfully and creatively. I'm not a person who has a difficult time with stress. When I work under pressure, I become much focused, methodical, and only want to get the job done. I always try to start on my assigned projects early so that I can avoid any last minute situations. I believe in any jobs in any industries, pressure is there. If a person has the tendency of procrastination, she/he is responsible for being the cause of her/his own stress and anxiety. Pressure might not be avoidable, but someone could always still manage to reach the finish line on time by being organized, self-disciplined, and having flexible thinking.

是的，當然。事實上，我覺得在有動力的壓力環境下工作很刺激。在我現在的職位裡，我不斷面對截止期限。我發現當我在一個有截止期限的壓力下，我能夠成功地和有創造性地做一些我的工作。我不是一個面對壓力有困難的人。當我在壓力下工作，我變得更專注，有條不紊，而且只想把工作做好。我總是試著早點開始我被指派的工作讓我能避免做到最後一刻的情況。我相信在任何行業的任何工作裡，壓力是存在的。如果一個人有拖延的傾向，她/他須為她/他自己的緊張和焦慮負責。壓力是不可能避免的，但是人始終仍能通過有組織、自律、並具有靈活的思維準時到達終點線。

Q 6 How do you feel about working on a team?
你覺得在一個團隊裡工作如何？

I enjoy working in a team environment, and I get along well with people. I like to communicate with people whom I can receive from and provide feedback. I believe that I have a lot to contribute to a team environment, and am comfortable in both leadership and player roles. I'm outgoing, friendly, and have strong communication skills. I like to make oral and written communication clear and easy to understand by effectively listening, conveying and receiving ideas, information and directions.

I always seek to clarify and confirm the accuracy of my understanding of unfamiliar or vague terms and instructions. I believe different team members contribute different perspectives and the synergy between team members can produce creative and productive results.

我喜歡在一個團隊環境中工作，而我與人相處的很好。我喜歡跟我溝通的人，我可以從他們身上接收和提供反饋意見。我相信我對團隊環境會有很多的貢獻，並且能同時發揮領導者與隊員的角色。我性格外向、友善、並具有很強的溝通能力。我喜歡藉由有效地傾聽，輸達和接收的想法、資訊與指示讓口頭和書面上的溝通清晰。我總是試圖澄清和確認我所不熟悉的或模糊的字語和指令的準確性。我相信不同的團隊成員會有不同面向的貢獻，並且團隊成員之間的合作可以產生有創造性與有生產力的結果。

7 Give an example of a successful project you were part of.
請給我們一個你有參與成功案子的經歷。

At ABC Enterprising, we were preparing to roll out the new release of our online corporate platform. Unfortunately, the developers ran into technical problems with the new reporting feature that was supposed to be the centerpiece of the release. In order to make the release date, they had to scale back and offer only limited functionality. We knew that some clients would be disappointed. After a lot of back and forth with the engineers and the senior people in Product, Customer Service, and Marketing; I drafted the announcement to customers. I emphasized the positive aspects of the new functionality, explained the delay, and laid out the timeline for the full functionality. We were then able to communicate strategically and proactively to clients before the release went live. Most customers got the realizations we were working our very best to in their best interest, and at the end they were pretty satisfied with the online platform we launched.

在 ABC 企業工作時，我們正準備推出網上企業平台的新版本。不幸的是，開發人員遇到了技術問題，而這正是要推出新的特徵的裡核心功能。為了在發布日期完成，他們不得不縮減並只提供有限的功能。我們知道有些客戶有感到失望。經過與產品、客服、與市場部門大量來回的溝通；我擬了一份公告給客戶。我強調的新功能的優勢、解釋了延遲的原因、並制定了全部功能會推出的時間表。在新功能推出之前我們這樣就能夠有方法地與積極地與客戶溝通。許多客戶了解到我們是在為他們的利益來盡我們最大的努力，並且在最後他們蠻滿意我們推出的網路平台。

8 Have you ever had a conflict with a former supervisor? How was it resolved?
你曾經與前上司發生過衝突嗎？它是如何解決的？

Yes, I have had conflicts with some of my supervisors very occasionally in the past. They were never the major ones but mostly involved in some disagreements that needed to be resolved. I've found when a conflict occurs, it usually two people cannot put themselves in each other's shoes and see both sides of the situation. In my past experience, I always first asked the other person to give me her/his perspectives, and at the same time, to allow me to fully express my viewpoints. At that point, I would work with the person to find out if a compromise could be reached. If not, I would submit their decisions because they were my supervisors after all. I think an employee should be willing to submit her/himself to the directives of the supervisor, whether she/he is in full agreement or not.

是的，我在過去曾與一些我的上司很偶然地發生衝突。這些衝突從來不會很嚴重主要是一些意見的分歧需要解決。我發現當衝突發生時，通常是兩個人不能把自己置身於對方的立場並看到的事情的兩面。在我以往的經驗中，我總是先請另外一方給我她/他的觀點，並在同時讓我充分表達我的意見。在這時，我會與這人合作來找出是否可以有辦法達成妥協。如果沒有，我想遵循他們的決定，因為他們是畢竟我的上司。我認為僱員應該願意提遵循她/他自己的上司的指示，即使他/她並不是完全同意。

1-2 臨場反應篇

Q **1** **What quality do you feel a successful manager should have?**
你覺得做一個成功的管理者應該有什麼樣的特質？

In my administrative work experience, I think the key quality should be strong and firm leadership. A successful manager should demonstrate the ability to be the visionary for the people who work under them. This person can set the course and direction for the subordinates. She/he should also be a positive role model for others to follow in many ways, at or after work. A true leader is being inspirational at all times to motivate others to reach the highest of their abilities. In my last job, my previous supervisors also tried to make personal connections with their employees; meanwhile, not to have any personal preferences to any of us but only to be professional. I also liked the fact that I was able to go to my managers if I had an issue at work or an idea I thought that could better facilitate our work.

在我行政工作的經驗，我認為最關鍵的特質應該是強大而堅定的領導能力。一個成功的管理者應該展現有遠見的能力給在下工作的人員。此人可以設定路線和方向給下屬。她/他應該是一個積極的榜樣讓其他人在許多方面可以跟隨，不論上班或下班後。一個真正的領導者是能夠隨時鼓舞人心去激勵他人達到自己最高的能力。在我的上一份工作裡，我以前的上司也會試圖與員工建立個人關係；同時，不會對我們有任何個人的偏好，只會專業的對待。我也喜歡如果我有一個工作上的問題或一個想法，我可以去找我的經理讓我們可以更好地促進我們的工作。

Q 2

Do you think you are overqualified for this job?

你覺得你做這份工作是大材小用嗎？

I'm flattered that you think I'm headhunter bait and will leap to another job when an offer appears. As you note, I've worked at a higher level but this position is exactly what I'm looking for. I'm here because this is a company on the move and I want to move up with you. I would say that I'm not overqualified but fully qualified. I can assure you that my experience will be an asset to the company and will help me be successful in this position. I have the education and experience to fit in readily with the exceptional team here. My maturity, along with my experience, will enable me to do a terrific job for the company. I will take directions well from managers of any age and continue to stay current on any technology my job requires.

我很受寵若驚你認為我是獵人頭公司的目標，可能另一個工作出現時將馬上跳槽。正如你所注意到的，我曾在更高階得職位服務過，但這個職缺正是我在尋找的。我來這裡是因為這是一家在成長的公司，我想和你們一起動起來。我想說的是，我不是大材小用只是完全合格。我可以向你保證，我的經驗將是公司的一個資產，將幫助我在這個職位上成功。我有所需的教育和經驗來馬上配合這裡卓越的團隊。我的成熟，以及我的經驗，將使我為公司做出了不起的貢獻。我會聽從任何年齡經理的指示，並繼續更新目前對我的工作需要的任何技術。

3 Tell me about a time you had a conflict on a team project.
請告訴我某次你在一個團體工作裡發生的衝突。

Once, I was managing the creation of our new corporate brochure on a very tight deadline for a big upcoming trade show. The designer unfortunately missed the deadline that I assigned. When I approached to him, he blew up at me. I remained calm, acknowledged that the tight deadlines and explained again the importance of having the brochure ready for the trade show. He relaxed when he saw that I wasn't attacking him. He told me about his other projects and how overwhelmed he was. I asked him if there was any way that I could help him. Eventually, we asked if his manager could better understand how important and time-consuming this project was. The manager ended up assigning some of his other projects to another designer, which took some of the pressure off of him. He apologized and thanked me for my help. As a result, the designer was able to focus on the brochure and meet the deadline. We successfully completed the brochure in time and received numerous compliments from both our own sales reps and potential customers.

有一次，在很緊的期限裡我負責管理做出我們為一個即將舉行的貿易展新的企業宣傳手冊。設計師很不幸地的沒在我指示的截止日期完成。當我去找他時，他向我發飆。我依然保持平靜，向他承認期限真的很緊迫，並再次解釋為貿易展完成手冊的重要性。當他看到我並不是在攻擊他時他放鬆了。他告訴我關於他其它的案子，以及他壓力如何之大。我問他是否有什麼辦法我能幫助他。最後，我們問他的經理能是否可以更體諒這個項目是如何的重要且耗時。經理最終分配他的一些其它案子給另一名設計師，讓他了減輕了一些壓力。他向我道歉，並感謝我的幫助。因此，這位設計師能夠專注於達成手冊的最後期限。我們在時限內成功地完成了宣傳手冊，並從我們自己的銷售人員和潛在客戶上獲得無數的讚美。

4   What is your greatest weakness?
什麼是你最大的弱點？

I am a single mother who has to raise two children on my own, and with some help from my family. As I'm coming from a non-conventional background, you may say that's a weakness. I've had to make a lot of sacrifices. For example, I had to do my most recent degree at night school while working a day job. However, I think my non-traditional background gives me an edge in many ways over my fellow colleagues. I've learned a sense of responsibility, good time management skills, and I've become much mature comparing to other people at my age. Sometimes, I also tend to be a bit of a perfectionist that I might get pretty hung up on the details of things. Actually this also works to my advantage in many situations because I can often spot problems that other people don't see.

我是一個單身母親獨力扶養自己的兩個孩子，加上我家人一些幫助。因為我從一個非傳統背景出身的，你可能會覺得這是一個弱點。我為此做出了許多犧牲。例如，我不得不在白天工作同時在夜校讀書來取得我最近的學位。不過，我認為我的非傳統的背景讓我在很多方面超越我的同事。我已經學會了負責，良好的時間管理技巧，並且我已經較其他同齡的人變得更加成熟。有時候，我也有些完美主義者的傾向，我可能會一直注意細節的東西。但這也其實在很多情況下變成我的優勢，因為我經常可以發現其他人看不到的問題。

1-3 我有疑問篇

Q 1

What are some responsibilities of this position?
這個職位上有一些什麼工作責任？

The work hours are technically 9-5. We have a tight system of phone coverage. It is imperative that phones be answered by the end of the first ring. You need to periodically check the emails and the calendar which we use the system of Google Office Calendar to see all the activities taking place in the department. You also need to support around 20 engineers in the department. At any given time, 10 of them could be traveling all over the world. You need to arrange, stay on top of their traveling plans, like hotels, cars, and get approvals for every portion of their traveling. If there's a meeting, you need to go to the Conference Room where the meeting will be held. Bring copies of the previous minutes of the meeting and today's meeting agenda. Inside the Conference Room, you need to prepare the laptop, projector and arrange the copies of the memorandum and agenda at the center of the table so that the attendees may easily get a copy each.

上班時間基本上是 9 點到 5 點。我們有嚴格的電話回覆系統。公司強制規定電話響第一聲後就要有人接起來。你需要定期檢查電子郵件和日曆，我們是使用谷歌辦公室日曆系統，來查看部門所有發生的活動。你還需要支持大約 20 名部門的工程師。在任何的時間裡，其中有可能有 10 人左右在出差。你需要安排及最清楚他們的旅行計劃，如飯店，汽車，並讓他們的旅行的每一個部分得到批准。如果有一個會議，你需要去舉行會議的會議室。準備好之前的會議紀錄和今天的會議的議程影本。在會議室裡面，你需要準備好筆電、投影機、並將大綱及議程的影本放在桌子的中央，使與會者可以很容易地拿到各一份影本。

Q 2 How does the company rate the performance appraisal?
公司是如何做績效考核？

You will get a detailed description of the appraisal during the hiring and training process. Basically all staff will have an appraisal with their line manager twice a year. The aim of the meeting is to have a chance to discuss your work over the past six months, such as your strengths, weaknesses, what's gone well, your training needs and so on. The company has been addressed several important qualities of the employees. You must have the adaptability and efficiency that you can work under stress and respond well to changes. We like to have our staff being receptive to changes and new ideas. Needless to say, we agree that the employee should pursue goals with commitment and take pride in accomplishment. Other more basic work requirements include your reports to work on time, willingness to assist co-workers, and job knowledge that demonstrates technical, administrative, or other specialized knowledge required to perform the job.

你會得到的招聘和培訓過程中拿到考核的詳細說明。基本上所有的工作人員會與他們的上司經理，每年兩次進行評估。這次面談的目的是為了有機會來討論你在過去的半年裡的工作表現，如你的優勢、缺點、什麼做得好、以及你的培訓需求等。公司有在強調員工的幾個重要特質。你必須具有適應性和效率，可以在壓力下工作，並對於變化反應良好。我們喜歡我們的工作人員能接受變化和新的想法。更不用說，我們同意員工應該追求目標並對於成就引以自豪。其他更基本的工作要求，包括你按時上下班、願意幫助同事、專業工作知識、以及展示了執行工作所需的技術、行政或其他的專業知識。

Q3 Where is the company going in the next five years?
公司未來五年內的發展方向在哪裡？

As we've grown over the years, both by expanding the scale of the company, but also by growing globally. Today we do business in Europe, North America, Latin America and obviously all around Asia. Growing globally has been a huge growth area for us over the last several years. Our goal is to open 8 new locations and to accommodate our clients growing needs and provide more job opportunities for our employees. The forecast by the beginning of 2014 is to have 2 offices in North America and to continue our expansion across the world. The second is we've expanded into different market segments. If you checked in on us 10 years ago, we were really only selling to the biggest companies in the world. Today we sign more deals with small companies than we do with big companies.

當我們已經經過多年的成長，無論是擴大公司的規模，或也在全球增長。今天我們在歐洲、北美洲、拉丁美洲、顯然在亞洲各地都有業務活動。在我們在過去的幾年裡我們在全球領域內有一個巨大的增長。我們的目標是開 8 個新分部，以滿足我們的客戶不斷增長的需求，並為我們的員工提供更多的就業機會。2014 年初已計畫在北美洲會有 2 個新的辦事處並且我們在世界各地繼續擴充。再來試是我們已經擴展到不同的市場區間。如果你在 10 年前知道我們，我們只賣給全球的大型公司。今天比我們來往的小公司比大公司簽了更多的交易。

4

Why did your last assistant leave the position? What were his/her strengths?
為什麼你的助理最後會離開這個職位？他/她的優勢是什麼？

My last assistant left her previous position for relocating to another area due to family circumstances in order to make the move. I would first praise her ability to maintain regular attendance and communicate schedule or any changes promptly to me. The best quality I found in her behavior reflected a desire to excel on the job. She always took initiative eagerly, demonstrated orientation to achieve results, and she worked steadily and actively. She possessed much self-confidence and positive attitude towards self and others. I could fully depend upon her to be available for work and to fulfill position responsibilities. She didn't need much supervision and could act independently within established guidelines. In fact, I have written the letter of references as being her former supervisor to her current company where she works now.

我最近的助理為了配合家庭因素離開了她的職位搬遷到另一個地區。首先我要稱讚她能保持良好出勤並和及時與我溝通任何時間表或其它的變動。我發現她最好的特質就是想把在工作做到最好的願望。她總是把熱切的採取主動，表明方向來取得成果，並且她不斷積極努力。她擁有很多的自信和以及對自己和他人積極的態度。我可以完全依靠她可以隨時工作，並履行崗位職責。她並不需要太多的監督，並可以在既定的規定下獨立行事。事實上，我以她前上司的身分寫了推薦信給她現在工作的公司。

自傳篇

1 範例

1-1. 自傳(1)

My name is Amy Lee, who is 27 years old. I was born in Hsinchu, a small city full of culture. I grew up in the well-off, warm family. My father is a governmental servant being an engineer, my mother is a housewife, the older sister is married having her own family, and my younger brother is graduated now has a steady job. We love, considerate, and respect each other very much, I am very fortunate to grow up in this happy, fabulous, and lovely family.（請閱2-1）

I graduated from Shi Chien University majoring in Business Administration. During my study, I participated in the program of food & beverage service, beauty assistant, etc as my part-time work. I also cooperated with my supervising professor and schoolmates on a project published as Business Related across Organizations in my junior year. I have had experiences of attending many competitions and performances when I joined the choir since elementary school to high school. I also have represented the school and won the national competition by second runner-up.（請閱2-1）

After graduation, I worked as an administrative assistant at a human resources company making recruitments in school campuses, and also worked part-time in a restaurant. These different work experiences that I couldn't be able to learn from school, such as the interpersonal skills, problem solving ability, crisis management and so on... （請閱2-1）

I love to learn, enhance knowledge and professional skills. I am interested in singing、watching movies and reading. I always aim high to realize my childhood dreams in the vision of my future, I will continue to travel to the different countries as possible as I can in order to see more and learn more from the knowledge and cultures all around the world! Thank you for your time and consideration.

我叫 Amy Lee，27 歲。我在新竹出生，一個雖小但很有文化的城市。我在一個小康溫馨的家庭裡長大。父親在公務機關當工程師、母親家管，姊姊已結婚有自己的家庭，弟弟也從學校畢業有份安定的工作。我們都非常相愛彼此，相互體諒、尊重，我很幸運能在這快樂幸福的家庭長大。

我畢業於實踐大學，主修企業管理學系。求學期間我參與過餐飲服務、美容助理等兼差工作。大三曾和同學及指導教授合作過企業跨組織合作相關專題發表。因從小學到高中都參與合唱團演唱，所以累積了許多比賽和表演經驗。更曾代表學校獲得過全國比賽得到季軍。

大學畢業後，我從事過人力資源公司的行政助理從事校園徵才工作，並在餐廳兼職。這些不同的工作經驗，讓我學習到許多在學校所學不到的經驗，如與人溝通技巧、面對問題的能力、危機處理…等等。

我喜歡不斷學習，增進自己知識與專業技能的人。我興趣於唱歌、旅行與閱讀。我對於未來願景就是完成從小在心中的夢想，我會繼續遊歷更多不同國家以增廣見聞。感謝你的時間與考量。

1-2. 自傳(2)

My name is May Lin. I grew up in a farmer's family. My parents teach us to be a person that has the sense of responsibility and conscientiousness, even they didn't study a great grade. (請閱2-2)

When I study at Taipei Unversity of Science and Technology, I majored in International Business. The teachers of this department always ask the student to improve our language skills, so I try to take many language exams, even the grades weren't very good, but I learned one thing—if you want success, you must be very diligent and follow through with your plans.

When I was work in the famous Formosa Freight and Logistics Corp., I need to communicate with forwarders, brokers, customs and clients of the company. I have to pay close attention on clearance of goods very much, and submit the payment of a monthly bill. It made me very careful in every case.

My last Job was an assistant in Kerry TJ Logistics now. I like my job because it combines the experience I've learned from the school and the work experience of my previous company. Working here lets me learn new things easier. I can finish my work in a very efficient way, and deliver the job performance my supervisor feels satisfied with.

I think the experience I have mentioned above will make great contribution in your department, and if you can give me a chance, I will do the job well. Thank you.

我的名字是 May Lin。我在一個務農的家庭長大。我的父母教導我們要成為有責任感與認真態度的人，即使他們沒有讀很高的程度。

當我在台北科技大學就讀時，我主修國際貿易。系上的老師總是邀學生去增進我們的語言技巧，所以我試著參加了許多語言考試。雖然考試成績不是很理想，但是我學到一件事，如果你想要成功，你必須要非常努力不懈並堅持你的計畫到最後。

當我在著名的台塑貨運及物流公司工作，我需要與發運人、經紀人、海關、顧客和公司客戶進行溝通。我必須密切關注非常多支付貨物通關的細節，並提交支付每月帳單。這讓我在每一個案件非常地小心。

我之前在大榮物流擔任助理。我喜歡我的工作，因為它結合了我在學校所學的和我以前的公司的工作經驗。在這裡工作讓我學到更容易新的東西。我能以一個非常有效的方式完成我的工作，並提供讓我的上司感到滿意的工作績效。

我覺得我上面所提到的經驗將能為你的部門做出很大的貢獻，如果你能給我一個機會，我會將工作做得很好。謝謝。

2 自傳寫作教室

2-1. 自傳(1) 寫作文法解析／小評語

第一段其中一句「I grew up in the well-off、warm family.」這很明顯是標點符號的誤用。英文中並沒有這些標點符號"、""，""。"常常見到學生將這些中文的標點符號放在英文寫作中。許多同學會形容自己的家庭經濟狀況狀小康，「well-off」已經是生活頗為富裕的程度，「comfortably-off」比較接近小康的狀況。冠詞是學生常見的文法錯誤。這裡因為 family 這個單字第一次被提起，先用不限定冠詞「a」。

所以這句應該改成「I grew up in a comfortably-off and warm family.」 另外一句「We love, considerate, and respect each other very much, I am very fortunate to grow up in this happy, fabulous, and lovely family.」是一個很常見的寫作錯誤 run-on sentence。兩個獨立的句子中間沒有連接詞就直接用逗號繼續。這裡可以用"and"連接或直接在中間做一句子的結束。

許多學生如果要提到參加比賽的經驗以及所得到的名次，如第二段的最後一句應該改成「won the third place in the national competition.」第三段最後一句 These different work experiences that I couldn't be able to learn from school, such as the interpersonal skills, problem solving ability, crisis management and so on...，「experience」如果統稱為一經驗，如果過往經驗，則為不可數單數，如「in my past work experience,」但如果是一次指許多不同的經驗，例如「among my traveling experiences,」則是可數複數。這裡「could」、「be able to」是同義不需重複，可改成「I couldn't learn」或「I wasn't able to」。最後 and so on 不可加…。請問最後一段第二句跟第三句又犯了以上哪些錯誤呢？

2-2. 自傳(2) 寫作文法解析／小評語

第一段的最後一句許多學生會直接把「even」當作是兩個句子的連接詞，其實「even」只是一個副詞，不能直接連接兩個句子。有包含「even」的連接詞有「even though」或「even if」。「they didn't study a great grade」是比較中式英文的講法，這裡英文正確的表達是「…, even though they were very well-educated.」。

第二段犯了一個也是在做常見的錯誤習慣，就是時態的不統一。其實這一段除了最後一句之外，所有關於時態動詞（標示底線）應該皆為過去時態。最後一句因為是以學到的事實，可以改為「I have learned one thing─if you want success, you must be very diligent and follow through with your plans.」被標示雙底線的連接詞代表這些句子雖然有用連接詞連接，但是也不能一直連下去沒有斷句。最後一句一樣是犯了同樣的錯誤，用「even」來做連接詞，這句應改成「…language exams. Even though the grades weren't very good, I have learned one thing…」或「The grades weren't very good, but I have learned one thing…」，記得「although,」「though,」「even though」同義，並且不能與「but」一起同時出現在同一句子造成兩個連接詞的出現。不過因為中文說「雖然…，但是…」所以這種錯誤非常經常出現。第三段的動詞時態也應該一致為過去動詞。「was work」是很明顯的文法錯誤，應改成「was working」或「worked」。

Get fit on Your Way to Work

Making cycling to work as part of your training will save you time, money, and many calories! Cycling is an easy and conveniently available form of exercise. By easy I mean almost anyone can do it. The plans of cycling to work have made cheaper to get a brand new bike through companies, ebay has made it even cheaper. You can find dozens of almost new, originally very expensive bikes at unbelievable decent prices on ebay. Governments and city councils around the world are putting extra effort into cycling systems to increase safety and break down barriers. Cycle lanes are now common places in most places. In numerous cities, renting a bike and locking up garages specifically for bikes are growing. The bike manufactures themselves are selling fold-up commuter bikes that can easily be carried. The barriers are shrinking.

On top of that, it is almost always quicker to cycle than it is to drive or get public transport admittedly more in cities. For someone training for a triathlon or a road race, cycle to work cannot only mean you can get out of bed a little later, but you won't have to go out and train again after you get back from work. It's a win-win situation. For the last benefit then, money. Once you have a bike, there is no daily cost of commuting.

在上班途中健身

將騎腳踏車上班工作作為你的健身的一部分，可以節省你的時間，金錢和許多熱量！騎自行車是一種簡單方便的運動形式。我覺得簡單的意思是幾乎任何人都可以做到這一點。騎一個全新的自行車上班的方案已經是便宜，eBay 更是讓它便宜。你可以在 ebay 上找到一點都不昂貴許多九成新，原本很貴的自行車。各國政府和市議會以提高安全性和打破障礙來將更多的精力投入到騎腳踏車通勤的計畫。自行車道變成是常見的地方。在許多城市租個自行車，跟可以鎖自行車的車庫是越來越多。許多自行車製造商在賣折疊式通勤自行車，可以很容易帶著走。許多障礙正在縮小。

最重要的是，固然比較起來多在城市中，騎腳踏車幾乎總是比開車或搭乘公共交通工具還快。對於有人在訓練鐵人三項或公路賽，騎腳踏車上班，不僅意味著你可以晚點起床，而且你下班回來不需要再出去訓練。這是一個雙贏的局面。然後最後一個好處，錢。一旦你有自行車，就沒有日常通勤的費用。

1-1 常遇到的考題

Q 1

Where do you get the information you share with tourists?
你從哪裡得到你與遊客分享的資訊？

I collect information from various sources, mostly from books and published guides. I have a very well-equipped library at home. I sometimes buy a book just because of a single page I might need for work. I also like to buy guide books about (Country name) written by foreign authors. They're often better than ours, more dynamic and informative and they're adapted to suit contemporary tourists. The Internet is also an available source of information. I like to hear and read stories about traditions and beliefs. I also like to read about legends and tell the stories that are the easiest to remember. Of course the visitors themselves constantly inspire me with their questions which then motivate me to research further. The most insight information is actually from the locals. I have made friends from (Country name) and kept in contact with them to get the most recent updates.

　　我會從各種管道收集資訊，大部分是從書上還有出版的旅遊指南。我在家裡有一個設備非常齊全的圖書館。我會因為一頁工作上有需要而去買了一本書。我也喜歡買不同外國作者寫的關於（國名）的導遊書，他們通常比台灣出版的好，也往往比我們的內容活潑跟資料豐富，來迎合現在旅客的需要。網路也是一個容易獲得資訊的來源。我喜歡聽和閱讀有關的傳統和信仰的故事。我也喜歡閱讀相關的傳說

並講一些最容易記住的故事。當然，遊客提出的問題不斷地激勵著我去進一步研究。最深入的資訊當然是從當地人身上獲得。我從（國名）交了一些朋友並與他們保持接觸，以獲得最新的情報。

Q 2 When did you want to become a tour guide?
你是什麼時候想要成為一名導遊？

I dreamed of traveling around the world from the time I was a child, and everything I imagined myself doing for a living one day was always related to travel. One step spontaneously led to another as I graduated. I was looking for Jobs, and saw a flyer for a course for tour guides and I enrolled. Friends from my early years at school who were already working as group leaders were taking the class. They recommended me to the agency where they were working for and that was how it all began. Its work still interests me and it has not become boring to me. The reason is that I still have things to learn. I can still stay excited every time I meet new people and places; that's stimulating and it pushes me forward. Reading something interesting about a place and then visiting it in person afterwards thrills me. It's enjoyable to make a tour filled with the history, literature and local culture.

我小時候就夢想要環遊世界，當我想像自己要靠什麼生活，總是會跟旅行有關。當我畢業之後這一切就很自然的發生了。我在找工作時，看到一張導遊課程的傳單然後我就去報名參加了。我早年在學校的朋友當時已經擔任領隊也在那邊上課。他們建議我去他們工作的地方上班，那就是這一切如何開始的。這份工作我還是很有興趣，也沒有感覺乏味。原因是我還有很多東西要學。我仍然對遇到心的人與拜訪新的地方感到興奮；這就是刺激我前進的動力。閱讀一些關於一個地方有趣的事情，之後親自拜訪它令我興奮不已。讓一趟的旅程充滿歷史、文學和當地文化，這是令人愉快。

3 Are there some groups more satisfying to work with? Which types of groups are most refreshing to work with or most interesting?
是否有一些團是讓你工作更滿意的呢?那一類型的團體是最令人精神振作或最有趣?

I can't set anyone apart as a greater or lesser pleasure to work for, if you mean pointing out the countries they come from. I can say that it's hard to work with groups where I feel I can't reach them who show no emotion either way. Sometimes there are groups which are uninterested, and it's hard to get my messages across to and make them accessible to them. I'm satisfied when a group leaves (Country name) with upbeat emotions and memories. A tour guide is an ambassador, and my goal is for visitors, after they leave, to pass on their impressions of the beautiful country. Guests like that are the best advertising. When the visitors are interested in the information that reaches them, and they'll share it with those closest to them.

我沒有辦法去特別指明說任何人是比較好或不好,如果你的意思是指出他們來自那一個國家。我會說如果這一團我覺得我不能打動他們的感覺,不管怎樣他們都沒有表情,這樣會很難帶。有時也有團會一點興趣都沒有,這會讓我很難傳達我想表達的訊息並讓他們接收。我很滿意當一群人(國名)時帶著愉快的情緒和記憶。一個導遊像是一位大使,我的目標是當遊客離開時,去告訴別人關於這國家美麗的的印象。這樣的客人是最好的廣告。當訪客對接受到的訊息有興趣時,他們會與那些最親密的人分享。

Q 4 What element of your job do you find most satisfying?
你最滿意你工作的哪一部分？

I think a great tour guide is one who knows how to feel out a group and adjust the tour to suit the group dynamic. She/he will always put herself/himself in it with lots of experience and stories; she/he is not just a narrator but an ambassador. What's most satisfying is the feeling that I'm doing something good not just for me but for others and for my country. In the business of tourism, we have direct contacts with tourists, so we also have a great responsibility. I take a lot of pleasure in the fact that I still don't feel the burden of that responsibility but rather find enjoyment in it. I love seeing the spark in the eyes and smile on the face of a guest after seeing more of Taiwan's beauties. I know then that I took part in the creating of an experience that is new for them.

我認為一個好的導遊是能知道如何感覺出團體氣氛，並調整遊覽內容來滿足該團的生態。她/他永遠把自己融入團體裡面並帶入許多經驗和故事；她/他的不只是一個解說者而像一個大使。最令人滿意的是，我不只是為我做了好事，而是感覺為別人以及為我的國家。在旅遊這一行中，我們與遊客直接接觸，所以我們也有很大的責任。事實上我得到了很多樂趣，不是感覺責任負擔，而是在裡面找到樂趣。我喜歡在介紹完更多台灣的美麗之後看到客人眼睛的火花以及臉上的微笑。我知道在那時我參與了他們一個全新的體驗。

5 Do you do anything else in addition to being a tour guide?
當導遊之餘你還有做哪些事情？

I work in a language school where I teach English when I'm off duty. I teach a lot of conversation classes especially about traveling English. I am also a member of a group with other traveling enthusiasts who wish to practice more English and share traveling experiences with each other. From time to time I do various types of translations, like the subtitles translation of American TV shows and films that are playing in Taiwan. I really enjoy that work for the reason that I can get to know more real life situations and cultures about the US. During the low seasons, I mostly spend more time teaching and working in the school. Also, I'm in charge of organizing expert lectures in the ABC Tour Guide Association. I have been interested in creating trips that haven't yet been introduced in the market. Lately, I've spent some free time organizing the ideas.

當我沒帶團時我在一個語言學校工作教英語。我教了很多會話類課程尤其是關於旅遊英語。我也是一個團體的成員，跟其他想多練習英語的旅遊愛好者互相分享旅遊經驗。有空時我會做各類的翻譯，像有在台灣播出的一些美國電視電影的字幕翻譯。我真的很喜歡這工作，因為我可以認識更多美國的現實生活狀況和文化。在淡季，我主要會花更多的時間在學校的教學工作上。另外，我還負責籌辦 ABC 導遊協會的專家講座。我一直熱衷於創造一些尚未在市場上見過的行程。最近我花了一些空閒時間整理點子。

Q 6 Tell us about your related qualifications and experiences.
請告訴我們你的相關資歷與經驗。

My first job was a resort representative working at Paradise Resort Company. I was primarily responsible for looking after holidaymakers at resorts. Every day at work I greeted people on arrival. I had to organize excursions and entertainment. Sometimes I acted as a tour guide. I needed to handle problems such as lost possessions or passports. In addition, I also dealt with illness of guests and liaised with hotel managers. I liked helping people, and working in a beautiful place. The pay was low though considering working in stressful and long hours. The work was mostly seasonal. By working there, I acquired people skills, strength, commonsense, enthusiasm, and language skills. I did my research on different certified schools for tour guides. I just enrolled in the program helping me pass the license test. In this program, we have classes for practicing different languages, and knowing the tour guide skills, tour guide law and tourism resources.

我的第一份工作是在天堂渡假村公司做一個渡假村工作人員。我主要負責照顧度假村的旅客。每天的工作要歡迎抵達的旅客。我必須安排短途行程和娛樂。有時候我會充當導遊。我需要處理的問題有像如丟失財物或護照。此外，我還必須處理生病的客人和擔任飯店經理的聯絡窗口。我喜歡幫助別人，並在一個美麗的地方工作。這份工作薪水不高但工時很長而且緊張。這項工作主要是季節性的。在那裡工作，我練習到了人際交往能力、耐力、常識、熱情與語言表達能力。我有去研究找出不同導遊的的認證學校。我剛剛報名了這個課程能幫助我通過導遊資格考試。在這個課程中，我們有練習不同的語言，並知道導遊實務，觀光法規和觀光資源概要。

7

What has been the greatest accomplishment in your career?
什麼是你職涯中最大的成就？

For about 3 years I've had a personal blog where I write about my trips and traveling experiences. A blog is online 24/7 and this means that you work with people across all time zones. It takes time to manage a blog. I need to regularly check and reply to all the e-mails which have come in; then I check my analytics. I look at how many people visited the blog the day before, where they came from, how they accessed the website and what the most popular post was. Then I get ready to go out and explore for stories I can write. I also update my Facebook page on a regular basis. Lately, many companies have been contacting me to ask me to try out their services since they can see I have a great number of visitors and followers through my website and my social media profiles. I believe I could be the best advertisement for the company if I were hired.

大約 3 年我有一個自己的部落格，我寫我的旅行和旅遊的經驗。一個網路部落格是全年無休，意味著你會與不同時區的人接觸。這需要花時間來經營。我需要定期檢查和回覆所有進來的郵件，然後檢查我的分析。我會去看有多少人在前一天拜訪了我的部落格，他們來自哪裡，他們如何發現該網站，還有什麼是最熱門的文章。然後我會準備好走發掘探索我可以寫的故事。我還會定期更新我的臉書頁面。最近，許多公司一直在聯繫我問我要不要試用他們的服務，因為他們可以看到我的網站與社群媒體有大量訪客和跟隨消息的人。如果我被錄用我相信我能成為公司最好的廣告。

8　What's your interaction like with the tourists?
你如何跟客人互動的？

Of course work which involves constant interaction with people is often draining, but fortunately I think it also renews me. It's true that I can sometimes feel like I'm on a constant repeat, but I've never felt burned out because I meet different people each time even at the same tourist spots. The interaction is always different. I always make my acquaintance with my clients on the first-name basis. I have some clients that I keep in touch with and a few of them are closer to my heart. I have received many messages written to me after the trips. I always appreciate with hosting clients who have a positive attitude. They are relaxed, willing to learn and follow me. They show with their non-verbal communication that they are enjoying the tour. Clients like that usually transfer their positive energy to the rest of the group.

當然涉及與人不斷互動的工作往往是很耗體力，但這也讓我有新的體驗。有時我會真的覺得我不斷的在做一樣的事情，但我從來沒有覺得職業倦怠，因為我每次都會遇見不同的人，即使一直到同一個觀光景點。每個團體的互動總是不同。我總是與我的團員像朋友般地打成一片。我有與一些客人保持聯繫而他們跟我私交甚密。我在旅行結束後都會收到客人寫給我的訊息。我總是很感謝可以帶到有積極態度的旅客。他們很隨意，也願意從我身上學到一些東西。他們用一些不是語言上的溝通來表達他們正在享受這旅遊的過程。這樣的客戶通常會把他們正面的能量傳達給該團的其他人。

1-2 臨場反應篇

Q 1 What is your most memorable trip?
你最難忘的一趟旅行是什麼？

Once I had a group to Phuket Island in Thailand. It was a group of college students for their graduation trip. One evening, everyone on our tour decided to get tattoos. They were not the permanent ones, but the henna versions that could be washed away after a couple of weeks. They were really trying hard on convincing me to get one too. I thought about the impression we must have made. Can you imagine a group of 25 people who were freshly tattooed walking through the island together? It was a night to remember. The next afternoon the owner of the hotel was very excited to speak with me. It seems that the maids discovered pictures of different animals and designs on the sheets of every single bed. He could not believe it. On every bed was an anchor, or a snake or a skull, even a kitten.

有一次我帶一個團到泰國普吉島。這是一群大學生到那裡做畢業旅行。有一天晚上，大家決定要刺青。不是那種永久的，而是經過了幾個星期可能被洗掉的指甲花刺青。他們很努力的想說服我一起刺。我想到我們會給人的印象。你能想像一群 25 人在島上帶著新的紋身走在一起嗎？那是一個難忘的晚上。第二天下午，飯店的老闆很興奮地跑過來跟我說。打掃的女傭在每一個床的床單上發現不同的動物和其它圖案。他簡直不敢相信。在床單上可能是一個錨、一條蛇或骷髏頭，甚至是一隻小貓。

Q 2 What would you describe your guiding styles?
你會怎樣形容你的帶團風格？

People tell me I am still a kid at heart. It's true. In fact, most tour members think I'm ten years younger than I really am. I don't take myself too seriously, I strive to be an extremely positive and happy person, and I love to have fun! At work, I try to intertwine history, lifestyle and funny stories from the past and present into my guided tours. I try to keep the listeners engaged, and can say I do succeed at that. A lot of time we have to sit on the tour bus for long hours to get to places. Usually, when I notice I've been talking for one or two hours, I ask them if they could be patient for another ten minutes, because there's something else I want to show them and tell them about. Nobody's ever said no. I think I'm a good storyteller!

人們跟我說我的內心還像個小孩子。這是真的。事實上，大多數團員都以為我比實際年齡年輕十歲。我不把自己搞得太嚴肅，我努力成為一個非常正向和快樂的人，我喜歡有樂趣！在工作中，我嘗試從過去到現在交織歷史，當地生活和有趣的故事在我的導覽中。我盡量保持聽眾參與的興趣，而且我可以說我在這方面是成功的。很多時候，我們必須長時間坐在遊覽車上才會到下一個地方。通常，當我發現我已經講了一兩個小時，我會問他們是否還有耐心再聽個十分鐘，因為我還有別的東西想告訴他們。從來沒有人說不好。我覺得我是一個很會說故事的人！

Q 3 **What's the dynamic like with a group of different ages on a tour together?**
帶一群不同年齡的團員出去是什麼樣的氣氛？

It's actually less stressful with a mixed age group. Having kids in the group helps to remind everyone that school is out and this trip is a vacation. In the evenings at many of the hotels, the adults might gather on outside and socialize over a glass of wine or beer. The kids get together to play games and sing songs. At group meals, the kids usually take over their own table. I believe the conversation improves considerably at both tables and I know the kids are having more fun. On the other hand, with a majority of the group is elderly people, it is really fun to see them feel young again. Traveling can make a person feel relaxed at the same time also adventurous. A lot of elderly people are willing to talk and laugh more than they usually do when they go on a trip.

實際上帶一團不同年齡出團是壓力比較小。有小孩子們在團中會讓大家感覺這是像學校遠足般的一次度假。到了晚上在飯店外面，大人可能會拿著一杯葡萄酒或啤酒在社交。孩子們則是聚在一起玩遊戲和唱歌。在團體用餐時，孩子們通常霸占在自己的桌子。我相信兩邊在聊天時都更愉快，而且我知道小朋友們會玩得更開心。在另一方面，團中大如果大部份是老人，看到他們再次感到年輕實在是也是很有趣的。旅行可以讓一個人感到輕鬆的同時也愛得敢冒險。很多老人家在他們出去旅行時都比平常時更願意聊天開玩笑。

Q 4

What do you think the pros and cons of being a tour guide?
你覺得成為一名導遊的優點與缺點為何？

I think being a tour guide is a really great job. I can get to go to places either I've always loved going to on vacation or have never been before. I also like researching the facts and the history behind the tourist spots and studying other languages. I get to interact with other people as well, which I enjoy a lot. If I work hard enough I could get good tips, making my salary very lucrative. Although being a tour guide has a lot of perks, there's also a lot of stress from work. There isn't always work available for us since most of our work depends on the season. We have to research thoroughly about the destinations, especially if they're new to us. Plus, not all clients are easy to get along with; some can be quite troublesome and harsh especially if they don't find us impressive.

我覺得當導遊是一個很棒的工作。我可以去任何我總是想要去渡假或從來沒有機會去過的地方。我也很喜歡研究旅遊景點背後的事實和歷史，以及學習其他的語言。我很喜歡可以與其他人互動，還有如果我夠努力，我能得到豐厚的小費，讓我的薪水很值得。儘管作為一個導遊有很多特殊待遇，這畢竟是一個壓力很大的工作。因為大多數我們的工作是季節性所以不會一直都有工作進來。我們要深入研究與目的地有關的資訊，特別是如果這些地方是我們沒去過的。另外，不是所有的客戶都很容易相處，尤其是如果他們沒有對我們的服務感到印象深刻，有些可能是相當麻煩和苛刻的。

1-3 我有疑問篇

Q

1 **What are some major job responsibilities of this position?**
這個職務有哪些主要工作職責？

For the full-time position working as a travel agent at ABC Tour Company, your main job duty first involves clerical and technical sorting of travel arrangements. Besides, you need to do financial and computer work after hours to ensure people and destinations match. You give advice to customers on travel matters anytime necessary and appropriate. You are also in charge in marketing holidays and travel, selling to customers, and meeting targets. You'll really enjoy seeing someone coming back from a good trip totally relaxed and changed. Well, I won't only show you the pretty side of the job. The travel agents have to deal with the stress of achieving turnaround of passengers in peak time, much paperwork, and the pay you might think not high enough for you hard work. You need to have skills of speaking, communicating, persuading, listening, and cooperating in this business to survive.

對於 ABC 旅遊公司這家旅行社的全職工作，你的主要工作職責首先是安排行程的文件和流程。此外，你需要帶團之餘做整理團費和電腦工作，確保人數和地點是無誤的。你隨時隨地必須要給客戶提供旅遊事宜相關的意見。你還負責節假日和旅遊行程的營銷，銷售給客戶，並達到業績目標。你會很高興看到有人來從一個愉快的旅行後完全放鬆回來。我不會只告訴你這工作好的一面。旅行社人員必須處理在旺季達到客人週轉率目標的壓力，很多文書工作，並且你可能會覺得努力工作但是薪水不夠高。在這行你一定要有說話、溝通、說服、聆聽和合作的技巧來生存。

2 What are some of the benefits for this position?
什麼是這個職位的一些好處？

You'll have a fixed monthly salary plus tipping. Tips are then added to these payments, so the larger the group, the more money you will make. Your benefits include travel opportunities, paid meals, transportation, and accommodation on tours, and days off. Let's look at these benefits in more detail. Travel opportunities exist for all tour guides. Whether you are leading domestic tours in Taiwan, or managing long distance or international tours, you still get the opportunity to travel and see new places. Visiting attractions, beautiful villages, restaurants that you wouldn't normally go to, attending shows and more can be realized as a tour guide. In this profession, the biggest incentive to travel to exotic locations and although you're working long hours, sometimes 12 to 15 per day, you have very few out of pocket expenses. I have to say it is a very stressful job; however, most tour guides here know how to have fun at the same time.

你每月會有固定薪水加小費。小費會被加到給薪中，所以帶得團越大，錢就越多。你的福利包括旅遊的機會、支付餐費、交通費，以及旅遊住宿，和月休。我們來看一下更多細節。在所有行程中都是旅行的機會。無論你是在台灣國內旅遊，或是長途的國外團，你仍然可以去旅行，有機會看到新的地方。當導遊可以實現去你通常不會去的景點參觀，或是美麗的別墅、餐廳、看表演以及更多。在這個行業，最大的誘因前就是前往有異國情調的地點，雖然你的工作時間很長，有時一天 12 到 15 小時，你很少會花到自己的錢。我不得不說這是一個壓力大的工作；然而，這裡大多數的導遊都知道如何同時找樂趣。

Q 3 What's most rewarding part about this job?
什麼是對這份工作最有價值的地方？

In general it's a 24/7 job once you're on a tour. As in case anything comes up, you are responsible. Meeting people is an exciting part of being a tour guide for many people. They enjoy hearing traveler's stories and networking with people from all over the world, whether they are CEOs, students, families, or retired couples. This is an integral part of being a tour guide and if you don't get along with people, then this job is not for you. It can be hard sometimes to juggle the responsibilities of finding lost luggage, keeping the group happy, organizing accommodation, booking shows and making restaurant reservations, while trying to find the time to travel, but you have to think that you will be doing all of these tasks while in Hawaii or Bali, India or Australia, so both can be accomplished at the same time in many instances.

一旦你在帶團時，一般來說這是一個全年無休的工作。你要負責任何可能出現的狀況。對一個導遊來說能夠遇到很多不同的人是令人興奮的部分。他們會樂於享受旅行的故事，並與來自世界各地的人們建立人脈，無論是公司的總裁、學生、一個家庭或退休夫婦。這是作為一個導遊的關鍵，如果你不喜歡與人相處，那麼這個工作不適合你。這工作有時很難同時兼顧很多事，要同時尋找丟失的行李、保持團員開心、安排住宿、預訂表演和預約餐廳，同時試圖找到時間去旅行，但你要知道你是在夏威夷或芭里島，印度或澳洲完成這些任務，這樣其實在許多情況下可以兼顧的。

Q 4 What qualities are the company seeking?
什麼是公司正在尋求的一些特質？

The definite requirement of this position is the license. The applicants must pass the license test for a foreign-language tour guide. We are looking for applicants who have passed the test in the category of English, Japanese, French, German, Spanish, and Korean. So you can see here we are finding tour guides who can speak a range of languages, including the local dialects. They should also speak clearly, audibly and with confidence. This person has to be punctual, friendly, and knowledgeable. A great tour guide must know how to share their knowledge in an engaging, illuminating and entertaining way, rather than repeating a list of facts by rote. We want each trip to our customers is like the best they have ever had. A certain level of friendly humor is essential in this business. Since your job is to take care of a group of people, you need relevance to a broad range of people, including different age groups. A good tour leader also needs to be aware of tour members with special needs.

這個職位是需要執照的。申請人必須通過外語導遊的執業資格考試。我們正在尋找在英語、日語、法語、德語、西班牙語和韓語類別通過測試的申請人。所以你可以在這裡看到我們需要導遊可以講各種語言，包括當地的方言。他們也應該有能力口條清楚，讓人聽得見與充滿信心。此人必須守時，友善跟知識淵博。一個好的導遊必須知道如何透過吸引人、具啟發性和娛樂的方式去分享他們的知識，而不是去重述死記硬背的事實。我們希望給我們客戶的每趟旅遊像他們有過的最好的。在這行中一定程度友好的幽默是必要的。由於你的工作是照顧一群人，你需要與廣泛的人群做連接，包括不同的年齡。一個好的領隊還需要懂得照顧有特殊需要的團員。

unit B 自傳篇

1 範例

1-1. 自傳(1)

I was born in Yunlin, and my father was a farmer. When I had free time, <u>I always helped him at farm that cultivated my hard-working personality.</u>（請閱2-1）My major was Hospitality & Tourism Management when I studied at JinWen University of Science & Technology. Once I was a class leader and an event planner in the student association of the department when I was a student. During my study, I got the license of an English tour guide. Furthermore, I won the intellectual instruction prizes in the class. Graduating from the university, I came to Taipei seeking <u>the employment of work development.</u>（請閱2-1）

My first job was an English tutor working at Melody English School. I assisted elementary school students with their homework and taught them English. In the summer and winter vacations, I was the teacher escort at ABC International Language School. <u>My main responsibility was to bring a student group to a language school in America.</u>（請閱2-1）I provided any necessary assistance during their study there. I was the coordinator between the language schools, students, sometimes the parents. Then I changed my job to ABC Traveling Corporation. Being a ticket operator, the experiences of this job helped me to know about the knowledge of the industry. Whatever my position is, showing the best working attitude is most important. I keep studying English to improve my English skills in order to enhance my competitiveness, and I have scored 790 on the TOEIC test. I am looking forward to serving in your company in the future. I appreciate that you open this resume in busy time and I expect that I can have an interview with you soon. （請閱2-1）

我出生在雲林，我的父親是一個農民。當我有空閒時間，我總是在農場幫他這培養了我吃苦耐勞的性格。我的主修是旅遊與酒店管理，就讀於景文科技大學。當我還是學生時我曾經當過班長和學生會的部門活動策劃。在我的就學期間，我拿到了英語導遊的執照。此外，我還得過智育獎。從大學畢業後，我來到台北尋找工作發展的就業機會。

　　我的第一份工作是在美樂蒂英語學校擔任一名英語家教。我協助小學生的功課以及教他們英語。在寒暑假，我是 ABC 國際語言學校的領隊老師。我的主要職責是將一群學生帶到美國一的所語言學校。我在過程中提供任何需要的協助。我在語言學校、學生、有時候父母之間作協調。然後，我換了我的工作到 ABC 旅遊公司。作為一個旅行社人員，這項工作經驗讓我了解這個行業的知識。不管我在甚麼職位，表現出最佳的工作態度是最重要的。我一直在學習英語以提高我的英語技能跟我的競爭力，並且我多益考試得分 790 。我期待著未來為您公司服務。我很感激您在忙碌的時候打開這個履歷並希望我很快能有面試的機會。

1-2. 自傳(2)

My name is Victor Lee. I am 27 years old. I come from a small family in Tainan. There are five people in my family, my parents and two brothers. My parents value it that children should have good habits. （請閱2-2）

I am honest, friendly and I always get along with everybody. I like to make friends with different people and build up relationships. （請閱2-2） I am happy to learn through working and applying my professional skills when facing challenges. There aren't any bad hobbies of me.

I graduated from the Department of Leisure Industry Management of National Chin-Yi University of Technology, Taiwan. At school, I have learned professions skills in tourism and passed the tour guide test. After serving in the army, I started working as an OP person. I worked with sales very closely. （請閱 2-2） I organized the documents and visa applications of the groups. I made all the necessary reservations and communications with airlines companies.

In my spare time, I like to do things related to English, such as listening to English songs and watching English movies. I think learning another language is very interesting, but I also feel it is very difficult to master it.

About planning for the future, I want to take on the challenge of being a tour guide. Although I'm currently still a beginner in the field, I believe that with my experience, I am ready to face any challenges in the future. I'm very diligent with training and improving myself in my professional abilities. I am looking forward to the opportunity to have outstanding performance at work.

我的名字叫 Victor Lee。我今年 27 歲。我來自一個台南的小家庭。有五個人在我的家庭裡，我的父母和兩個兄弟。我的父母非常看重孩子應該有良好的生活習慣。

我很誠實、友善，我總是每一個人相處的很好。我喜歡與不同的人交朋友，並建立關係。我很高興能運用我的專業技能通過工作時面臨的挑戰來學習。我沒有任何不良的嗜好。

我畢業於台灣國立清雲大學休閒產業管理系。在學校裡，我學到了關於旅遊業的專業技能，並通過了導遊考試。當兵後，我開始工作當票務人員。我跟業務人員工作關係密切。我負責整理團體的文件和簽證申請。我安排所有需要的預訂跟與航空公司接洽。

在我的業餘時間，我喜歡做與英語相關的事情，比如聽英文歌曲跟看英文電影。我認為學習另一種語言是很有趣的，但我也覺得很難去把它學得很好。

關於對未來的規劃，我想藉此挑起身為導遊的挑戰。雖然我目前仍然在該領域仍是一名新人，我相信憑我的經驗，我已經準備好去面對未來的任何挑戰。我很勤奮的訓練和提高自己的專業能力。我期待著有機會擁有出色的工作表現。

2 自傳寫作教室

2-1. 自傳(1) 寫作文法解析／小評語

　　英文寫作中習慣一個段落就是敘述一個重點，像這裏只有兩個段落，這樣會造成一段裡會放入太多資訊而讓人比較每有停頓的空間。建議這一份文章要再分多幾段。台灣學生英文介系詞是很容易犯錯的地方。常用的介系詞 in, at, on 用於不同的地方與時間，建議這方面的文法練習要多做，至少把時間、地方、位置的幾個常見介系詞使用正確。第一段第一句應該是用「in the farm」。自傳履歷中一定會提到畢業科系與學校，建議一定要查詢正確的英文名稱，而不是直接由中文翻譯。許多學生連自己就讀的學校與科系的英文講法都不知道。第一段最後一句「Graduating from the university, I came to Taipei seeking the employment of work development.」。這個句子前一子句省略了"I"這個主詞，然後將「graduated」改成「graduating」。這是算比較有程度的寫法，可惜還是要加一個連接詞「After」。像這樣的句子可以省略的連接詞有「when」或「because」。如果是指美國這個國家，一般比較常用「the United States」。另外「the employment of work development」在英文中正確的表達方式為「the employment opportunities」。第二段最後一句「that you open this resume in busy time」這是比較中式的英文，應該改成「that you take time on reading my job application while busy」，然後「expect that I can」語氣會聽起來有點強迫，如果用「hope that I could」會聽起來比較禮貌。

2-2. 自傳(2) 寫作文法解析／小評語

　　在此建議學生真的不需要再去說明從哪裡來，家裡有幾個兄弟姊妹等。這樣的自傳開頭會顯得太過制式，而且對所應徵的工作內容無關。第一段地第二句建議可以拿掉。而下一句首先是文法上有些問題，「it」應該要拿掉，讓「that…」後的子句變成動詞 value 的受詞。這一句在英文中比較通順的講法是「My parents put a high value on our education.」或「My parents have high expectations for the children. They would like us to have social responsibility and positive pursuit of the future.」。在結構上，建議將下一段直接拉到這一句的後面來強調父母的教育是如何讓你塑造這些正面的人格特質。既然是應徵導遊領隊的工作，當然要強調自己喜歡與不同人相處的個性特質。第二段第二句建議就寫這一特質，不用說到還要建立關係，在英文裡聽起來也有些奇怪。這一句可以改成「I like to make friends with people from different backgrounds and areas.」。而最後一句沒有壞習慣也建議拿掉。OP 人員是台灣票務人員的講法。在英文中這樣的職稱是用「a tour operator」。在台灣常見的另外一個錯誤是直接將業務人員稱作「sales」。「sales」是指業務範圍或工作內容，業務人員應該是「a sales person」，複數為「sales people」或「sales representatives」。這裡建議多加一些轉折句子的連接詞像「In addition,」、「Furthermore,」或「Moreover,」來讓文章比較不會一直只是以「I」開頭。第四段講英文學習提到覺得很難就建議不用多提。

激勵小故事

Office WORK

How Does a Dream Come From?

"Whatever the mind can conceive and believe, it can achieve."Would you agree with the statement that a dream is born from a simple idea conceived in the mind?

The Wright brothers were great thinkers. They enjoyed learning new things. Initially, they recycled broken parts, built a printing press machine and opened their own printing office. Their interest moved to bicycles and they opened the Wright Cycle Company where they sold and repaired bicycles in 1893. But Wilbur (the older brother) had his mind set on something more thrilling. He decided to seriously pursue flying.

The dream started with an idea that was planted in their minds by a toy given by their father. In the words of the boys, "Late in the autumn of 1878, our father came into the house one evening with some object partly concealed in his hands, and before we could see what it was, he tossed it into the air. Instead of falling to the floor, as we expected, it flew across the room till it struck the ceiling, where it fluttered awhile, and finally sank to the floor." This simple toy, which was made of bamboo, cork and stretched rubber bands, captivated the Wright brothers and sparked their lifelong interest in human flight.

After unsuccessful attempts at human flight, the brothers spent many hours researching, testing their machines and making improvements. What started out as a hobby soon became a passion. With determination and patience they made their dream come true in 1903.

In the 19th century two brothers had an idea which eventually became their passionate and dream. Their persistent pursuit of that

> dream became the ultimate accomplishment that changed how the people traveled the world.

夢想是由哪裡而來？

「人類的思想可以設定任何目標，並相信它可以實現。」你同意這個說法一個夢想是從一個腦海中簡單的想法裡誕生嗎？

萊特兄弟是偉大的思想家。他們喜歡學習新的東西。最初，他們回收破損的零件，建了一台印刷機，並開了自己的印刷廠。他們的興趣後來轉到自行車，並於 1893 年，他們開了萊特自行車公司，他們出售和修理自行車。但威爾伯（哥哥）對一些更令人興奮的事物執著。他決定認真追求飛行。

這個夢想開始於他們的父親給他們一個玩具栽在他們心中的想法。男孩們敘述著，「在 1878 年的晚秋，一晚我們的父親走進房子拿著一個東西部分被遮蓋住在他的手裡，在我們看清楚它是什麼之前，他把它丟到空中，而不是掉在了地上，如我們所料，它在房間裡飛了，直到它擊中了天花板，在那裡飄揚一段時間，最後掉到地板上。」竹子、軟木和橡皮筋作成的簡單的玩具，著迷著萊特兄弟，並引發他們對人類飛行的終身興趣。

這對兄弟花了很多時間研究，測試他們人類飛行機器後失敗中作出改善。開始只是一種業餘愛好很快成為一種激情。只要有決心和耐心，他們在 1903 年實現了自己的夢想。

在 19 世紀有兩兄弟的一個想法最終成為他們的激情和夢想。他們不懈怠地追求的夢想最後成為改變旅行世界方式的成就。

英文老師

1-1 常遇到的考題

Q 1

Tell us some of your teaching experience.
請告訴我們一些你的教學經驗。

I have taught English in Taiwan starting from July 2010 at a private language school after my study in Seattle. Since I have both child and adult students, I am able to gain a wide variety of practical teaching experiences. The open policy regarding the curriculum of the school allows teachers to design their own lesson plans. The subjects I have taught range from conversation skills, pronunciation, grammar, and vocabulary classes. Even with my academics training and theoretical knowledge of language teaching, I still went through a number of trial-and-error processes. However, I learned to keep records as my teaching portfolios that I used as reflective resources. These accumulated materials helped me shape up my teaching from scratch to become more proficient. Co-teaching with foreign teachers from different countries and sharing experiences with colleagues at work also have greatly improved my teaching skills.

我在西雅圖畢業後，我從 2010 年 7 月在台灣一所私立語言學校開始教英語。因為我同時有兒童和成人學生，我得以在我教學中獲得各種實務的經驗。學校對於課程是以開放政策允許老師去設計自己的教案。我所教的課程包含會話技巧、發音、文法和字彙。即使我有學術上的訓練和語言教學的理論知識，我還是經歷了一些嘗試錯誤的過程。然而，我學會了記錄教案在我的教學檔案中我可以再利用的教學資源。這些累積的教案幫助我的教學從毫無經驗到變得更加熟練。與來自不同國家的外籍教師合作教學和在工作中與同事分享經驗也有相當地提昇了我的教學技能。

2 What is your teaching philosophy?
你的教學理念是什麼？

My students may come to my class with various purposes, but my goal is always to inspire them a lifelong interest in English learning. I believe that bringing authentic materials into class is very important in teaching English. According to my past learning experiences, I realize that the better efficiency of learning comes from meaningful learning. I grew up in a generation when most of the learning was executed by drilling and memorizing. With very few opportunities for meaningful language practice, English was only one of many subjects in my studying until I applied it in a meaningful context. That is why I advocate using English for communicative function in my teaching. English should be applied for fulfilling certain purposes in life. In sum, my goal is to let my students develop the capability to apply English well outside the classroom in unrehearsed situations.

　　我的學生可能帶著不同的目的來到我的班上，但我的目標始終是激發他們英語的終身學習興趣。我相信帶進生活化的材料是對英語教學非常重要的。根據我以往的學習經驗，我了解到更好的學習效率來自於有意義的學習。我生長在一個世代，當大部分的學習是通過不斷地操練和記憶。因為有意義的語言練習機會很少，英語對我而言只是我許多學校科目之一，直到我把它應用在一個有目地的環境下。這就是為什麼我主張我的教學是在使用英語做溝通的功能。英語應適用於完成某些生活上的目的。所以，我的目標是讓我的學生在課堂外未經練習的情況下有使用英語的能力。

3 What's the most important quality that makes a good teacher?
一個好老師有什麼最重要的特質？

A good teacher must love to teach. The single most important quality that every teacher should possess is a love and passion for teaching young people. Unfortunately, there are teachers who do not love what they do. This single factor can destroy a teacher's integrity quicker than anything else. Teachers who do not enjoy teaching cannot possibly be successful in their profession. There are too many discouraging factors associated with teaching that is difficult enough on a teacher who absolutely loves teaching; not to mention that teaching could crash someone who doesn't have the drive, passion, or enthusiasm for it. On top of that, kids are smarter than what we think they are. Children are very candid and honest when it comes to people they are dealing with. They will spot a teacher with no enthusiasm quicker than anyone and then wipe out any credibility that the teacher may have.

一個好的老師必須熱愛教學。每位老師應具備的最重要的特質是對教育年輕人的熱愛和激情。不幸的是，有一些老師不喜歡他們做的工作。光靠這一點就比什麼都快地摧毀一個老師的誠信。不喜歡教學的老師是不可能在他們的職位上成功的。對於熱愛教學的人，教書這份工作已經有太多令人沮喪的因素，更何況是對於教學沒有動力，激情或熱情的人。最重要的是，孩子們比我們想像地更聰明。孩子們對與他們打交道的人都非常坦率和誠實的。他們會很快地發現一個沒有積極性的老師，然後抹去老師可以有的任何公信力。

Q

4

What are your strengths and weaknesses as a teacher?
你身為一位老師有什麼優勢和缺點？

I'd say my greatest strength is my constant strive to be better. I believe no matter how long a teacher has taught, she/he should always want to grow as a teacher. Every year there is new research, new technology, and new educational tools that could make us a better teacher. I always seek out professional development opportunities and try to apply something new to my class every year. I also always make my lessons well planned and organized. I like to plan ahead, look for aspects that my students might have issues with, and proactively find solutions to solve those problems. My biggest weakness is most definitely time management. I usually have too many things going on at the same time and struggle to juggle them all. It is something that I am actively working on; however, and am making some progress.

我會說我最大的優點是我總是努力做到更好。我相信無論一個老師教的多久，他/她應該總是要成長。每年都會有新的研究，新技術和新的教育工具，可以使我們成為更好的老師。我總是尋找我專業上發展的機會，並每年嘗試新的東西應用到我的課程上。我也總是讓我的課程是精心策劃和有組織的。我喜歡事前將課程準備完善，以及先去找出我的學生在那方面可能會有問題，並積極尋找解決方案來解決這些問題。我最大的弱點絕對是時間管理。我平時上課會有太多的活動想在一堂課中進行與完成。我正在這方面積極努力改善，並已經取得一些進展。

Q

5 How do you accommodate various levels of students within a class?
你如何在一個課程中迎合不同程度的學生？

I use different techniques and class materials to give comprehensible input to students of different levels with various learning styles and interests. As I get to know them, I begin to develop different expectations from different students based on their abilities. The students can work on the same materials and all can contribute, but at different levels. For the materials, I always bring in different levels of practices with specific language skills I'd like to practice with them. I always start the easiest practice as the warm up activity at the beginning of a class. As the class proceeds, the students work on materials that get more difficult and challenging. I also very often put my students in pairs and groups when students of different levels of language proficiency can work together. I particularly mix students who possess stronger language abilities with the weaker ones so they can help out, and sometimes encourage their own confidence and others' motivation.

　　我使用不同的技巧和課堂材料給不同程度、學習風格和興趣的學生可理解的練習。當我足夠了解他們程度時，我對他們的期望會基於他們能力的差異。學生可以在做相同的練習，但有不同程度的回饋。對於教材，我總是在練習時帶來不同程度但具有特定語言功能的材料。我總是從最簡單的開始當做類似熱身活動。當課程進行時，學生會得到更困難和挑戰的練習。我也經常把我的學生們分組所以不同程度的學生可以一起練習。我會特別把比較強的學生跟程度較弱的分在一組，使他們能夠互相幫忙，並且鼓勵自己的信心和他人的動機。

6 Why do you enjoy being a teacher?
你為什麼喜歡當老師？

I've been a teacher for over 5 years. I never stop enjoying my students. I love it when I have been teaching a concept that is very difficult and suddenly they "get it." It makes teaching worth it, even if just a few get a difficult problem solved because you showed them the way. I never just tell them the answers; I like to show them how to get it. My students always feel touched by my enthusiasm and hard work at my teaching, because I believe that such passion can be passed on and penetrate into my students. I also like knowing about my students and taking care of them. I believe I'm molding these young minds to live their lives to the best of their abilities, to solve problems in a logical and good ways, to love and to understand others and to be good citizens. It isn't just about the subject you teach. It's all about the students.

我當老師已經超過 5 年了。我從來沒有停止欣賞我的學生。我喜歡當我教一個非常困難的概念，突然間他們「懂」了。它讓我的教學變的值得，哪怕只是幾個學生理解，因為你教給學生如何找答案。我從來不會直接告訴他們答案，我想讓他們知道如何得到。我的學生總是覺得被我的熱情和對我的認真的工作態度所感動，因為我相信這樣的激情可以被傳遞和滲透到我的學生。我也很喜歡了解我的學生和照顧他們。我相信我在塑造這些幼小的心靈，以他們最大的能力來以邏輯和方法解決問題，並去關愛和了解別人，以及成為好公民。教學不只是關於你教的主題。而是關於學生。

Q 7

What are your classroom rules and how do you make sure your students know them?

你的課堂規定是什麼，以及你如何確保你的學生了解這些規定？

I am a strong believer that ground rules must be laid down in the classroom from day one if I plan to maintain order and control in the classroom. I keep my rules simple and make sure that they are in a format that the student can understand. The rules aren't lengthy so as not to overwhelm the students or confuse them. I give each student two copies of my classroom rules on the first day of class; one they will sign and return to me, the other is for their reference. I always ask the students to raise their hands when they need help. Others are like "walk don't run," "follow directions," and "treat others as you would have them treat you." It's that simple. These rules may seem simplistic, but they can cover a lot of incidences that might occur.

如果我打算維持良好秩序，我非常相信基本規則必須從第一天上課就說明清楚，並在教室裡實現。我把我的規則訂得非常簡單，並確保學生可以理解。我的規則並不冗長，以免讓學生覺得不知所措或困惑。我在上課的第一天給每個學生我的課堂規則兩份影本，一份讓他們簽好並交回給我，另一份則是供他們參考。當他們需要幫助，我總是要求學生舉手。其他像「用走的不用跑的」，「按照指示」和「對待別人用你希望他們對待你的方式。」就這麼簡單。這些規則看似簡單，卻可以涵蓋了很多可能發生的問題。

8

In what ways do you help students prepare for their school tests?
你在哪些方面曾幫助學生為自己學校的考試做準備？

I find that using practice exams and sample questions throughout the terms is a great way to prepare students to get ready for their school testing. I try to implement questions that are similar to what the student will be answering on the test into my lessons whenever possible. To prepare the students for the writing requirement on any standardized tests, I usually ask my children to write various pieces during the school year and then grade those pieces based on the criteria that will be used. This gives students a heads-up on testing so that they are more comfortable and prepared for school tests each term. This is not only good for the students, but is also good for the parents' satisfaction. A lot of the parents have told the school they were so pleased to see their children perform better on their school English tests.

我發現在學期中使用練習卷和模擬考題是一個很好的方式來幫助學生做好學校考試的準備。在我課堂中我嘗試著使用類似學生考試可能出現的問題。為了準備學生在任何統一考試中的寫作要求，我通常會請小朋友在學年中寫各種練習，然後根據考試標準來批改這些練習。這給學生一個試前準備，讓他們可以更有自信每學期為學校的考試來準備。這不僅對學生有益，父母也很滿意。很多家長都告訴學校，他們很高興看到自己的孩子在學校的英語測試中有更好的表現。

1-2 臨場反應篇

Q 1

What is your opinion about grammatical accuracy versus fluency?
你對文法的準確性與流暢性有什麼意見？

I think we need both. The practical grammar that students can use as they speak does not only come from an obsessive focus on being accurate, but also fluent. I definitely agree that using correct grammar helps students make communication clear; however, I've found most grammar usages are acquired and expressed instinctively. Drilling and exercising repetitively might help students be more accurate in forms, but hearing meaningful language is how students become fluent according to the language acquisition research over the past years. If there is enough input in the language by listening and reading, students will develop a sense of what right usage is. When a teacher merely focuses on forms in teaching, it leads to students that focus on forms only when they speak. This makes them use the language more like a machine and they have less spontaneity with native speakers. The result might be great on their accuracy but less fluency especially outside of the classroom.

我認為我們兩者都需要。學生應該要可以實用文法觀念，因為他們說話並不僅僅是在執著於準確的文法重點，但也要可以流暢地表達。我絕對同意使用正確的文法可以幫助學生清晰地溝通；然而我發現大部分的文法用法是本能地獲得和表達。反覆地訓練和做練習可能有助於學生在形式上更準確，但根據過去幾年的語言學習研究聽到有意義的語言是讓學生變得流暢的方式。如果有足夠的聽力和閱讀的語言輸入，學生將發展出語感知道如何正確的使用。當一個老師僅僅注重於形式的教學，它會導致學生也只注重於形式，這會使得他們在使用語言時像是一台機器，而且他們在與母語人士說或時感覺很不自

然。結果就是可能他們可以變得準確性高但不流暢，尤其是在課堂之外的環境。

Q2 Have you had experience boosting a student's self-esteem?
你有過什麼經驗來體驗提升學生的自我成就感？

There are some particular class techniques I have implemented in class and found them successful. As always, I give my students much praise and I try to be as specific as possible. Rather than saying "I'm proud of you," I try telling them what it is that they have done to make me proud. That way, they know which behaviors or work skills to repeat in the future. The other way to boost a student' esteem is to post the student's work. I always try to find the best work sample for every student and post it in some area, such as a bulletin board where everyone can see it. It is amazing how displaying a student's work will increase their tendency to complete work and do it to their best ability. Working one-on-one with students is also a very effective way to boost self-esteem as they feel recognized as an individual, not overlooked in the classroom, and pride in their achievement.

在我的課堂裡有一些特定的技巧我曾經使用也發現他們是成功的。我總是給我的學生們最大的讚美，並盡可能試著將它具體化。不單只是說「我為你感到驕傲」，我會試著告訴他們做了什麼來讓我感到引以為榮。這樣一來，他們在未來就知道要重複甚麼樣的行為或技能。另一種提高學生的自尊心的方法是張貼學生的作品。我總是試圖找出每一個學生的最好的作品，並張貼在一些公共區域，如公告板所以每個人都可以看到。張貼一個學生的作品會非常激勵他們的來完成工作的意願，並去盡他們最大的能力。與學生一對一也是一種增進自我成就感的方式，因為他們會覺得自己被重視，不會在課堂上被忽略，並對他們的成就感到自豪。

Q 3 In what way do you make your teaching more effective?
你用什麼方式讓你的教學更有效率？

I think an effective teacher understands the content that they teach and knows how to explain that content in a manner that their students understand. I know there are teachers who do not know the content well enough to effectively teach it. I've seen teachers who are truly experts on the content, but struggle to explain it to their students. I always try to both understand the content and explain it well. This sometimes can be difficult to accomplish, but surely maximizes my effectiveness as a teacher. I also try to use a variety of media in my lessons. This generation of students was born in the digital age, and has been bombarded by modern technology unlike any other generation. They have embraced it, and if we as teachers do not, then we are falling behind. I'm not saying that we should eliminate textbooks and worksheets completely, but we should not be afraid to implement other forms of media within our lessons.

我認為一個有效率的老師能徹底了解他們教的內容，並且知道如何解釋這些內容讓他們的學生理解。我知道有一些老師可能不是很清楚知道內容來有效率地教學。我見過一些老師是某方面的專家，卻不知如何解釋觀念給他們的學生。我總是試圖理解內容同時清楚地解釋。這有時是很難達成的，但確定的是我的教學帶來最大的效率。我也嘗試在我的課程裡使用各種媒體。同於其他任何一代，這一世代的學生出生在資訊化的時代，已被現代科技不斷轟炸。他們完全接受，如果我們作為教師不這樣做，那麼我們就落伍了。我不是說我們應該完全捨棄教科書和課堂練習，但在我們的課程中我們不應該排斥使用其他形式的媒體。

4

**What have you done for attracting students'
interests in learning?
你曾做了什麼去引發學生的學習興趣？**

I always work hard to figure out how to relate to each of my students. Common interest sometimes can be hard to find, but I think an exceptional teacher will find a way to connect with the students. For instance, I may have a student who likes watching sport games. I can relate to that student if I do something playing video clips of sport games and then going through them with that student. Even if I have no actual interest in sports, the student will think I do and thus naturally create a connection. Also, I think every kid learns differently so we have to find and utilize different strategies and differentiated learning to reach every student. What works for one student, will not work for every student. I am always willing to be creative and adaptive in my lessons, and thinking outside the box on a continual basis.

我總是努力地找出如何與我的每一個學生來產生連結。有時可能很難找到共同的興趣，但我認為一個優秀的老師總是會找到一個方法來與學生有連接。舉例來說，我可能有一個學生喜歡看體育比賽。我可以通過像撥放體育比賽的影片，然後透過他們去與學生產生共同興趣。即使我對運動沒有實際的喜好，學生也會覺得我有，從而自然地與我建立連接。另外，我覺得每個孩子學習的方式不同，所以我們必須找到和利用不同的策略和差異化的學習，來針對每一個學生。對一個學生有用的方法，不會對每一個學生也都可行。我總是願意勇於創新，在我的經驗教訓找到對應的方式，並在持續的跳脫框架去思考。

1-3 我有疑問篇

Q 1

What are some qualities of a good teaching candidate the school is looking for?
什麼是學校在應徵者上尋找的一些特質？

Of course we're gathering the applicants who have a good attitude in teaching. An educator with a positive attitude inspires students to look at the world in the same way. We're looking for the best candidate who has good communication and organization skills to start with. A teacher's job is to discuss key concepts and explain them in more than one way so learners all understand the idea and how to apply it to future problems. To achieve this goal, this teacher must be able to communicate clearly and effectively. She/he must be able to keeping track of student's papers, grades, and any kinds of schoolwork as well. The school wants to have a teacher who has a forgiving heart. Children make mistakes everyday in behaviors and schoolwork. A teacher must be able to move forward and allow a child to grow. We also need the teacher to have strong willingness to communicate with the parents.

當然，我們正在網羅教學態度較好的申請人。一個教育者應以積極的態度去激發學生以相同的方式看待這個世界。我們正在尋找擁有良好的溝通和組織能力的最佳人選。教師的工作是去討論關鍵的概念，並用不同的方式去解釋它們，使學習者都明白這個想法，以及如何將它應用到未來的問題。為了實現這一目標，這位老師必須能夠清楚和有效的溝通。她/他必須能夠整理學生的試卷，成績，以及任何種類的功課。學校都想擁有一位有一顆寬容心的老師。孩子每天都會在學業和日常行為犯錯。老師必須能夠繼續前進，讓孩子成長。我們還需要老師有很強的意願與父母溝通。

2 What resources does this school have that I can use to help me?
這所學校有什麼樣的資源我可以用來幫助我的嗎？

For your teaching, there is a predetermined curriculum you can follow when you first get started. However, the school strongly encourages the teacher to develop their own lessons. The school wants the teachers to demonstrate their willingness and ability to be a proactive educator who supplies their own materials for the specific needs of the students. We don't want to kill a teacher's creativity by asking she/he to follow a predetermined and constructed day-by-day lesson plan for her/him; in the meantime, we also understand it's bad if there is nothing at all for a teacher to use as a guidance. The school has a very good balance between the two. There is a teacher mentor program that you can be a part of. It's important that the teachers here to demonstrate that they are an enthusiastic teacher who is willing to learn from other educators. The newcomers can observe and partner with an experienced teacher who will help show you some professional tricks in this profession.

對於你的教學，學校有設計好的課程，當你剛上手時你可以照著教。然而，學校強烈鼓勵老師們編寫自己的課程。學校希望老師們有這份能力及意願為學生具體的需求去積極主動提供自己的材料。我們不想要求她/他每天跟著預定的課程計劃而去扼殺了一名老師的創造力；在此同時，我們也知道如果老師什麼導引都沒有可以拿來參考是不好的。學校在這兩者之間擁有一個很好的平衡。你可以參加老師學習課程。對這裡很重要的是老師願意展現他們可以熱心老師的與其他教育工作者學習。新人可以觀察與有經驗的老師合作夥伴去學習一些在這個行業的專業技巧。

Q 3 If I am hired, what would your expectations be for me?
如果我被錄用，你對我有哪些的期望？

The school wants a highly qualified teacher who understands her/his subject area inside and out. The teacher should be able to apply concepts in their certification area, offer students real-life examples and show how students can apply what they learn to the everyday world. We know well that teachers want their students to respect them, but teachers who get the most respect are the ones who give the most respect to their students. We expect the teacher who can foster an atmosphere of mutual respect in class. Of course we'd like you to be dependable. A teacher can be the most entertaining, brilliant, supportive educator ever, but if she/he does not show up for work, students will suffer. Students need the assurance that their teacher will be present at all times. This keeps distractions from learning and interruptions in the natural flow of a classroom at a minimum.

學校想要一個高素質的老師能徹底了解她/他的教學內容。這位老師應該能夠應用他們所學的概念，為學生提供現實生活中的例子，並展示如何能運用所學到日常世界中。我們深知老師希望自己的學生尊重他們，但真正能得到尊敬是那些給予他們的學生尊重的教師。我們期待這位老師可以促進課堂中相互尊重的氣氛。當然我們希望你是可靠的。一位教師可以是最有趣的，聰明，給予支持的教育者，但如果她/他不來上班，學生將會受到影響。學生需要確定他們的老師在所有時間將會出現。這會讓學生在學習中分心與受影響的程度降到最小。將影響減到最小。

Q 4 Can you tell me more features of your programs here?
你能告訴我這裡課程的更多特色嗎？

All classes are taught through the medium of English and students are expected to and encouraged to communicate in English at all times within the school. Students are reminded by the staff and teachers to speak English when they are heard using their first language. The school has 7 levels of ability and the students are divided into classes based on ability in English. Each level is either 9 or 10 weeks long. Most levels start and finish at the same time, although some levels, particularly popular ones, run staggered to ensure that incoming students can be placed more exactly into the most appropriate class. All levels can be best described as mixed syllabus design. Grammar items and vocabulary are integrated into skills work through a topic based approach. Each level has a level descriptor. The level descriptor describes the key skills, knowledge and 'can-do' statements that each student should have achieved to successfully complete the level.

這裡所有課程均以英語為教學媒介和學生被要求並鼓勵他們在學校內的任何時候都要用英語進行溝通。學生被學校人員和老師使用聽到他們使用母語時會提醒他們說英語。學校基於學生英語能力將他們分為 7 個級別。每個級別大約是 9 或 10 週之久。大多數課程可以同時開始結束，儘管有些級數，尤其是人多的，會分開上課，以確保新生可以更準確地放到最合適的班級。各等級最好地設計是為混合不同的內容。文法項目和字彙希望能基於主題式教學都能融入課程。每個級別都有一個等級說明。每個等級說明會描述關鍵技能，知識和每個學生應該已經成功取得這個等級所能「做到」的陳述。

unit B

自傳篇

1 範例

1-1. 自傳(1)

I graduated from Ching Yun University with a degree in Business administration in 2002. After my graduation, I worked for David's English Center as an administrative secretary. From 2002 to 2005, I taught English at ABC Cram School in Chupei and learned people skills, scheduling and organizational skills. From 2005 to 2006, I taught English at Bell's Language School in Chunan; from 2005 to 2013, I worked for Koala Bear English Language School in Hsinchu as an English teacher for elementary and junior high school students; from 2011 to 2013, I taught English for elementary and junior high school students at XYZ Cram School. I have learned teaching skills, classroom management and how important lesson planning is. <u>With all the past work experiences, I can solve problems more easily when I am faced with difficulties.</u>（請閱2-1）

The English ability of my students has been greatly improved through my systematic and organized teaching methods. Moreover, the enrollment at my school has been steadily increasing because of my consistently enthusiastic attitude. My goal has always been to keep my classes highly interactive about learning in order to keep students interested and excited.

I am a very responsible person that I do my best to finish my job well every day. I realize that students will not be responsible unless their teacher is very responsible. Also, I am patient and conscientious. I always teach my students over and over again until they totally understand. In my leisure time, I enjoy traveling, hiking, reading, gardening, watching movies and listening to music.

After work, I am a motivational learner as well. I studied English and Spanish at the Language Center at National Tsing Hua University for seven years. In addition, I have passed high-intermediate level of GEPT and scored high on TOEIC. In my opinion, I believe a good teacher should not only have professional skills, but also possess multiple interests and hobbies to be creative.

我在 2002 年畢業於清雲科技大學，主修工商管理。我畢業後，我曾在大衛美語中心作行政秘書。從 2002 年到 2005 年，我在竹北 ABC 補習班教英語，學習到人際交往能力，計劃和組織能力。從 2005 年到 2006 年，我在竹南貝爾語言學校教英語；2005 至 2013 年，我在新竹的無尾熊英語學校擔任小學和國中學生的英語教師；2011 至 2013 年，我在 XYZ 補習班針對小學和國中的學生教英語。我已經學會了教學的技能，教室管理能力，以及課程規劃的重要。有了所有過去的工作經驗，當我面對困難時我可以更容易地解決問題。

我的學生的英語能力已經通過我有系統，有組織的教學方法大大提高。此外因為我的一貫熱情的態度，我的學校的招生一直在穩定地增加。我的目標是一直讓我的班級有高度的互動學習，以保持學生的興趣和熱情。

我是一個很負責任的人，盡我所能每天將我的工作完成做好。我了解到，學生不會學會負責任的態度，除非他們的老師也是非常負責的。另外，我有有耐心以及認真。我總是一遍又一遍地教我的學生，直到他們完全理解。在我閒暇的時候，我喜歡旅行、健行、閱讀、園藝、看電影和聽音樂。

下班後，我也是一個有動力的學習者。我在清大的語言中心學英語和西班牙語有七年。此外，我還通過全民英檢的中高級，並在多益考試取得高分。在我看來，我認為一個好老師不僅要具備專業技能，而且還具備多種興趣和愛好，勇於創新。

1-2. 自傳(2)

Life is a journey full of surprises. （請閱 2-2） The period, from my studying in college to developing a profession after graduation, was a major transition in my life. During my experiences at school and later on, I have developed skills necessary for teaching and also gained a desire to become an English teacher.

I graduated from Shih-Hsin University, a school famous for mass media and communication. During my study there, classes such as journalism and various workshops provided me the opportunity to practice the skills of communication and public speaking. At the last semester, I participated in the preparation of the graduate exhibition. It was my first experience of working in a publicity campaign by contacting and negotiating with administration about implementing the exhibition.

I was accepted by the Washington & Jefferson College in September 2011. I completed a one-year non-certified program in Washington, Pennsylvania. The experience there later became enormously helpful for my profession. First of all, staying and studying in America significantly improved my English which evolved from a textbook style to a more fluent style that could be used in daily life. Secondly, the language problems I encountered in a real-life setting provided me with a great deal of inspiration to design teaching materials for my classes.

After returning from the United States in 2012, I have started teaching at Gram English. My students come to my class with specific purposes and expectations. I need to implement a great deal of practical and intriguing class activities to keep students' learning interests. My class subjects cover conversation skills, pronunciation, grammar, and test preparation.

The more I become involved in this profession, the more I feel like dedicating myself to teaching English as a second/foreign language. In this field, my journey has just begun. Thank you for your consideration.

生命是一個充滿驚喜的旅程。從我在大學畢業之後到成為一個專業老師的期間，是我人生的一大轉變。在我在學校和後來的經驗裡，我發展出必要的教學技能，並渴望成為一名英語教師。

我從世新大學畢業，是一所以大眾媒體和傳播著名的學校。在我念書期間，如新聞和各種研討課程提供了我練習溝通和公開演講技巧的機會。在最後一個學期，我參加了畢業展覽的準備工作。這是我的第一次經驗，去與有關單位進行聯繫與準備有關展覽的宣傳工作。

我在 2011 年 9 月到 Washington & Jefferson 學院就讀。我在賓州的華盛頓完成了為期一年的非學位認證課程。這些經驗後來對我的專業有很大的幫助。首先，在美國居住與學習大大地提高了我的英語能力，從教科書式的語言發展到可以在日常生活中更流暢使用的風格。其次，我在現實生活中遇到的語言問題為我提供了很大的啟發來設計我的教材。

在 2012 年從美國回國之後，我開始任教於格蘭英語。我的學生來上課都有特定的目的和期望。我必需要運用很多實用和有趣的課堂活動，以保持學生的學習興趣。我教的科目包涵會話技巧、發音、文法和考試準備課程。

我越深入這個行業，我越想投身於英語教學的領域。在這一行中，我的旅程才剛剛要開始。感謝您的考慮。

2 自傳寫作教室

2-1. 自傳(1) 寫作文法解析／小評語

　　每份自傳都應該仔細校對標點符號、拼字和文法，確定都正確無誤。這是一份英文老師的自傳，當然其中更需要準確地使用單字文法和標點符號。自傳的起頭很重要，第一段應該要有一個主要論點，表明你是這份工作的最佳人選，並補充履歷中不足的部分。這裡的第一段雖然無太大錯誤，但是每一句子結構都很類似，而且這些資料履歷中一定都已經說明，不需在自傳中累贅地重複敘述一遍。建議把時間與工作地方全部拿掉，只需說明過往的工作是獲得了哪些與現在所應徵工作相關的經驗。每一段的第一句盡量要讓讀者很快地知道這一段的重點為何，最後一句則是做一個有力的結尾，或是與下一段的關聯轉折。這裡第一段最後兩句在強調這些工作經驗帶給這位應徵者哪些有利的特質，這樣的句子顯得語氣有些薄弱，如果是像這樣的句子，「With all the past work experiences, I have become a strong problem solver whenever I deal with difficulties.」聽起來是不是有力多了？像第三段的最後一句，很明顯地跟本段其它內容無關，讀起來變得突然很突兀地出現這一句，而且其實跟下一段反而比較有關聯，所以建議就直接一到下一段的第一句。這整個自傳再一次缺少有力的結尾去做一結論為何會有自信申請這份工作。至少真的不知如何結尾，至少可以用「Thank you for your time and consideration.」或甚至一個簡單的「Thank you.」即可。

2-2. 自傳(2) 寫作文法解析／小評語

　　寫自傳的要點盡量不要抄襲他人的自傳，也不要抄襲書中的範本。多數業者沒有時間一一檢視每位應徵者的自傳，所以自傳應以一頁為限。就像面試一般，每個人只有簡短的時間不僅介紹自己甚至推銷自己。這時有個引人注意的開頭就像一個良好的第一印象讓業者想多了解你。學生很容易將整篇自傳塞滿跟自己家庭、學校、工作經驗和嗜好等的繁瑣細節，自傳中所提的細節重點應都與你所應徵的工作有關。這一篇自傳以一簡短的開頭「Life is a journey full of surprises.」來吸引讀者的注意，更重要的是，這一文章的第一與最後一段以 journey 來互相呼應，讓這篇文章像敘述一有趣的人生經歷，達到引人注意的目的。中文寫作裡有著起承轉合的技巧，而英文寫作其實也可以運用同樣的方式讓文章生趣，但學生常忘記的是在英文中更重視的是句子與段落間的連結與轉折。像這篇文章想要表達在大學畢業之後沒有從事自己主修科系的工作，反而變換跑道轉向英語教學。但是這中間並沒有看到任何說明這轉折的原因。在寫作時，應該先將方向與結構先訂出來，再去做句子編寫等的細節工作。如果對自己的文法或寫作沒有太大的自信，寫完一定要請人潤飾修改。但是寫出來的程度還是要符合自己的英文程度。書中提供的範例有不同程度的文章，如果無法寫出很進階程度的文章，至少要簡單扼要，並且要言之有物。仔細研究每個應徵職位的特色和對應徵者特殊的要求，寫出符合每個公司需要的自傳，這樣才能增加面試的機會，甚至是工作的機會。

激勵小故事

What are the "Big Rocks" in Your Life?

One day, an expert in time management stood in front of the group of high-powered overachievers he said, "Okay, time for a quiz" and he pulled out a one-gallon, jar and set it on the table in front of him. He also produced about a dozen fist-sized rocks and carefully placed them, one at a time, into the jar.

When the jar was filled to the top and no more rocks would fit inside, he asked, "Is this jar full?" Everyone in the class yelled, "Yes."

The time management expert replied, "Really?" He reached under the table and pulled out a bucket of gravel. He dumped some gravel in and shook the jar causing pieces of gravel to work themselves down into the spaces between the big rocks. He then asked the group once more, "Is the jar full?"

"No! " the class yelled.

He said, "What is the point of this demonstration?" One eager student raised his hand and said, "The point is, no matter how full your schedule is, you can always fit some more things in it if you try really hard!"

"No," the expert replied, "that's not the point. The point of this demonstration shows us that if you don't put the big rocks in first, you'll never get them in at all."

What are the "big rocks" in your life, time with your loved ones, your faith, your education, your dreams, your career or simply yourself? Remember to put these big rocks in first otherwise you'll never get them in at all. So whenever you are reflecting on this short story, ask yourself this question: What are the "big rocks" in my life? Then, put those in your jar first.

你生命中的「大石塊」是什麼？

有一天，一位時間管理專家向一群資優學院學生說：「好吧，我們來做個測試。」他拿出一個一加侖的玻璃瓶，把它放在桌子面前。隨後，他取出一堆拳頭大小的石塊，將它們小心翼翼一次一個放進瓶子裡。

當瓶子裝滿到頂並放不下更多的岩石時，他問道，「瓶子滿了嗎？」班上同學喊著，「是的！」

時間管理專家反問，「真的？」再一次，他伸手從桌下拿出一桶碎石。首先，他搖一搖瓶子讓石頭間產生空隙。他將一些碎石倒進使砂礫填滿到大石塊的間隙。然後，他又問道，「瓶子滿了嗎？」

「不！」學生們大聲說。

他說：「這個例子說明什麼意義呢？」一個心急於表現的人舉起手說，「問題的關鍵是，不管你的行程安排是多滿，如果你確實努力，你總是可以在裡面塞滿一些更多的事情！」

「不是，」專家回答，「那不是重點。這個例子告訴我們的是如果你沒有先有大石塊，你永遠不會得到全部。」

在你的生命中你的「大石塊」是什麼？與你所愛的人相處的時間、你的信仰、你的學業、你的夢想、你的事業還是就只是你自己呢？記得先去處理這些大石塊，否則你將永遠不會得到全部。所以不論什麼時候你想著這個小故事，先問自己這一個問題：什麼是我生命中的大石頭呢？然後，把那些先放在你的瓶子裡。

1-1 常遇到的考題

Q 1

Describe how your work experience relates to this job.
請描述跟此工作你的相關工作經歷。

First, I'd like to cite some of the experience in regard to scheduling, dealing with inquiries and information related to the management in the department. My regular work duties include maintaining department schedules by keeping calendars for department personnel, arranging meetings, conferences, teleconferences, and travel. Next, I am also in charge of maintaining office supplies inventory by checking stock to determine inventory level, anticipating needed supplies, placing and expediting orders for supplies and verifying receipt of supplies. My job is to keep equipment operational by following manufacturer instructions and established procedures. Lastly, I would also like to highlight my ability in writing and editing correspondence. I am very good at transcribing, formatting, and editing texts, data, and graphics. As the secretary of the department, I also have to secure information by completing database backups. After work, I have consistently updated my technical knowledge by attending educational workshops and reading secretarial publications.

首先，我想舉一些經驗關於安排行程，處理查詢及管理部門中相關的資訊。我的日常工作職責包括維護部門的進度保藉由維持部門人員的行事曆，安排會議、討論會、電話會議和出差。接下來，我也負

責維護辦公用品庫存藉由檢查庫存，確定庫存數量，預計所需的物資，訂購及發送用品訂單和驗證耗材的收據。我的工作是依照製造商的指示和既定程序保持設備運行。最後，我也想強調我的寫作和編輯信件能力。我非常善於記錄，設計和編輯文本、數據及圖形。作為該部門的秘書，我也必須完成資料庫的備份以妥善保管部門資訊。下班之餘，我一直透過參加教育講座和閱讀秘書相關出版物來更新我的專業知識。

Q 2 What sort of correspondence were you responsible for generating?
你有負責做什麼樣的商業文件呢？

I performed tasks such as creating and editing tables, columns and charts as well as sorting table data and performing calculations in tables. I created and formatted forms by using a variety of software packages, such as Microsoft Word, Outlook, Powerpoint, Excel, Access, etc., to produce correspondence and documents and maintain presentations, records, spreadsheets and databases. I was also in charge of organizing and storing work-related paperwork, documents and computer-based information. I provided historical references by utilizing filing and retrieval systems. The systems were well designed and maintain during the time I worked at the position. I was responsible for sorting and distributing incoming mail and organizing and sending outgoing mail for my manager. Since I had to attend all the managerial meetings, I took minutes and kept notes. Lastly, I was responsible for managing and maintaining budgets, as well as invoicing. In my work experience working as a secretary, I have always maintained a high level of written communication skills, accuracy, spelling and grammar ability.

我執行過像是建立和編輯表格、欄列和圖表，以及整理表格資料與進行表格計算。我透過使用多種軟體來建立和格式化形式包括如

Microsoft Word、Outlook、PowerPoint 、Excel 和 Access 等，用於編寫信函和文件，保存演講文稿，記錄，電子表格和數據庫的。我還負責整理和儲存與工作相關的紙本，文件和電腦資訊。我利用歸檔和檢索系統提供參考舊有文件。我在那職位時該系統是由我精心設計和維護。收到給我的經理的郵件我負責整理和分發以及向外組織與發送。由於我必須參加所有的管理會議，我負責會議記錄與摘要。最後，我也負責管理和維護預算，以及發票。在我作為秘書的工作經驗工作裡，我一直保持高水平及準確拼寫和語法的書面表達能力。

Q

3 | What do you like most and least about your current or last job?
你目前或上一份工作你最喜歡和最不滿意那一部分？

I like new challenges, interacting with people, growth and learning opportunities. In my previous job, I had implemented and improved a number of the systems including the order processing system. I also enjoy taking the initiative, working as part of a team and meeting the set objectives and goals. Unfortunately, there was very little opportunity for me to use my potential and initiative at the company I worked before. I regard this as one of my strengths and found it frustrating that I was unable to get past the bureaucracy of such a big company to implement any improvements. There was a lack of growth opportunities in such as large corporation. That is why I am enthusiastic about working for a smaller company like this which I know the management oftentimes encourages employees to use their full potential and initiative.

　　我喜歡新的挑戰、與人互動、成長和學習的機會。在我以前的工作，我已經實施並改進了一些工作系統，包括訂單處理系統。我也喜歡採取主動，作為團隊工作的一份子，並達成既定目的和目標。不幸的是，在我以前工作的公司很少有這樣的機會讓我發揮我的潛能和積

極性。我認為這是我的優點，並發現在這樣的大公司裡的官僚作風令人沮喪，因為我無法實施任何改進。在一個大型企業裡工作會缺乏成長的機會。這就是為什麼我很熱衷於在這樣的小型企業工作裡服務因為我知道管理階層常常會鼓勵員工發揮自己全部的潛能和主動性。

Q

4 How would you describe your previous manager or supervisor?
你會如何形容你以前的經理或主管？

I liked my former manager as a person, respected him professionally, and appreciated the time I worked with him. My manager was very experienced. He had managed a big number of staff over the past 12 years. He liked his staff to be able to work independently and I had to learn quickly to become independent about analyzing problems and finding solutions. I have never thought of our relationship in terms of like or dislike. I have always focused on getting along together and getting the job done. However, my former manager wasn't used to give sufficient support to his staff due to his amount of experience. On the other hand, I actually took this opportunity to be proactive and deal with this situation. It was the time I learned to work independently and solve problems in a timely fashion.

　　我喜歡跟我的前任經理相處、尊重他的專業、並感激我與他共事的時間。我的經理相當地有經驗。他在過去 12 年管理眾多員工。他喜歡他的員工不僅要能獨立工作，所以我必須迅速學會獨立分析問題和尋找解決方案。我從來想過喜歡或不喜歡我們的關係。我一直專注與他共事，並完成工作。不過，我的前任經理因為他豐富的經驗所以不習慣給予他的員工太多的支持。不過另一方面，我利用了這個機會變成積極主動處理這樣的狀況。這段期間我學會了獨立工作，以及即時去解決問題。

5 What experience do you have with planning meetings?
你有沒有規劃會議的經驗？

I have taken to set up and co-ordinate meetings such as organizing the venue and times, informing participants, preparing agendas and organizing documentation. As the secretary, I have to ensure that the notice of the meeting is given, and copies of the agenda are prepared. If there are any traveling arrangements, I have to make sure that any suitable accommodation has been arranged and confirmed. At the meeting, I arrive in good time before the meeting with all the relevant correspondence and business matters for that meeting. I have much experience in taking minutes, typing them up and distributing them. After the meeting, I send a reminder notice of each decision requiring action to the relevant person. This could be done by telephone, or by email. I also have to promptly send all correspondence as decided by the Management Committee. I believe I have excellent organizational and planning skills that sometime I feel I was born for being a secretary.

我曾經計劃和協調會議，如舉辦地點和時間，告知與會者，準備議程和組織文件。作為一位秘書，我要確保會議通知已經發出，並準備議程的影本。如果有任何旅行的安排，我必須確定合適的住宿已經安排及確認。在會議上，我要會議前準時到達準備好所有相關的文件和業務事宜，該次會議。我在會議記錄、打字和分發資料上有豐富的經驗。會議結束後，我寄提醒通知給每一個決定需要採取行動的有關人士。這可以通過電話或電子郵件來完成。我也必須及時發送所有管理階層所決定的相關通信。我相信我有出色的組織和規劃能力有時我覺得我天生就適合作為一個秘書。

Q 6 **How did you make your opinions known or get your messages across with your former supervisor?**
你是如何將你的意見讓你的前上司知道或了解？

My last manager made it clear that she valued my opinion by welcoming my input anytime appropriate. If the opinions were sought in a meeting, I would offer some constructive suggestions by being aware of not turning them into any criticism. I never criticized any coworkers or supervisors based on my personal feelings and preferences. At work, I only thrived on professionalism and work ethics. Sometimes my manager and I had private meetings discussing work issues more closely related to both of us. If there was something I felt uncomfortable in our work relation, I usually addressed the matters right away and asked for her input to what I could do to make the improvement. I considered I was the person who took the responsibility for any communication problems and it was my job to make them clear. Since I was also in charge of liaising with staff in other departments and with external contacts, I reminded myself always implementing clear but diplomatic communication methods.

　　我上個經理很清楚表示她隨時歡迎我適當發表並重視我的意見。如果這意見是在一個會議上被尋求，我會盡量提供了一些有建設性的建議有意識地不能把他們變成任何批評。我從來沒有基於我個人的感受和喜好來批評任何同事或上司。在工作裡，我只專於發展敬業精神和職業道德。有時候，我的經理和我會面會討論更密切相關於我們倆工作的問題。如果有些事情我在我們的工作關係上就感到不舒服，我通常會說出來並馬上問她自己能做什麼來改進解決。我認為有任何溝通上的問題這是我的責任使事情清楚。由於我還負責與其他部門員工以及與外部的接觸聯絡，我是始終提醒自己實施清楚但有手腕的溝通方法。

Q

7

How do you prioritize your work when things haven't gone as planned?
當事情按沒有按照計劃進行你如何優先安排你的工作？

I always focus on key aspects like finding out the urgency of the task, determining deadlines, working out how long the task will take and setting realistic targets for myself. I always make a list of activities completed at the start of the day or before you go home ready for the next day. When situations arise that demand a change in my priorities, especially things aren't gone as planned, I pause for a few minutes making some reflections thinking what went wrong and why. I'll come up alternative approaches and solutions as soon as possible; in the meantime, get together with my colleagues and boss to review the whole situation and my new proposed solutions. However, I'm also careful to look for the things that went right, too. I believe every urgency even mistake is a good lesson to learn.

我總是專注於關鍵方面，如找出任務的緊迫性、確定最後期限、計畫工作將花費的時間和為自己設定實際可行的目標。我總是在一天的開始或在前一天回家之前完成工作行程。當突發狀況出現我需求改變工作的重點，尤其是事情都不按計劃進行時，我會停下來做一些思考想一下什麼地方出了錯以及為什麼。我會盡快拿出替代方法和解決方案；在此同時，我會集合我的同事和上司來審視整個形勢和我的新提出的解決方案。不過，我也仔細去找出那些有做對的事情。我相信每一個緊急事件甚至錯誤都是一個很好的教訓。

Q 8 **Describe how you handled your manager's work schedule.**
請描述你是如何處理你的經理的工作行程。

First of all, I have to say my manager was the most relaxed manager in the company that she could solely focused on her managerial tasks without worrying the details. As her secretary, I sat down with her every month and found out the dates of all the appointments and meetings. If there were any travel arrangements, I first thing made all the reservations and communicated with other subsidiaries or people I had to contact with. I always made sure that every detail of her traveling went smoothly. I well organized her calendars by synchronizing all her electronic devices, including her company computer, laptop, and iphone. For arranging an in-house meeting, I first found out how long it would take to prepare the meeting materials and get in contact with all the attendees. Then I come up with a deadline. I put the deadlines in her and my calendars two weeks in advance to ensure everything was done on time.

首先，我不得不說我的經理是公司裡最輕鬆的經理，因為她可以只專注於她的管理任務，不用擔心太多細節。作為她的秘書，我每個月坐下來與她一起找出所有的約會和會議的日期。如果有任何旅行的安排，我第一件事就是作所有的預約和與其他分部或需要接洽的人來聯繫。我會一直確認她出差的每一個細節都很順利。我也通過同步她所有的電子設備，其中包括她的公司電腦，筆記本電腦和 iphone 整理她的行事曆。在安排一個內部會議上，我會先出找出它需要多長時間準備會議資料，並與所有與會者接觸。然後我會訂出了一個最後期限。我把最後期限的時間在她和我的行事曆上提前兩個星期以確保一切都按時完成。

1-2 臨場反應篇

Q **1** **Tell me about a time that you had to use your judgment to make a tough decision in your previous job.**
請告訴我某一次在你上一份工作你必須使用你的判斷做一個艱難的決定。

In my previous job, I was responsible for ordering office supplies for the company. The company always ordered a month's supply at a time to keep inventory costs low. I had to decide whether to keep doing this or buy six month's supply and get a discount for ordering such a big volume and escape possible future price increases. I did some research and worked out we could reduce our costs by buying for six months, especially since the amount we used remained practically unchanged every month. I had to make a logical decision and take action. I wrote a proposal to my manager showing all the relevant facts that helped her weigh up the alternative and commit to the most appropriate action. It turned out that I was right with the result that the prices went up by 3% during those six months.

在我以前的工作的公司，我負責訂購辦公用品。公司始終在同一時間訂購了一個月的供應量，以保持庫存成本低。我必須決定是否要繼續這樣做或買六個月的供應量，並得到訂購這麼大量的折扣和避免將來可能的價格上漲。我做了一些研究，並制定了可以通過購買半年的量來降低我們的成本，尤其是因為每個月我們的使用量基本保持不變。我必須做出一個合乎邏輯的決定並採取行動。我寫了一個提案顯示所有的相關事實來幫助我的經理衡量這個替代方案，並採取最適當的行動。後來證實我是正確的，其結果是在這 6 個月中價格上升了 3 ％。

Q

2 | How well do you take directions and criticisms? 你接收受指示和批評的能力好嗎？

In general, I take directions well. Of course there are directions easy to follow when they are well explained in detail and people have sufficient time to execute them. However, it's not usually the case in most real life work scenarios. There are times with deadlines and other pressures, the directions are being brief and even vague. While some people might get upset with the situation, I always try to find out other considerations or aspects. I'm not aware of without feeling offensive. I've always held the same attitude when I deal with criticisms. I try to listen carefully and ask questions for clarification. Then I give my feedback to make sure both parties get the same facts. I also ask for advice, and ideas that we could mutually agree with the solutions means of improvements.

　　一般情況下，我很能接受指示。當然有了詳細很好的解釋，有些指令很容易跟隨，人們有足夠的時間來執行。然而在真實生活的工作場景裡，它通常不是這樣的狀況。在期限及其他壓力下，指令是簡短暫，甚至是含糊的。雖然有些人可能會這這種情況下不高興，我總是試圖找出其他因素或面像，我不會感到反感。當我處理批評時，我總是持相同的態度。我試著仔細聆聽並提出問題進行澄清。然後我會提供我的回饋意見，以確保雙方都得到相同的認知。我也請教他們的想法，來共同解決與改進的辦法。

3 Why have you changed your jobs so often?
你為什麼如此頻繁的換你的工作？

For my very first job, I had to do a lot of commuting. Even though I acknowledged the fact soon I started the job, I wanted to gain the valuable experience as a novice secretary first worked in a corporation. Frankly, the long commuting was very time consuming and exhausting. After I gained adequate experience as I moved up from the entry-level position to a senior secretary. Then, I found a job much closer to my place. It was a new company that was just starting up. Just when I thought I had the chance to help a company starting from the scratch, I realized it was a mistake. The management was not experienced enough to make prompt executive decisions and judgments. All the staff felt we were led by the blinds and I couldn't make any contributions there. I have been with my current company for a reasonable length of time. Now I want to settle down and make my diverse background pay off in my contributions to my new employer.

對於我的第一個工作，我不得不做很多的通勤。雖然我一開始工作我就很快就面對了這個現實，在公司第一次擔任一個新手秘書，我希望能獲得寶貴的經驗，坦白說，遠距離上下班是很耗時和花體力。之後我獲得了足夠的經驗，我從初階級的職位置昇到秘書。然後，我找到一份更接近我的地方的工作。這是一個剛起步新的公司。就在我以為我有機會來幫助從一家公司從頭打拼，我意識到這是一個錯誤。管理層並沒有足夠的經驗來迅速作出行政上的決策和判斷。所有的工作人員覺得我們被盲目地領導，這樣下來我做不出任何貢獻。我已經與我目前的公司合作一段合理的時間長度。現在我想安頓下來，提供我不同的背景給我新的雇主。

Q 4 Have your career motivations changed over the years?
幾年之後你的職業動力有何改變？

When I first graduated from school, I didn't have much practical work experience as a novice administrative assistant. It took me much time and effort to realize the differences between the school and the real world. When I was a student, I was more concerned about myself instead of having any team spirit. To be honest, I was more self-centered driven by being the center of the attention. Over the years, I've realized nothing happens with a one person team. We all have to function with one great goal in mind as being a part of meaningful contributions with each individual's professional presence. I've gained more and more enjoyment working as a team member in a department, having the sense of collaboration, and seeing a group of professionals working together in different roles. I've moved up the corporate ladder being the secretary of the department now. I'd like to use my past experience to facilitate and motivate others more as being a real team player.

當我剛從學校畢業，我並沒有多少實際工作經驗，作為一個新手行政助理。我花了很多時間和精力去了解學校與現實世界之間的差異。當我還是一個學生時，我更關心的不是有任何的團隊精神而是我自己。坦白說，我之前比較以自我為中心關心的是成為大家注意的焦點。幾年工作下來，我已經意識到一個人的團隊是不會有沒有任何的成績。我們都必須在心中有一個偉大的目標，共同與每個人的專業有意義的去貢獻的每一部分的功能。我已經獲得了越來越享受作為一個部門的團隊成員的工作，及合作的意識，看到一群一起工作的專業人才扮演不同角色。我晉升到了成為一部門的秘書了。我想用我過去的經驗，來促進和激勵他人以作為一個真正的團隊人員。

1-3 我有疑問篇

Q

1 **How would you describe your ideal employee?**
你會如何形容你心目中理想的員工？

I would always like my staff to come to work on time, not just to come in right at the second but 5 minutes early. This person can keep good attendance by not calling in sick at the last minutes or leaving the work unfinished at the end of the day. My ideal employee should be honest, trustworthy, hardworking, and optimistic. This person should learn things quickly, promote teamwork and take pride and ownership in her/his work. She/he also takes responsibility when she/he makes a mistake and genuinely works to fix it. Better yet, this person also has a positive attitude and a great sense of humor to help get through the day. I'm expecting who can get the job done without extensive hand holing. I'm an aggressive and ambitious leader, so I'd like everyone in my team, especially my secretary, to be action-oriented. While chances might lead to failure, this person much be able to lead to success and mold confidence while generating new ideas and taking actions.

我總是希望我的員工來上班的時候，不只是準時到而是提早 5 分鐘。此人可以保持良好的出勤率藉由不在最後幾分鐘才請病假還是在一天結束的時候工作未完成就離開。我的理想員工應誠實、值得信任、勤奮跟樂觀。這個人應該要學習東西很快，發揮團隊精神，以及在她/他的工作中感到自豪和掌控。她/他也需要在她/他犯了錯誤責任的時候，真正致力於解決它。更好的是，這個人也有一個積極的態度和幽默感來以幫助度過工作的每一天。我期待這人能夠沒有完全的輔助下把工作完成。我是一個積極的和雄心勃勃的領導者，所以我希望大家在我的團隊，尤其是我的秘書，也是行動派的。雖然冒險有時可能會導致失敗，這個人應該在產生新的想法和採取行動時，同時能夠導向成功和建立信心。

2 What responsibilities are included in this position?
這個職位包含的責任有哪些？

We're looking for the best candidate equipped the various writing skills for any necessary administrative and reporting work involved preparing and organizing reports, correspondence, and telecommunications. This person must provide strong support to the management in any shapes or forms that needed. She/he has to do all the scheduling of the meetings and makes sure everything run smoothly where there is very little margin of careless errors. Strong Microsoft Office skills are required for this position with the responsibility for devising and updating office systems, websites and internal databases. She/he also needs to possess high level of professionalism and confidentiality for maintaining customer confidence and protecting operations by keeping information confidential. We would also like to have this person to have excellent verbal communication skills for answering or referring inquiries. A lot of traveling arrangements need to be made at this job. This person has to liaise with colleagues and external contacts to book travel and accommodation.

我們正在尋找最佳人選具備各種寫作技巧，對於任何關於以及準備部門報告，信件，和電信的行政與書寫工作。此人必須提供強有力的支持給管理者在任何需要的形式下。她/他必須要做會議的所有行程安排，並確保一切運行順利，其中只有很小的空間容許粗心大意的錯誤。這個職位負責需要熟悉微軟的 Office 軟體來建立和更新辦公系統，網站和內部資料庫。她/他還需要具備高水平的專業性和保密性以維持客戶的信心和保持訊息的機密性與保護系統。我們也希望這個人具有良好的口頭表達能力回答或轉接部門查詢。在這個崗位需要大量的安排出差的運行。這個人需要聯絡與同事和與外部聯繫，預訂旅行和住宿。

3 How would you describe your management style?
你會如何形容你的管理風格？

I would say I'm the type of manager allows the employees to take part in some decision-making process; therefore everything is agreed upon by the majority. The communication is extensive in both directions, from employees to leaders and vice-versa. I constantly ask for input from my staff especially when a complex decision needs to be made that require a range of specialist skills. Take the new IT system for example, I knew my IT subordinates were more computer-literate. I fully delegated the project to them with regular reporting of process in return. The new system has greatly improved the job satisfaction and quality of work. I'm very good at reading people's characteristics and finding their potentials as being a very experienced manager in this business. I know very well how to motivate different people by tapping their potential that they didn't even realize existed. I use much positive reinforcement for well job performance with knowing everybody's strength and weakness.

我會說我是會允許員工參與一些決策過程的經理類型；因此所有事情都得到了大數的同意。溝通是在廣泛在雙向的，從員工到領導者，反之亦然。我不斷地問我的員工提出意見，尤其當需要一系列的專業技能來做一個複雜的決策時更是如此。就拿公司新的 IT 系統來舉例，我知道我的 IT 下屬更有電腦方面的知識。我將這個專案在過程中完全委託給他們，以定期報告來交換。新的系統大大地提高了工作滿意度和工作質量。作為一個在這一行非常有經驗的經理，我很善於讀出人的特點以及找到他們的潛能。我非常清楚地知道如何通過挖掘他們甚至沒有意識到存在的潛力來激勵不同的人。我對好的工作績效使用很多正向鼓勵同時知道每個人的實力和弱點。

Q 4

What are some job performance issues have become your concerns?
有哪些工作表現上的問題曾成為你的擔憂？

I once had a staff member who was much careless on handling his documentation. He didn't proofread his emails or reports so his written work constantly consisted of typos and even informal usage. I first gave him some moderate verbal warning asking him to correct this problem until the mistake had gone externally. He sent out the wrong quote to an overseas client with other incorrect information. I asked him to stop handling any external correspondence and started monitoring more of his writing myself. I told him to build up a system which gave himself a constant reminder to double or even triple check his documentation. He still makes mistakes here and there but they become more acceptable. I fired a few people for not showing up for work for days without noticing me or the HR department. The company has the policy that an employee is deem to quit for being absent from work for three consecutive days or more without giving notice.

我曾經有一個工作人員處理他的文件太過馬虎。他沒有校對他的電子郵件或報告，造成他的書面工作裡不斷出現錯別字，甚至是非正式語法。我剛開始給他一些溫和的口頭警告，要求他更正此問題，直到錯誤發生到外部。他送出了錯誤的報價給海外的客戶以及其它不正確的資訊。我要求他停止處理任何外部通信，並開始監視更多他的寫作。我要求他建立的一個時刻提醒兩次甚至三次檢查他自己的文件的系統。他還是會出現些許的錯誤但是這些錯誤變得比較可以接受。我開除過幾個人好幾天沒有來出現來上班，也沒有給我或人力資源部門任何通知。公司政策規定任何員工曠職連續三天以上不給予通知是被認為辭職。

1 範例

1-1. 自傳(1)

My name is Helen Lu. I graduated from the Department of International Business at Providence University. For me, I believe only we love ourselves first. Then, we are capable enough of loving others. Learning and doing exercises has played important roles in my daily life.

I used to take on many different challenges during my school life. One of them was to be the class representative. This gives me feel pleasure and full of the sense of achievement because I enjoy helping people. Also, I do many different kinds of exercise, like jogging, basketball and golf etc... （請閱2-1）Basketball is especially my favorite. After years of practicing, I think It's the best way for me to release my stress when I feel frustrated and stressful.

The main reason why I apply for the opening position is I would like to be a successful manager so I have to learn how to keep a good relationship with my employees and make proper decisions in various situations. I want and I will be a manager one day. This is like my dream job. I believe that ABC Enterprising can help me make my dream come true. That is why I choose to work here.

I would like to have the opportunity to have the interview. I will do my best to be a successful employee. I will let you know that choosing me is the right decision. Thank you kindly for your time and consideration.

我的名字叫盧海倫。我畢業於靜宜大學國際商務系。對於我來說，我相信只有我們愛自己第一。那麼，我們有足夠的能力愛別人。學習和運動在我的日常生活中扮演了很重要的角色。

我曾經在我的學校生活裡接受許多不同的挑戰。其中一個就是成為班代。這給了我快樂和充滿成就感因為我喜歡幫助別人。此外，我做很多不同種類的運動，如慢跑，籃球和高爾夫球等⋯籃球尤其是是我的最愛。經過多年的練習，當我感到沮喪和壓力的時候我覺得這是釋放我壓力的最佳方式。

主要我申請這個職缺的原因是我想成為一名成功的經理，所以我必須學會如何保持與我的員工一個良好的關係，以及在不同的情況作出適當的決定。我想，而且我會有一天成為一個經理。這就像我夢想中的工作。我相信 ABC 企業可以讓我的夢想成真。這就是為什麼我選擇在這裡工作。

我希望能有面試的機會。我會盡我所能成為一個成功的員工。我會讓你知道我的選擇我是正確的決定。真摯的謝謝您的時間和考慮。

1-2. 自傳(2)

My Chinese name is 林佩妮 and my English name is Penny Lin. This letter is in connection with my application for the job vacancy of the Project Secretary.

I hold a bachelor's degree with a major in Business Administration which was awarded to me by Fu-Jen University in Taipei in 2013. （請閱2-2）Although I am just graduated this summer, I believe I am qualified for this position according to the job requirements. First, I have good command of English because my university minor subject was English. Moreover, my TOEFL test score is 89. These two facts provide the evidence that （請閱2-2）I have adequate qualification to work in an international company like yours.

Even though I did not major in computer, there were many chances I had to make class presentations by using computer science when I was a university student. I am familiar with some software package such as Word, Excel, Front Page, Power Point, etc. I won't have great resistance when I encounter the new things about computer. It makes me flexible when I face the surrounding which computer is indispensable. （請閱2-2）

I am from a middle-class family which is composed of four members: my parents, my younger sister and I. My father is a businessman who deals with international trades. My mother used to work at a bank, but she has retired recently. My sister studies nursing and she is going to work in a hospital. The life in my family is calm and steady. My parents love their children and have great expectation that one day we can have our own careers and live a happy life. My hobbies include watching movies, listening to music and playing sports. I am an enthusiastic, initiative and interesting person.

I can confidently say that I am ready for having my future career at your company. I am looking forward to having a good opportunity in which I can make a contribution to the welfare of the company where I will work for. （請閱2-2）

我的中文名字是林佩妮以及我的英文名字是 Penny Lin。這封信是與我應徵專案秘書的職位相關。

我在 2013 台北輔仁大學授予給我一個學士學位主修企業管理。雖然我這個夏天才剛畢業，我相信根據工作要求我能勝任這個職位。首先，我有良好的英語水平，因為我在大學副修科目是英語。此外，我的托福測驗成績是 89。這兩個事實提供證據證明我有足夠的資格如貴公司的在國際公司裡工作。

雖然我沒有主修電腦，但當我在大學時我有很多機會我必須使用電腦作課堂發表。我熟悉一些軟體，如 Word、Excel、Front Page、Power Point 等。當我遇到有關電腦的新事物我將不會有很大的阻力。這讓在我面對電腦是必不可缺的環境時是靈活的。

我來自一個中產階級家庭，有四名成員：我的父母，我的妹妹和我。我父親是一個做國際貿易的商人。我的母親曾經工作在一家銀行，但她剛剛退休。我妹妹學習護理，她將會在醫院裡工作。在我家的生活是平靜和穩定。我的父母愛自己的孩子，對我們有很大的期望希望有一天我們可以有我們自己的事業和幸福的生活。我的嗜好包括看電影，聽音樂和玩運動。我是一個熱情、積極性和有趣的人。

我可以自信地說，我已經準備好在貴公司發展未來的前途。我期待著這個機會在這我能為公司的福利做出好的貢獻。

2 自傳寫作教室

2-1. 自傳(1) 寫作文法解析／小評語

　　這上下兩篇自傳都是大學畢業生剛出社會所寫的自傳。第一篇是使用比較像口語的語句與單字，而第二篇寫作就使用比較正式的英文。不管學生英文程度為何種程度，通常在沒有許多工作經驗之下，一般學生寫的不外乎是關於自己的家庭跟學校生活。雖然比較沒有比較多可以著墨的地方，但是還是要切記所提到的所有個人特質與學校活動對於這份所應徵的職位有何相關之處。像第一段所提到的學習與運動，在第二段就有繼續闡述相關之處。但關於愛自己與愛別人這一點就像天外飛來一筆的句子，也不見有繼續說明之處，更不知與此職務有和相關。建議可以改成像「I've grown up in a loving family where I learn to be considerate and compassionate.」我在一個充滿愛的家庭中長大學會了體諒和富有同情心。

　　第二段中就有敘述到一些比較吸引雇主的個人特質，譬如喜歡接受挑戰、幫助別人與懂得釋放壓力，建議可以用更直接有利的語句譬如「thrive on challenges,」「good leadership skills,」或「work well under pressure」來形容自己。「etc」是拉丁文「et cetera」，指的是「and so on」。這裡犯的一個常見的錯誤就是在使用「etc」時，不用在前面加 and，更不可以在後面加…。

　　充滿自信與直接了當也許是大多數現在年輕人的特質，但在求職時，台灣的雇主依然希望看到求職者是以一個謙虛的態度但願意展現進取心來爭取這份職位，這中間的平衡也是撰寫自傳時要留心的地方。

2-2. 自傳(2) 寫作文法解析／小評語

　　第二篇自傳的句型較為正式，在寫這樣的文章時，要小心的是不要將句子直接用複雜的中文句子想要的寫出一樣對等且流暢的英文。程度較好的同學常寫出過於複雜的句子，不僅文法已經出錯，也變成是中式英文的講法。像第二段中的一句就是一個很好的例子，「with a major in…」或「which was awarded to me by…」都只是讓句子看起來很累贅，而不是讓這一句英文很流利又很有程度。「I earn a bachelor's degree in Business Administration at Fu-Jen University in Taipei in June 2013.」這樣的句子還是有一定的寫作水準但是簡潔清楚多了。另外一個句子「These two facts provide the evidence that…」以中文念起來似乎通順，但是在英文中這語氣似乎像是在 CSI 辦案，就把 facts 換成 factors 就已經好一些了，或直接用「As a matter of fact,…」才聽起來像流暢語氣又正確的英文。

　　其它中式英文的句子包括「make presentations by using computer science」，直接用「make presentations on computer」就可以了。「I won't have great resistance when I encounter the new things about computer.」建議改成「I am a fast learner when it comes to the latest computer technology.」。「It makes me flexible when I face the surrounding which computer is indispensable.」可以改成「I am a very efficient person when I work at a place where computer skills are needed.」

　　英文寫作的正確度與流暢度可以透過多閱讀任何英文書籍、報紙、雜誌或是網頁來加強。這樣在選擇單字或片語時才有足夠的英文語感知道這樣才是真正在英文中會這樣去使用，而不是先用中文思考，然後寫出複雜但累贅的句子，甚至是變成中式英文。像最後一句的後半段，建議直接改成「having the great opportunity that I can make a contribution to the company.」

Keep Your Goals Ahead

When she looked ahead, Florence Chadwick saw nothing but a concrete wall of fog. Her body was numb from swimming for nearly sixteen hours in the ocean. In the morning of that Fourth of July in 1952, the sea was like a giant ice bath and the fog was so dense that she could hardly see her support boats. Sharks cruised toward her isolated body, only rifle shots could drive them away. Against the frigid grasp of the sea, she struggled on for hour after hour while millions of people watched her on television nationwide.

She was already the first woman to swim the English Channel. At her 34, she set the goal to become the first woman to swim from Catalina Island to the California coast.

Her mother and her trainer offered encouragement alongside Florence in one of the boats. They told her it wasn't much farther, but all she could see was fog. They begged her not to quit. She kept swimming until a half mile to go, she asked to be pulled out.

She told a reporter after still thawing her chilled body several hours later, , "Look, I'm not excusing myself, but if I could have seen land I might have made it." It was not fatigue or even the cold water that conquered her. It was the fog. She could not see her goal.

She tried again two months later. This time, regardless of the same thick and solid fog, she swam with her faith intact and with her goal clearly pictured in her mind. She knew that somewhere behind that fog the land was there and this time she made it! Florence Chadwick became the first woman to swim from Catalina Island to the California coast, eclipsing the men's record by two hours!

保持你的目標在前

當她看著前面，佛羅倫·查德威克什麼也沒看見，只有霧所構成堅實的牆。她的身體一直在海中游了快 16 個小時已經麻木了。在 1952 年七月四日早上，大海就像一個大冰浴，霧是如此密集，她幾乎看不到自己的支援船。鯊魚朝她孤獨的身影逼近，只有被步槍射擊才能趕走。她一小時又一小時地掙扎對大海的寒冷的緊握，而數以百萬計的人在全國電視上觀看著。

她已經是第一位遊過英吉利海峽的女性。在她 34 歲時，她的目標是成為第一個從卡特林娜島游到加利福尼亞州海岸。

她的母親和她的教練之一在佛羅倫邊的船上提供鼓勵。他們告訴她離岸已經不遠，但她的眼前只見得到霧。他們勸她不要放棄。她一直遊直到只有半英里的距離，她退出了。

在她的解凍冰冷的身體幾個小時後，她告訴記者，「你看，我不是為自己辯解，但是如果我能看到陸地，我是可以成功的。」這不是身體的勞累，甚至寒冷的海水擊敗了她。這是霧。她無法看到她的目標。

兩個月後，她再一次嘗試。這一次，儘管同樣的濃霧，她帶著她堅持的信念不變地游著，而且她的目標清晰地呈現在她的腦海裡。她知道濃霧後的某個地方就是陸地，而這次她成功了！佛羅倫·查德威克成為第一位遊過卡塔利娜海峽，打敗男子紀錄快兩個小時！

英文客服

1-1 常遇到的考題

Q 1

Tell me your skills and experience.
請告訴我你的技能和經驗。

I have a Bachelor's degree in Business Administration. My equivalent work experience is my 3 years experience in the customer service department with high volume of transactions in ABC Healthcare Center. I have high computer system proficiencies in Microsoft Office programs and an Internet based environment, including the operating knowledge of Word, Excel, Outlook and Internet Explorer. I am able to work efficiently in a fast-paced, high-volume environment. I have demonstrated excellent customer service skills such as developed phone skills, customer relationship management, multi-tasking etc. I also have tremendous oral and written communication skills and problem solving or analytical skills. In addition, I possess strong leadership and organizational skills. I am motivated and thrive in a fast paced environment and have no problem to work non-standard hours. I am a fast learner, so I believe I have the ability to demonstrate detailed knowledge of specific product offerings, internal systems and company service processes once I get onboard.

　　我有工商管理學士學位。我的同等工作經驗是 3 年在 ABC 保健中心的客服部處理多人次的轉接。我對 Microsoft Office 程式系統和網路工作環境非常熟練，包括 Word、Excel、Outlook 和 Internet Explorer 的操作知識。我能夠在一個快節奏，高人次的環境中有效地工作。我展現出色的客服務能力，如熟練的電話技巧、客戶關係管理、同時處

理多項任務等。我也有很好的口頭和書面溝通能力和解決分析問題的技巧。另外,我具備有力的領導和組織能力。我在快節奏的環境下可以得到動力及成長,並且我在任何時段工作都沒有任何問題。我學得很快,所以我相信我有能力一旦開始上班就可以展現特定產品種類,內部系統和公司服務流程的詳細知識。

2 How do you explain your job successes?
你如何定義你的成功?

To begin with being a successful customer service rep, I always take the initiative to meet internal and external customer needs in a timely and courteous manner. I respond to customer requests on contact date or within 24 hours. Being customer focused at work, I examine customer requests to properly identify and resolve customer concerns. I like to help my customers to increases their confidence and knowledge to resolve their own problems. I advise the customers bearing with their wants and needs in mind and acknowledge them the shortcomings appropriately. I never assume our customers have a satisfactory experience solely by purchasing our products, so I make much customer service efforts through follow-up. Their feedback has provided valuable insight into the qualities and characteristics of our products. The customers always appreciate the follow-up, especially when something hasn't gone right. That gives me the opportunity to correct it on a timely basis.

首先要成為一個成功的客服人員,我總是主動有禮貌及時地去滿足內部和外部客戶的需求。我會在與客戶接觸的當日或 24 小時內回覆。在工作中我永遠以客戶為中心考察客戶的要求來正確地識別和解決客戶關心的問題。我喜歡為客戶增加他們的信心和知識來解決自己的問題。我給予客戶建議時總會考慮他們的需要和需求,並適當跟他們承認缺點。我從來不認為我們的客戶僅通過購買我們的產品就有一個滿意的經驗,所以我通過大量的後續服務為客戶工作。他們的回饋

在我們的產品的品質和特點中提供了寶貴的見解。客戶總是喜歡後續服務，尤其是當事情沒有發展順利。這使我有機會在及時去糾正。

Q

3　**Tell me about a time when you worked on a team.**
請告訴我一個你在團隊工作的經驗。

My role was to manage the communications to customers about the new release, which involved coordinating with dozens of people from Technology, Operations, Customer Service, and Marketing. It was my job to get everyone's input on how to communicate it to customers. I had to do it quickly because the decision was made right before the release date and we wanted to give customers the some heads up. The communications were received positively by clients. Though some customers were disappointed with the limited functions, many were more pleased with the benefits of the new features and appreciated the timely and clear communications. I received nice comments from the senior managers in Technology and Customer Service. They told my boss that I was doing a very good job at keeping everybody focused on the customer experience and making the tight deadline.

我的角色是去向客戶介紹與溝通新產品，其中涉及協調幾十個在技術、營運、客服和行銷不同的人員。我的工作是去知道每個人想要如何跟客戶介紹。我動作要很快，因為這決定是要在產品發表之前就要做好，並且我們想給客戶一些一手訊息。客戶對於我們的溝通有很正面的回應。雖然有些客戶對於一些有限的功能感到失望，但更多人新功能帶來的好處覺得高興，並讚賞我們及時和清楚的溝通。我從技術和客服的高階主管那裡得到了不錯的評語。他們告訴我的老闆我在保持每個人都專注於客戶體驗與及時完成方面做得很好。

Q 4 Why are you applying to work here?
你為什麼要申請在這裡工作？

This has been one of my favorite stores for years. When I saw there was a job opening here, I was very excited at the possibility of becoming part of the team. I really enjoy working with people in a store setting, helping customers, organizing stock, and changing displays. This seems like a really interesting place to work with the variety of items and services that you offer. I feel that if I were given the opportunity, I could be an asset to the team. I have a lot of experience in helping customers satisfy their needs, and would welcome the opportunity to learn a new business, and share my expertise in customer service. I've seen most of your competitors have tried to do many similar things. Nonetheless, your store has remained the leading role in the market for years while keeping expanding and maintain consistent quality.

多年來這一直是我最喜愛的商店之一。當我看到這裡有個職缺，我感到非常興奮可能可以成為這團隊的一部分。我非常喜歡在一家店裡與別人一起工作、協助顧客、整理庫存、以及更換展示商品。根據各項您所提供的產品和服務這似乎是一個非常有趣的工作場所。我覺得如果我得到這個工作機會，我會是這個團隊很有利的資產。我有很多的幫助客戶滿足他們需要的經驗，並希望有機會學習新的業務，以及分享我在客服的專業知識。我見到您們大多數的競爭對手都試圖做很多類似的事情。不過，您的商店一直在市場上的多年保持主導，同時持續擴張，以及維持穩定的質量。

Q

5

How do you handle the situation when you have to deal with an angry customer?
你在必須處理憤怒的客戶這個情況下是如何處理的？

Customers get rude or angry for a variety of reasons. Since I'm in the business to serve customers, I have a good system that can make a customer who feels satisfied with the resolution. First, I always remain calm even when a customer starts yelling or being rude. What they want the most is to vent and they need someone to listen. Listening patiently can defuse a situation, as long as the customer feels acknowledged in her or his complaint. After the customer vents, s/he wants to know if you understand how she/he feels. I always express sympathy for their unpleasant customer experience and apologize gracefully. Of course, the most important part is to find a solution. I'd ask them what should be done or put forward my own fair and realistic answers. In most cases, that's all customers are looking for.

客戶變得粗魯或生氣的原因有很多種。既然我在客服這一行工作，我有一個好的系統可以解決一個不滿意的顧客。首先，我始終保持冷靜即使當客戶開始大喊大叫或者是變得粗魯。他們最需要的是發洩，而且他們需要有人傾聽。只要客戶感覺在她或他的投訴有被理解，耐心聆聽是可以化解這樣的情況。當客戶發洩後，他/她想知道你是否了解她/他的感覺如何。我總是會對他們不愉快的客戶體驗表示同情以及得體地道歉。當然，最重要的是要找到一個解決方案。我會問他們應該要怎麼做或提出了我自己覺得公平和現實的答案。在大多數情況下，這是所有客戶所期待的。

Q 6 How do you keep yourself organized?
你是如何保持自己有條理？

First, I keep a clean desk to ensure that important paperwork doesn't get lost, and set up zones on my desk to organize materials, such as telephone and message pads, mail and files. Zones help me get to things quickly and facilitate multitasking by keeping tasks from overlapping. I also have a small reception area. I keep it neat and well-stocked with courtesy items for visitors, such as company business cards, brochures, magazines and tissues. One of my daily duties is to start each day checking that refreshments are available to serve to visitors. For being able to efficiently transfer telephone calls, greet visitors and help facilitate meetings, I need to know the whereabouts of employees. I use an electronic calendar system to track vacation and sick leave for employees. I like to keep things neat and accessible. I label separate inbox, filing trays, and filing cabinets to keep paperwork from becoming overwhelming and I don't need to rely on memory to find things.

首先，我保持我的工作台面一個乾淨以確保重要的文件不會丟失，並我的桌子上分不同區域來整理不同材料，例如電話或留言紙條、郵件及文件。不同區域能我拿東西時很快速，也方便我在進時多項任務時讓工作不會互相重疊。我也有一個小的接待區。我會整齊精心擺放著迎賓項目，如公司名片、宣傳手冊、雜誌和面紙。我的一個日常工作是每天一開始檢查茶點以服務客戶。為了能夠有效率地轉接電話、迎接賓客、並幫助安排會議，我需要知道員工在什麼地方。我用一個電子日曆系統來跟蹤休假和病假的員工。我喜歡保持整潔和方便。我會在不同的收件箱、文件盤和檔案櫃上貼標籤來保持文書工作不要變得亂七八糟，這樣我就不需要靠記憶找東西。

Q 7

Tell me about a time that you went above and beyond at a previous job.
請告訴我你曾經在之前工作做出超越自己的表現。

The company where I worked for before the customer retention was poor. I thought we should understand and improve this situation by thoroughly researching our customers. I proposed that we could conduct a customer behavior, attitude, and satisfaction survey. My manager thought that was a total waste of time. I tried to approach him more aggressively and persuaded him by showing him how our competitors using customer surveys to their advantages. He agreed that our customer retention had been gone worse and we should really find the causes and reasons. After the surveys were designed and implemented and analyzed, we had discovered the changes we had to make in how we deal with our customers. For example, some customers were really frustrated with not being able to receive the orders fast enough, neither to get some prompt responses in the customer service department. We immediately improved on the efficiency of the delivery system. Not long after, we got more positive customer feedback once we addressed the issue.

　　我之前工作的公司在那裡客戶的保留度很差。我想我們應該要藉由徹底研究我們的客戶去了解改善這種狀況。我建議去做對於客戶行為、態度及滿意度的調查。我的經理認為那只是浪費時間。通過展示競爭對手是如何使用客戶調查來成為自己的優勢，我試圖更積極地說服他。他同意我們客戶的保留率已經越來越差，而且我們真的應該找出原因和理由。經過調查、設計和實施、並進行分析，我們發現我們必須在我們調整如何與客戶互動。例如，有些客戶對不能夠快速下訂單，也無法在客服部門得到一些迅速的回應感到失望。我們立即將遞送系統的效率提高。一旦我們解決了這個問題之後沒多久，我們得到了更多正面的客戶回應。

Q

8 How do you do stress relief especially after handling some tough situations?
在處理一些棘手的情況後，你是如何緩解壓力？

I always take a few minutes on my own. After the situation has been resolved and the customer is on her/his way, it's helpful for me to take my own "time-out." Even if I've handled the situation in the most professional way possible, it's still a stressful experience. Rather than let the stress linger inside me, I usually take a short walk, treat myself to a snack or find someone to talk to who makes me laugh. Then I'll be ready to once again engage with my customers. I've personally found the best stress relief is to keep a laugh diary. When I'm feeling stressed and depressed after a call or service, I look at my laugh diary to neutralize negative emotions. When I'm not at work, I stay alert for funny incidents from movies or reality and add to my laugh diary. While it can be helpful to decompress with colleagues by talking about difficult situations, it's healthier not to spend lots of time reliving stress.

我總會跟我自己相處個幾分鐘。在情況已經解決，客戶已經離開時，「中場休息」總是對我有幫助。即使我已經以最專業的方式來處理完狀況，它仍然是一個緊張的經驗。與其讓我內心的壓力揮之不去，我通常會去散步，吃一些零食或找能使我發笑的人傾訴。然後我可以再次準備好與我的客戶互動。我個人覺得最好的緩解壓力是保持一個微笑日記。當我在一通電話或服務後感到壓力或鬱悶，我會看我的微笑日記中和消解我的情緒。當我下班時，我會留意電影或現實的搞笑事件，並加到微笑日記裡。雖然跟同事一起討論難解決的狀況可以幫助減壓，不需花大量的時間消除壓力相對比較健康。

1-2 臨場反應篇

Q

1 **How do you respond when you don't know the answer to a question?**
你如何回應當你不知道一個問題的答案？

My strategy in this type of situation is to place the emphasis on the customer's needs over my own situation, and to let them know that I'm going to do whatever I need to in order to find out the answers for them. First, I repeat the question and let the customer know I'm writing it down. I tell the customers exactly when I will get back to them. I make sure to get the customer's contact information if I don't have it. I also state whom I'm going to immediately refer or consult and that usually brings the customers some comfort because they can see I'm taking action and I know what I'm doing. I see this is an opportunity to go the extra mile, expand my knowledge, and impress your customers showing the extra effort I put on finding the answers for them.

　　我在這種情況的策略是把重點放在客戶的需求超過我自己的情況，並讓他們知道我會做什麼，我會為了他們找出答案做出任何需要的動作。首先，我會重複問題，並讓客戶知道我把它寫下來。我會告訴客戶我確實會在什麼時候跟他們連絡。如果我沒有客戶的連絡資料，我會確認有拿到。我也通知客戶我會立即跟誰轉介或諮詢這往往會帶給客戶的一些安慰，因為他們可以看到我有馬上採取行動，以及我知道我在做什麼。我會認為這是一個機會，去加倍努力，擴大我的知識，並打動你的客戶展示了額外的努力去把找到的答案給他們。

Q

2

What excellent customer service do you think we can provide to outshine our competitors?
你認為哪些卓越的客戶服務我們可以提供來超越我們的競爭對手？

I think first we should determine what makes us special by studying the competition. If I were the customer, I would compare the competitors' customer service and the service we provided. What can we offer our customers that is "better" than the competition? There are sure to be aspects of our customer service that we can promote as our special or unique features. Then we should make a list of all these ideas for providing customer service. After we study the customer service ideas on the list, it's the step to examine the feasibility. We have to make sure we can provide the kind of service that carries that same kind of guarantee; it cannot be done only "sometimes." We need to choose what we can definitely do one hundred percent of the time to maintain the same highest level of our customer service. Last but not least, I would say we should always stay proactive and keep gathering customer service ideas.

我覺得首先要特別通過學習競爭對手確定是什麼讓我們跟他們不一樣。如果我是客戶，我會比較競爭對手的客戶服務與我們提供的服務。我們是哪方面可以為客戶提供比競爭對手「更好」的服務？在我們的客服方面肯定是有我們可以提升成我們特殊或獨特的特質。然後我們應該將這些所有提供客務的想法列表。經過我們研究名單上的客服理念，下一步是檢查它的可行性。我們必須確保我們可以提供一種服務，它同種具有一種保證；它不能只是「有時候」去做。我們要選擇我們絕對可以百分之百地做到來維持相同的最高客服水準。最後很重要的一點就是我們應該始終保持積極地去不斷收集客服的想法。

Q 3 **Do you consider yourself a leader or a follower?**
你認為自己是一個領導者或跟隨者？

I believe I am a little of both. People often say that in order to become a good leader, one must be a good follower. A person needs to learn how to follow and obey orders from people who are in a higher position than her/him. I think by being a good follower, I can gain a lot of wisdom and knowledge from others and that can help me become a better leader. I acknowledge that being a leader requires motivating, disciplining staff, and molding a team. That involves a number of delicately sophisticated skills. I don't think there's anyone who was born as natural leader. Leadership is a skill required first by desire and it's a lifelong learning process. I can see myself be prepared to complete any given tasks and learn new things. I have much willingness to adapt any types of situations. I believe one day, once I've gained enough experience, will be assigned a leadership position, I'll be ready to take on the responsibilities of being a leader.

我相信我是兩者都有一點。人們常說，要想成為一個優秀的領導者，必須先是一個好的跟隨者。一個人需要學習如何從一個比她/他更高的位置的人那裡遵循和服從命令。我覺得藉由當一個好的跟隨者，我可以從別人身上獲得了大量的智慧和知識，那並能幫助我成為一個更好的領導者。我知道作為一個領導者需要去激勵、管教員工、塑造一個團隊。那涉及了一些微妙老練的技巧。我不認為有任何人出生就是作為天生的領導者。領導力首先需要有欲望去培養的一個技能，以及一個終身學習的過程。我覺得自己是已經準備完成任何指定的任務和學習新事物。我非常願意去適應任何類型的情況。我相信有一天，當我已經獲得了足夠的經驗，我將被分配到一個領導地位，我會準備好承擔起作為一個領導者的責任。

4

What was your most important contribution to the previous company?
什麼是你對以前的公司最重要的貢獻？

My last position was the receptionist serving for the ABC Enterprise. I believe receptionists are the first people clients see and speak to during a visit or a call. They are the connection between the clients and the company; they are the front line of the business. Thus, receptionists should possess a high degree of professionalism and efficiency in order to represent the company well. Speaking of my contribution, I was always able to finish tasks and obligations under time pressure even before the deadline. By being able to finish my work earlier than expected, I could also help other personnel achieve their goals. As a receptionist, I always had a good attitude toward clients and coworkers. I had a lot of experience that I was in charge of teaching and training new receptionists. I believe my skills and abilities to do the job well were a major asset to the company.

我的最後一個職位是服務於 ABC 企業的櫃檯人員。我相信櫃檯人員是客戶最首先看到和交談的人。他們企業的第一線連接客戶和公司之間的關係。因此，櫃檯人員應具備高度的專業和效率以良好地代表公司。說起我的貢獻，我總是能在截止日期前或時間壓力下提早完成工作和責任。由於能夠比預期提前完成我的工作，我也可以幫助其他人完成他們的目標。作為一名櫃檯人員，我一直對客戶和同事保持一個良好的心態。我有很多的經驗所以我負責教學和培訓新的櫃檯人員。我相信我的技巧和能力做好這份工作是一項公司重要的資產。

1-3 我有疑問篇

Q 1

What's the latest development the company implementing in the customer service department?
什麼是公司的客服部門實施的最新發展？

The company now is seeking the ways to boost the customer service satisfaction via social media sites. The rise of social media has given consumers a powerful new way to talk about or to interact with our company. Not every satisfied or unsatisfied customer will contact you directly. They'll often simply share their opinions with their friends and followers through social media channels. We've have tuned into these conversations by using social monitoring tools such as Google Alerts and Twitter searches. You have to monitor them regularly for individual conversations that may require customer service attention, such as a customer complaining about a late order or a bad experience. Look for larger trends in customer opinions that might require more specific attention, such as complaints about your service, product quality or the work you deliver. Most social media users expect a response within a day so make sure you give prompt follow-up and respond to the issues.

公司目前正尋求通過社交媒體網站，以提高客戶服務的滿意度。社群媒體的興起，給了消費者一個有力的新方法來談論或與本公司互動。不是每一個滿意或不滿意的客戶會直接與你聯繫。他們通常只是會通過社群管道的朋友和追隨者分享他們的意見。我們已經利用社群監控工具，如谷歌快訊和 Twitter 搜索來接收到這些談話。你要定期監控可能需要客服重視的個別談話，如客戶抱怨超時訂單或不好的經驗。去尋找客戶意見的趨勢，尤其是需要更具體的注意，比如你的服務，產品質量或交付你的工作的投訴。大多數社群媒體用戶期望在一天之內回應，所以確保你及時作出針對問題作出回應。

Q
2
What type of qualities are you looking for in the best job applicants?
你在求職者身上尋找什麼類型的特質？

It's all about the soft skills. There are some key things I am looking for in a potential hire. First I'd definitely say personality. They need a great personality to start. I want someone upbeat, cheerful, and always smiling. They need to be able to win over angry customers. Next is communication. They need to communicate clearly and concisely. Every customer you have is unique and every trouble they find themselves in is different. That's why I want to have a rep that's creative; they'll use their best judgments to figure out how to make the customer happy. I also want someone who is driven, able to work on their own, and such. I can teach anyone how to reply to an email, but I can't teach them how to empathize with a customer. It's about certain personal traits make you the best candidate.

這一切跟特質技巧有關。我在潛在的僱員上尋找一些關鍵的東西。首先，我會說是關於個性。一開始他們需要很好的人格。我希望這個人樂觀、開朗、總是面帶微笑。他們需要能夠籠絡憤怒的客戶。接下來是溝通。他們需要清楚準確地溝通。你擁有的每一個客戶是獨一無二的，而他們找出的每一個麻煩是不同的。這就是為什麼我希望有一個客服代表是有創意的，他們能運用他們最佳的判斷來找出如何讓顧客高興。我也希望這個人積極、能夠獨立的工作跟其它別的。我可以教一個人如何回覆郵件，但我不能教他們如何去同情一個客戶。是否為最佳人選這一切關係於某人特質。

3 How much training will be done when I get started?
當我開始時會有多少員工訓練？

You'll have a one-day orientation the first day you start working here. You need to go first complete some forms in the HR department and get the employee handbook. The HR staff will walk you through the company policies. If you have any questions about them, you can mostly find the answers in your handbook. You'll meet the manager of your department and someone will give you the basic training to get you situated. We have a training program that allows our reps to shadow every department within the company. This instills a big picture view of the company's process and gives the reps the knowledge they need to think though problems. This benefits our customers because they are interacting with reps that have a wide range of knowledge. All of your outgoing messages could be seen by a manager or an experienced rep that is in charge of your shadowing. This allows the new hire to see valuable feedback about their actual responses.

　　當你開始在這裡工作的第一天，你將會有一個為期一天的新進人員報到。你需要去先人力資源管理部門完成衣些表格，並且你會拿到員工手冊。人資部的工作人員會介紹一些公司員工政策。如果你有任何相關的問題，你可以幾乎全在你的員工手冊裡找到答案。你會見到你的部門經理，會有人給你一些基本訓練讓你進入狀況。我們有一個培訓方案讓我們的客服在公司每一個部門見習。這可以介紹公司完整的結構，並給了客服代表他們需要思考問題時所需的知識。這有利於我們的客戶，因為他們是與具有完整知識的客服互動。在你見習時所有你發出的郵件經理或負責你見習的資深客服是可以看到。這可以使新員工在他們的實際反應中得到寶貴的回饋意見。

4 How does the company see its concept of customer service?

公司如何看他們的客戶服務理念？

That's a very good question! As you can see here, the company has brought the top of the line quality customer service over the years to the level our competitors have never reached. We always make sure the executives of the organization know that customer service is serious business to the company. It cannot be lip service; senior management must take service very seriously. All of our executives and managers are also interacting with customers. We know the employees observe management and how it supports this culture. They will act accordingly. We keep the key issues of the company's service beliefs and principles alive via regular meetings and discussions. The company treats the customer service reps as importantly as any other employees. New employees should have no question regarding the importance of service in the organization. The focus on customer service is reinforced during any orientation as well as the natural mentoring that will take place with new hires.

這是一個非常好的問題！正如你在這裡可以看到的，公司多年來有最優質的客戶服務是我們的競爭對手從來沒有達到過的水準。我們始終確保公司的管理人員知道客服是對企業非常重要。它不能只是嘴巴說說；高階主管理一定對客服非常重視。我們所有的主管和經理也都與客戶交流。我們知道員工會去觀察主管理如何支持這樣的公司文化。他們會採取相同的行動。我們通過定期的會議和討論關鍵問題來維持公司的服務理念和原則。公司將客服代表與任何其他員工視為同等重要。新僱員應該對於客服務在公司的重要性是毫無疑問的。新進員工會在報到時與見習時再加強專注於客服的所有過程。

1 範例

1-1. 自傳(1)

My name is Rosa Chen who was born in Taichung City. My family consists of five members and I am the second child among three. I feel lucky that I grew up in a liberal family where everyone is all open-minded and supportive to each other.

I studied in the Department of Applied English at Ming Chuan University. During my four years of study, not only did I learn knowledge but also unity.（請閱2-1）We had the graduation performance that we had to write the story and play on stage in English. Although everyone had different opinions at first, but we overcome difficulties and finally did a great job.（請閱2-1）I also participated in the Student Association. After my graduation from university, I have been to America for two months, I like to experience different cultures and make friends all over the world. Until now I still keep in touch with them.

I worked in a trading corporation as an assistant in Taipei for three years. I have learned how to communicate with the customers, and also to know some basic accounting. Moreover, I have met some foreign businesspeople in order to develop new customers who were interested in our products. During my first two years of college, I also had a part-time job in a fast-food restaurant, it was a good chance for me to learn about customer service.（請閱2-1）Sometimes customers had strange requests about the food or the service, but I would try my best to satisfy their demands. I always treated customers like my friends and hoped they would feel comfortable.

I am an easy-going person who always gets along well with my friends. In my free time, I like jogging, reading or going to the movies. For me, doing exercise benefits every part of my body, including my mind. I can release my stress and feel more peaceful. When I am on vacation, I like to travel abroad to experience the different cultures and stay in different countries. It's really an unforgettable, priceless experience and memory to enrich my life.

I deeply believe the saying, "where there is a will, there is a way." Being the customer service representative at your company is my dream job; I hope my dream will come true soon. Thank you.

　　我的名字是 Rosa Chen，出生於台中市。我的家庭由五名成員組成，我在三個孩子中排名第二。我覺得很幸運我在一個自由的家庭長大，每個人都是開明的並互相支持。

　　我就讀於銘傳大學應用英語系。在我四年的學習中，我不僅學到知識還有合作。我們有畢業演出，在其中我們要用英語寫故事並在舞台上演出。雖然每個人在第一次有不同的意見，但我們克服困難終於做了很棒的演出。我還參加了學生會。之後在我大學畢業，我曾去過美國兩個月，我喜歡體驗不同的文化，與來自世界各地的人交朋友。直到現在我仍然與他們保持聯繫。

　　我曾在一家台北的貿易公司做過三年的助理。我學會了如何與客戶溝通，也了解一些基本的會計。此外，我也遇到了一些對我們的產品感興趣的國外商人以開發新的客戶。在我大學期間前兩年，我也在一個快餐店打工，這是對我來說，是了解客戶服務的一個很好的機會。有時客戶對食物或服務有一些奇怪的要求，但我會盡我所能來滿足他們的需求。我總是對待客戶像我的朋友，希望他們能感到很舒服。

　　我是一個隨和的人總是與我的朋友們相處得很好。在我有空時，我喜歡跑步，看書或看電影。對我來說，做運動有利於每一個部分我的身體，包括我的心智。我可以釋放我的壓力並感覺更平靜。當我度假時，我喜歡出國旅行體驗不同的文化並待在不同的國家。這是一個令人難忘無價的經驗和記憶，豐富了我的生活。

　　我深信這句話「有志者事竟成」。在您的公司作為客服代表是我夢寐以求的工作；我希望我的夢想能夠盡快成真。謝謝你。

1-2. 自傳(2)

Hello, my name is David Wang. I'm very pleased to have this opportunity to introduce myself to you. I have confidence in both of my own abilities and work attitude. They are the important factors in my belief that I can be the best candidate for this position.

My first job was in ABC Computer in Hsinchu Science Park starting from 1999/11/2. My main job function was preliminarily analyzing the defective products that customers returned. (請閱2-2) When I worked in ABC, I had won the outstanding employee for 2 times in the third quarter of 2000 and in the second quarter of 2001.

Due to I would like to continue learning, I left ABC in March, 2003 and switched my gear in XYZ IT Corporation. (請閱2-2) For this job, I worked in the Customer Service Department answering the hot line of end-users' requirement. I also needed to respond end-users' question, duplicate their problem, and coordinate with our staff member in the production line. I appreciate that XYZ offered me a very good working environment and allowed me to pursue my further education after work.

I left XYZ in December 2007 and started at OPT Displays Corporation at the same month. I worked in supplier quality engineering department. My main job was controlling the material quality.

In July 2008, I went back to XYZ IT Corporation and continued to work in the Customer Service Department. I had the same duty doing the preliminary analysis for the defective products. In addition, I needed to go to the customer's company to double check the failures, and then brought back the flawed products to do further analysis. After the analysis, I needed to provide a report to the customer and solved the issue.

I have been worked for nearly 13 years. (請閱2-2) I think being responsible and having a good attitude are the keys to success. I believe I can make a great contribution at this position. Thank you for taking the time reading my job application, and thank you for your interest.

你好，我的名字是 David Wang。我很高興有這個機會介紹自己。我在自己的能力和工作態度這兩方面都有信心。他們是我相信我可以成為這個職位的最佳人選的重要因素。

我的第一份工作是從 1999 年 11 月 2 日開始在新竹科學園區的 ABC 電腦。我的主要工作職務是初步分析客戶退回的瑕疵品。當我在 ABC 電腦時，我在 2000 年第三季和 2001 年第二季兩次獲得優秀員工的獎項。

因為我想繼續學習，我於 2003 年 3 月離開 ABC 電腦轉換跑道到 XYZ 資訊公司。我在這份工作在客服部負責接聽終端用戶的需求熱線。我還需要應對終端用戶的問題，複製他們的問題，並我們在生產線的工作人員協調解決。我感謝 XYZ 給了我一個很好的工作環境，並讓我下班後持續進修。我在 2007 年 12 月離開 XYZ 並在同月開始在 OPT 顯示器公司上班。我曾在供應商質量工程部門。我的主要工作是材料控制。

2008 年 7 月，我回到了 XYZ 資訊公司，並繼續在客服部工作。我的責任同樣是為有缺陷的產品做初步分析。另外，我還需要去客戶的公司要仔細檢查錯誤，然後將瑕疵品帶回了做進一步的分析。經過分析，我需要提供一份報告給客戶，並解決問題。

我已經工作了將近 13 年。我認為有負責心以及有一個良好的心態是成功的關鍵。我相信我可以做在這個職位上有很大的貢獻。感謝您抽出寶貴的時間閱讀我的求職申請，並感謝您的興趣。

2 自傳寫作教室

2-1. 自傳(1) 寫作文法解析／小評語

在第二段裡的其中一個句子，「…,not only did I learn knowledge but also unity.」，中文裡我們會覺得知識是學來的，但在英文中 knowledge 很少跟 learn 搭配。這中觀念稱為 collocation。collocation 指的是單字間的習慣的一些組合，譬如說 knowledge 常搭配的動詞是 acquire, gain, have, demonstrate, test, apply 等。在英文中，知識 knowledge 是用取得 acquire 或獲得 gain 的，而不是用學習 learn。對 學生來說，知道 collocation 英文單字的習慣組合是克服中式英文的最 好辦法之一。而 unity 也是中式英文，這又關係單字選擇 word choice 的習慣，當然如果用中文直翻就是會有這種問題。這一句子建議可以 改成「…, not only did I gain professional knowledge but also sense of teamwork.」我不僅得到專業知識，也獲得了團隊工作的精神。 「Although…, but…」也是常犯的文法錯誤，中文中常講「雖然…但 是…」，但在英文中一個句子中只能有一個連接詞，所以 although 或 but 只能二選一。

第三段中間的這一句「During my first two years of college,…」 則是缺了連接詞。這裡連接句子可以用不同的種類的連接詞，最簡單 的就是使用「and」，變成「… in a fast-food restaurant, and it was...」，不然就是直接在「… in a fast-food restaurant. It was...」結 束句子，變成兩個完整的句子。

2-2. 自傳(2) 寫作文法解析／小評語

　　這個自傳是出自一位較有工作經驗的求職者，所以重點會放在以往的工作敘述。第二段中英文日期的講法是「Month date, year」，所以這裡建議改成 November 2, 1999。但在英文履歷跟自傳中一般只要提到月跟年就可以了。在第二句中，首先「function」應該改成「duty」。負責甚麼職務有不同的講法，可以用「I was in charge of…」或「I was responsible for…」等，記得後面是加名詞或動名詞。讓文章有變化的其中一個方式就是相同意思的表達可以試著在英文中用不同的說法，像這裏要一直提到自己所負責的工作職務，就可以試著不要一直重複「my main job duty was…」。

　　第三段第一句前半段「Due to…」是一個介系詞片語，後面只能加名詞或動名詞，這裡建議改成「For the pursuit of the continuous improvement in my professionalism,…」。其它畫底線的名詞則也是學生常犯的錯誤，在這裡它們應該全部都是複數形式。「requirement,」「question,」跟「problem」都是與 end-users 有關，不可能為只有一個為單數，而「member」前面是「staff」，本身「staff」就是指一群員工，所以後面的「member」也應該是複數。

　　最後一段的的第一句則是時態的錯誤。這一句可以用現在完成式「I have worked for nearly 13 years.」，或現在完成進行式「I have been working for nearly 13 years.」來強調 13 年不間斷地工作。不過這一句應該是要強調多年的工作經驗，所以更好的講法是「I have 13-year work experience.」。

激勵小故事

A Lesson Worth Million Dollars

I've been to seminars where motivational speakers charge thousands of dollars to impart training to corporate executives and staff. Once, a cab driver taught me a million dollar lesson in customer satisfaction and expectation. It cost me a $15 taxi ride.

I had flown into Chicago for the only purpose of meeting a client. Time was very important and my plan included a quick turnaround trip from and back to the airport. A squeaky clean cab pulled up. The driver came out rushed to open the passenger door for me and made sure I was comfortably seated before he closed the door. As he got in the driver's seat, he reminded me that the tidily folded newspaper next to me was for my use. Then he showed me several CDs and asked me what type of music I would like. Well! I looked around for a "Hidden Camera!" I could not believe I was receiving this type of service! I took the opportunity to say, "Apparently you take great pride in your work. You must have a story to tell."

"Of course," he replied, "I used to work in Bank America, but I got tired of doing my best would never be good enough. I decided to find my position in life where I could feel proud of being the best I could be. I knew I would never be a brain surgeon, but I love driving cars, providing my service and feeling like I have done a full day's work and done it well. I evaluate my personal assets and... voila! I became a taxi driver. One thing I know for sure that if I want to be good in my business I could simply just meet the expectations of my passengers. However, if I want to be great in my business, I have to go beyond the customer's expectations! I like to be constantly told that I am being 'great' better than just getting by on 'average' in return."

Did I tip him like big time? Oh, yah! Bank America's loss now is the best company a passenger could ever ask for!

一個價值百萬的課程

我曾經去過許多研討會勵志演講要價數千美元傳授訓練給企業管理人員和工作人員。在一次機會裡，一個計程車司機在客戶滿意度和期望給我上了寶貴的一課。而它只花了我 15 美元的計程車費。

我曾經飛到芝加哥的唯一目是要與一位客戶接觸。時間很重要，而我的計劃包括快速地來回機場。一輛一塵不染的計程車停在我面前。司機隨即出來打開車門，並在他關上了門之前確保我舒服地坐好。當他在駕駛座上，他提醒我在我旁邊折疊整齊的報紙是給我使用。接著，他拿了幾個 CD 出來，問我喜歡什麼類型的音樂。好吧！我環顧四周想找出一個「偷拍」的攝影機。我簡直不敢相信我在享受這樣服務！我趁機說：「很明顯，你在你的工作上感到非常自豪，你一定有一個故事。」

他回答「當然，「我曾經在美國銀行上班，但我厭倦了怎麼努力也永遠不夠好。我決定要將我的生活立基在我能盡我所能去做並感到驕傲。我知道我永遠也不會成為一個大腦外科醫生，但是我喜歡開車，為別人服務，就感覺像我已經做了一整天的工作而且把事情做好，我評估了我個人的條件……瞧！我成了一個計程車司機。有一件事我可以肯定知道，要做好我的生意，我只需簡單地滿足乘客的期望，但是要把我的生意做得傑出，我就必須超出顧客的期望！我想要不斷有回應告訴我做的『很棒』而不只是『還好』。」

我有給他很多的小費嗎？當然！美國信用公司的損失成為了乘客的良伴!

1-1 常遇到的考題

Q 1

Tell me about yourself?
請自我介紹。

My name is Thomas. I graduated from XYZ University with Bachelor degree in English. After graduation, I have traveled to several countries in Europe. Getting to know other cultures and people is a fascinating experience. I'm a great communicator. I get along well with almost everyone and I have no trouble getting to know new people. My friends think I am helpful and dependable.

After 2 years working as a product promoter, I have well knowledge of principle and methods for showing, promoting, and selling products to customers. When I worked in ABC company, I met and deal with all kinds of people every day. I was excited to suggest specific product to meet customers' needs.

I know AAA Company operates in the U.S. I found that you have recently entered the Europe market. I would love to become part of your team, helping to develop the new market by utilizing my promoting skills.

我是 Thomas。我畢業於 XYZ 大學，英語學士學位。畢業後，我到歐洲幾個國家旅行，了接當地的名俗風情是極好的經驗。我是個絕佳的溝通者，我能夠與大多數人相處，剛認識的人也沒問題，我的朋友認為我很熱於助人，並且值得依賴。

擔任 2 年的產品解說員，我具備應有的規範與方式，像是展示方

式、推廣及銷售產品。我在 ABC 公司工作期間，我每天要面對各式各樣的客戶，我很樂意向客戶推薦適合他們需要的產品。

　　我知道 AAA 公司主要美國。我發現最近貴公司已進入歐洲市場，我很希望成為貴公司的一員，運用我的推廣技巧幫助拓展新市場

Q 2 What do you know about the position of Product promoter?
你對產品解說員這個職位知道些甚麼？

　　The duties of product promoters are someone who creates public interest in buying products or service. They must greet and catch the attention of possible customers and quickly identify those who are interested and qualified. They inform and educate customers about the features of products and demonstrate their use with apparent ease to inspire confidence in the product and its manufacturer. Product promoters also try to build future sales by gathering names of prospects to contact at a later date.

　　For me, I think the product promoter has abilities to listen to and understand information and ideas presented through spoken words and sentences; to promote products, provide good services; to work under pressure.

　　Therefore, product promoters need knowledge of showing, promoting, and selling products or services. This includes marketing strategies and tactics, product demonstrations, sales techniques, and sales control systems. Knowledge of providing customer and personal services. This includes customer needs assessment, meeting quality standards for services, and evaluation of customer satisfaction.

　　產品解說員的職責是引起大眾購買產品或服務的興趣，必須要能夠吸引潛在客戶注意，快速的辨別出會購買產品的客戶；他們要能夠傳遞及教育客戶產品的功能，並且示範使用方式，使客戶對產品與製造商有信心；產品解說員也要試著利用蒐集的客戶名單，在之後連繫以建立未來的銷售。

對我來說，我認為產品解說員要有傾聽與理解的能力、推廣產品、提供好的服務，並且能夠在壓力下工作。因此，產品解說員要有展示、推廣與銷售產品或服務的知識，包含了行銷策略與戰略、產品展示、銷售技巧與銷售控制系統；客戶服務的知識，包含客戶需求評估、與客戶開會時的服務標準流程，以及顧客滿意度衡量。

Q 3 **Why should we hire you as Product promoter?**
為什麼我們公司要僱用你呢？

I'm a good fit for the position because of my past experience, my personality, and my education. I have the determination and necessary skills for this job. For personality, I am a self-starter, highly motivated, enthusiastic and goal-oriented, independent and also cooperative and a team player. I have good communication skills and good listening skills. Also I have extensive knowledge of principles and methods for showing, promoting, and selling products and services. This includes marketing strategies and tactics, product demonstrations, sales techniques, and sales control systems; have remarkable ability to listen to and understand information and ideas presented through spoken words and sentences; have great ability to persuade others to change their minds or behavior; have profound ability to promote products, provide good service; have pleasant, patient and friendly attitude and hard working. My track record during my 3 years with AAA Company proves that I possess all of them. I am impressed with ABC Company and would feel privileged to work here.

我過去的工作經驗，個性與教育程度可以說明我非常適合產品解說員。我具備這份工作要有的能力；就個性來說，我是個做事主動，有衝進、有熱誠、目標導向，可以獨立作業也可以與團隊合作。 我具有良好的溝通與傾聽能力。我也對展示、促進、和銷售的產品和服務的原則方法，有廣泛的瞭解，這包括行銷戰略和策略、 產品演示、銷售技巧和銷售控制系統；有出色的能力理解傾聽說話者的字裡行間的

訊息；有能力說服他人改變他們的思想或行為；有令人深刻的能力，推廣產品、提供良好的服務；能用令人愉快、耐心、友好的態度努力工作。從我過去 3 年在 AAA 公司的工作經歷可以證明擁有這些能力。可以加入 ABC 公司並在此工作，是我的榮幸。

Q

4 **How many years of experience do you have for Product promoter position?**
你擔任產品解說員的職位有多少年？

I have had 3 years of working for Tom Electrical where I was in charge of product promoter position. My experiences and duties are includes, such as: Visiting homes, community organizations, stores, and schools to demonstrate Tom Electrical products and services. Attending various trade, traveling, promotional, educational, and amusement exhibit, answering visitors' questions and protecting exhibit against theft or damage. Setting up and arrange display to attract attention of prospective customers. Suggest improvements of management and products. Answer telephone and written requests from customers for information about product use and writing articles and pamphlets on product. Lecturing and showing slides to users of electrical products. Advising customers on homemaking problems related to products or services offered by Tom Electrical. Instruct customers in alteration of products. Develop list of prospective clients from sources, such as newspaper items, company records, local merchants, and customers.

我曾在 Tom Electrical 擔任產品解說員 3 年。我的經驗與職責包括：前往各家庭、社區組織、商店和學校展示 Tom Electrical 產品和服務。出席各種貿易、旅遊、宣傳、教育、和娛樂等展覽、回答訪客的問題和保護展場秩序防止盜竊或損壞。布置和安排產品展示來吸引注意的潛在客戶。建議產品和管理的改進方法。答覆客戶來電或書面

詢問關於產品使用方式，撰寫文章，產品型錄的想關資訊。向使用者用幻燈片演示講授電器產品。通知客戶 Tom Electrical 產品使用或服務上的問題。指導客戶在產品修改。從報紙專案、公司記錄、本地商家和客戶等來源，開發潛在客戶名單。

Q 5 What are top 3 knowledge/top 3 skills for Product promoter position?
產品解說員的首要三個技能是甚麼？

I believe clear speaking, active listening, and great comprehension are top 3 skills to succeed in Product promoter position. First, this position requires clear speaking skill. Because a product promoter need to demonstrate and explain products or services in order to persuade customers to purchase products or utilize services. What I think talking to others to convey information effectively is very important as a Product promoter. A good Product promoter also requires active listening skills. Giving full attention to what customers are saying, taking time to understand the points being made, asking questions to be aware of their queries. In addition, a great comprehension is essential. A Product promoter must have ability to understand information and ideas presented through spoken words and sentences from customers; and further, must identify interested and qualified customers in order to provide them with additional information.

　　我認為清楚的談話、積極的傾聽與良好的理解力是身為一位成功的產品解說員需要的前三種能力。首先，這個職位應具備清楚的說話技巧，因為需要藉由展示與介紹產品或服務，以說服客戶購買。所以我認為有效傳遞資訊是非常重要的。同時一位好的產品解說員也需具備傾聽的能力，客戶在說話時要專心聆聽，適時給予回應，詢問以了解客戶需求。除此之外，要具備良好的理解能力，要從客戶的話語中理解訊息，釐清客戶喜好以提供他們額外的資訊。

Q 6

How to measure/appraise your position: Product promoter?
要如何評定衡量產品解說員的職位？

Product promoters most concerned with promoting products to create a lasting impression among customers to improve product sales and market preference of a brand name. I think a good product promoter should do these well. Write down the benefits of the product you are promoting, so that you will have a clear idea of why other people should pay attention to your demonstration. Approach the target audience for the product you are promoting in a nonthreatening, relaxed, and friendly way. Answer questions honestly, and present information in a forward, confident way. Use your people skills to become more trustworthy and likable. Discuss only the positives, and act responsibly. Prepare for any questions or eventualities that might arise when promoting. Take every opportunity to promote, and do it in a fresh way every time. To be a good product promoter you need to be aware of the different approaches, angles and products that compete with yours.

　　產品解說員要關注的是產品的推廣，在顧客心中建立一個長久印象，增加銷售和市場品牌知名度。我認為好的產品解說員應該做好這些：寫下推廣該產品的好處，你會清楚地了解為什麼其他人應重視你的展示。以不具脅迫感的、輕鬆和友好的方式向目標聽眾，推廣產品。用熱誠自信的方式，誠實地回答問題，提供資訊。

　　運用你的人際關係技巧，令人覺得可信任和討人喜歡。用積極態度與人討論，並表現負責行為。對展示中，任何可能會出現的問題與突發事件做好準備。不放過任何解說機會，而且每次都以耳目一新的方式。好的產品解說員，需要用不同方法和角度了解競爭者的產品。

7 What are key tasks for a Product promoter?
產品解說員的主要任務是？

From my experience, the key tasks for a product promoter are: Demonstrate or explain products, methods, or services to persuade customers to purchase products or use services. Provide product samples, coupons, informational brochures, or other incentives to persuade customers to buy products. Keep areas neat while working and return items to correct locations following demonstrations. Record and report demonstration-related information, such as the number of questions asked by the audience or the number of coupons distributed. Set up and arrange displays or demonstration areas to attract the attention of prospective customers. Suggest specific product purchases to meet customers' needs. Transport, assemble, and disassemble materials used in presentations. Identify interested and qualified or prospective customers to provide them with additional information. Learn about customer's interests and design products as per their needs. Develop lists of potential clients from sources. Practice demonstrations to ensure that they will run smoothly.

　　就我的經驗，產品解說員主要任務包含：

　　展示或解釋產品、方法或服務，以說服客戶購買產品或使用服務。提供產品樣品、優惠券、產品說明、或其鼓勵說服客戶購買產品。工作時保持整潔的區域和在產品示範後放置在正確的位置。要記錄和報告與展示有關的資訊，如觀眾提問數量或優惠券分發數量。布置和安排產品展示或示範區，以吸引潛在客戶的注意力。建議購買特定的產品來滿足客戶的需求。運輸、裝配、和拆卸在展示時要使用的材料。確定感興趣的和符合資格或潛在客戶，為他們提供的額外資訊。了解關於客戶的喜好，或依據需要量身訂做產品。從各種資源中尋找潛在客戶名單。演練展示，確保正式展示時可以順利運行。

8

What made you choose to apply to Product promoter?
為何要應徵我們公司產品解說員？

Alok Group has been enjoying an incredible standing in the food industry for the last 60 years. You have created a special world of healthy, natural products for customer to get the most refreshing flavors. I always read about your company involving in "Go Green" activities. I am impressed by this and want to be part of such an admirable culture. Now, I learned that you are looking for a pleasant and competitive product promoter that thrives in attracting new customers.

Alok Group 在過去的 60 年，在食品工業享有特殊地位。貴公司建立了一個健康，天然產品的特殊世界，讓客戶能夠嚐到令人耳目一新的口味。我總是讀到有關貴公司公司投入「綠色」活動的消息，令我印象深刻，且想要成為這種令人敬佩的文化的一員。現在，我得知共公司正在尋找有親和力和有競爭心，能夠吸引新的客戶的產品解說員。

I have Bachelor degree in Marketing and have more than two years of experience as a promoter preferable. I have ability to understand customer needs and handle different types of personalities; have strong listening, communication, presentation and social skills. I know how to play a fundamental role in achieving your ambitious customer acquisition and revenue growth objectives. I am comfortable making numerous product presentations, generating interest and qualifying sales prospects.

我有市場行銷學士學位，並有超過兩年的產品解說員經驗。我有能力瞭解客戶的需求和處理不同類型的客戶；我有很強的傾聽、溝通、展示和社交技能。我知道如何扮演好我的角色，實現貴公司的開發新客戶的抱負和增長營收的目標。我很習慣於做產品展示、引起興趣和滿足銷售目標。

1-2 臨場反應篇

Q

1

Try to imagine that I am a customer.
Demonstrate this pen to me.
試想我是一位客戶，向我展示這支筆。

What kinds of pens do you use now? I am going to present you a pen doesn't use an ink cartridge; my company develops a special composite tip that gives the appearance of ink but lasts for years and doesn't smudge at all. Once you get one, you don't need to replenish it for years. It will save your purchasing department a lot of time and cost. Right now, if your order quantity is over 100 units, we will mark your Brand on it to well promote your image.

您現在使用哪種產品呢？我正展示給您的筆不需要使用墨水夾，我們公司研發出一種特殊合成的鋼筆頭，字跡如同用墨水寫出一般，維持多年不會消失，而且不暈開。您只要購買一次，好幾年都不需要再補充，可以大幅節省貴公司採購部門的時間與金錢。現在，如果你的訂單量有超過 100 隻，我們將會在筆身打上貴公司商標，可以推廣貴公司形象。

I am sure you will agree with me that a pen is vital to your day-to-day work. This pen is solidly constructed so as to be durable for everyday use, even if it rolls off your desk onto the floor. It fits comfortably into the hand and even has a clip so you can safely attach it to your jacket pocket when you're on the move. I can offer you this pen at the very reasonable price of 20 dollars.

我相信你會同意我筆是對您的日常工作至關重要，這支鋼筆是做的扎實用適合日常使用，即使它從桌子滾到了地板上。他拿在手上非常貼合，甚至筆上有個安全夾，當你在行動時，可以夾在你的夾克口袋。我可以給你這支筆 20 美元的價格，非常合理。

2

It seems that you don't have any experience in this position.
似乎你沒有具備這個職位該有的任何工作經驗。

I do admit that I don't have as much experience in product promoter. However, before I graduated from university, I have worked a part-time job at XXX, a well-known company. I am a rep and marketing assistant. My job is let customers know our products during the product trade show. My boss was impressed by my communicate skills and the ability to respond effectively.

我承認我未曾擔任產品解說員的工作，但是，我在大學畢業之前，我曾在一家知名的 XXX 公司打工，我是業務與行銷部門的助理。我的工作是在展會時，讓客戶知道我們公司的產品。我的主管對我的溝通技巧與快速的應對能力印象深刻。

No. Although I do not have directive experience in product promoter, because of my educational background in biomedical engineering, I have a good understanding of what customers need and how to communicate effectively with them. My biomedical knowledge would add value. In addition, I worked as an interpreter at international trade fairs. I learned the importance of effective communications, especially in an intercultural setting like that. I believe my background, intercultural experience and skills will be an asset in a global cooperation like yours.

雖然我並沒有產品解說員的經驗，但是我在生物醫學工程的教育背景，使我非常瞭解客戶需要什麼，以及知道怎麼有效地與他們溝通。我在生物醫學的相關知識是一種附加價值。此外，我曾在國際貿易展覽會，擔任一名口譯員。我學會了有效的溝通的重要性，特別是在跨文化的環境中。我相信我的教育背景，跨文化經驗和技能，對公司這樣的跨國企業能有所貢獻。

3 How do you handle difficult customers?
你如何處理難搞的客戶？

As a Product promoter, I often had to deal with unexpected situations. I have a few tips to help me cope the rude customers. Keep smiling and set the tone by responding calmly and politely, no matter how the client spoke to me. Not only does this establish me as a professional, my calm tone will prompt my client to respond in kind. The client may not have even realized his behavior was rude. Be patience. Allow the client to finish speaking before responding, then summarize what I heard and ask for verification that I heard correctly. Sometimes, all the client needs is to feel like you have paid attention to his concerns. Control the conversation. Firmly guide the conversation toward the client's needs and if the client wanders off topic, politely guide him back to the point. If I am unable to satisfy the customer with my own power, I will contact my supervisor for help.

身為一個產品解說員，我時常必須處理突發狀況，我有幾個方法作應對這類客戶。保持微笑，用平靜和禮貌的語調回應，不管客戶怎麼說。這樣，不只會建立我專業的形象，我平靜的口氣將提醒客戶作出同樣的反應，客戶可能沒有意識到他的行為是不禮貌的。有耐心，在回應客人之前，讓他先完整說完，然後總結我聽到的，並且問問題檢查我聽到的是否正確。有時客戶只是想要覺得你有留意他的關注。控制談話，堅定地引導談話往客戶需求，如果客戶離題，禮貌的引導回正題。如果我的處理權限不能滿足顧客，我會向我的主管尋求幫助。

Q

4

While you are introducing products to potential customers, one of your existing customers comes and very upset about your product. What would you do?
當你正在對潛在客戶群介紹產品時，一位你的現有客戶出現並且對產品表示不滿，這時你會如何處理?

When the situation happened, I will first call a help from my team member to replace my presentation and then take my current customer to a quiet place and take several steps to deal with this situation. First the most important thing is listen thoroughly to the customer's complaint and avoid interrupting him while he is speaking. I will ask some questions once the customer is finished to clarify issues. Remaining professional during this time keeps the customer calm and prevents the situation from becoming complicated or out of control. Usually I will say something like "I apologize that this occurred, John." to agree with the customer that a problem exists. I will not disagree or argue whether the customer is right or wrong. If the problem will take multi-step process to resolve, I will completely explain the procedures or steps necessary to solve the problem. Customers want to know that their problems will be resolved in a reasonable amount of time, if the complaint cannot be handled immediately.

當情況發生時，我首先會尋求我的組員接替產品介紹的工作，然後我會將現有客戶帶到相對安靜的地方。首先，最重要的是仔細地傾聽客戶的投訴，當他在說的時候，避免打斷他。當客戶說完後，我會問一些釐清澄清的事情。在這過程中，維持專業形象，讓客戶冷靜下來，避免情況變得複雜或是超出過控制。通常我會說些像是「我很抱歉發生這樣的事，John」的話，同意客戶問題的存在。不管客人對或錯，我不會提出異議或辯論。如果問題將採取多個步驟來解決，我會完整向客戶解釋處理過程或解決問題的必要步驟。客戶想要知道如果不能立即處理的話，要花多長時間解決他們的問題。

1-3 我有疑問篇

Q 1 **What will my responsibilities be?**
請問我的工作內容？

Generally speaking, you will need to visit community organizations, stores, and schools to demonstrate XXX products and services; attend trade, traveling, promotional, educational, and amusement exhibit to answer visitors' questions; develop a list of prospective clients from sources. Here is our detailed job description for your reference.

Demonstrate product to customers during a show, or another venue. Market product to clients or companies who displays a need for the product. Show how product is best-used. Show how product should be cleaned and properly stored. Use graphics and slideshows during presentation. Answer questions about the product. Give product samples. Visit customer's home to demonstrate product. Set up booths, including pictures and samples. Conduct guided tours. Tell customers why product is better than competitors. Suggest specific product purchases. Visit trade shows to demonstrate product. Contact businesses and arrange for demonstrations or exhibitions. Recommend product improvements to maker. Improvise product demonstrations depending on audience size and attention span.

Produce coupons and informational brochures. Take orders from companies for products.

大致上，你會需要到各地，例如社區組織，店面及學校，示範產品與服務;參加展示會、出差、產品推廣、教育與娛樂展示、回答參觀者問題；利用不同資源，開發潛在客戶名單。這是我們的詳細工作說明供你參考。

在展會期間或一個地點，向客戶在展示產品。向對公司產品表示有興趣的客戶或公司行銷產品。示範如何最佳使用產品。示範產品清

理和妥善保存方式。在演示過程中使用的圖片和幻燈片。回答有關產品的問題。給產品樣品。到客戶家中拜訪展示產品。設置展覽攤位，包括圖片和樣品。導覽。向客戶說明為什麼產品比競爭對手更好。建議購買特定產品。參觀展會展示產品。請聯繫業務並安排展示或展覽。向製造商建議產品改進。根據觀眾大小和注意力即興產品示範方式。

發送優惠券和產品宣傳文宣。遵守公司對產品的指示。

2 **What training do you provide?**
貴公司提供甚麼樣的員工訓練？

The ABC Company has several innovative XXX products in the pipeline. And that is why we welcome enthusiastic, talented individuals to help us extend our global market. We treat our staff as our asset. On-the-job training is the standard method of obtaining the knowledge and skills required for product promoter jobs. As a product promoter, you are given special training that is product oriented. These training sessions are designed and tailored with the intention of equipping employees with thorough understanding of products and services. So, product promoters are able to familiarize themselves with the product and demonstrate it properly. You will also receive knowledge of the ABC Company's corporate vision, customer services, and sales strategies. Moreover, ABC company will offer extensive training sessions to employees. We will invite experts to guide employees and reinforce your skills.

ABC 公司在領域中有幾項創新 XXX 產品。這就是為什麼我們歡迎熱心、有才華的個人，來協助我們拓展的全球市場。我們把我們的員工當作我們的資產。對產品解說員，在職培訓是獲取知識和技能的標準方法。身為產品宣傳員，你會有產品方面的特別培訓。這些培訓課程設計，專門產品解說員量身訂作，主要是能夠完整瞭解的產品和服務，能夠熟悉產品並且正確地展示。您還會接收有關 ABC 公司的企

業願景、客戶服務和銷售戰略的相關知識。此外，ABC 公司將為員工提供廣泛的培訓課程。我們會邀請專家到公司指導員工增強職能。

Q 3 **What qualities do you look for in this position?**
你對這個職務的要求條件為何？

The stress tolerance is quite important. Because, a product promoter, usually, has to work under stress as it is likely to come while working in crowded trade atmosphere. You have to deal with a number of customers in limited amount of time. This job also requires accepting criticism and dealing calmly and effectively with high stress situations. So, adaptability and flexibility is also very important. We are looking for a qualified candidate who are able to self-motivated, work alone and a member of a team. The candidate must be comfortable with public speaking and interacting with perfect people skills. The person we want must be happy and friendly and also be able to talk to customers about the benefits of the product they are demonstrating to help sell the products. Also the candidate must able to learn about customer's interests and suggest suitable products as per their needs.

壓力的承受力是相當重要，因為一個產品解說員，通常會在壓力下工作，譬如是在擁擠的展會氛圍之下，你必須在有限的時間中，要處理大量的客戶；這份工作也需要能夠接受批評，有效的自我緩和高壓，所以適應力與保持彈性也是很重要的。我們在尋找的合格候選人，能夠自我激勵，可以單獨做事也可以在團隊中工作。候選人必須能夠自在的公眾演講和客戶完美互動的技能。我們要找的人必須能快樂和友善的與客戶暢談展示正在推銷的產品的好處。候選人還必須能夠瞭解客戶的喜好，根據他們的需要，建議適合的產品。

4 What is your competitive edge?
貴公司的競爭力為何？

Top-quality products, outstanding customer service, quick and reliable delivery times that makes Danny Inc. difference. For over 50 years, we have not only designed, built and installed the finest custom shutters in the world, we also build futures. Danny Inc. is a patent-holding shutter manufacturer and innovator. Quality has always been the focus at Danny. All of our products are 100% custom-made, and we can build shutters to fit any type or shape of window and match the decor of your home interior. Danny is staffed by highly trained, competent professionals. Our goal is to guide our clients through the whole shutter process as smoothly as possible. To keep control of the immense workflow in our production facilities, Danny created a proprietary shutter software program enables our staff to schedule all aspects of the manufacturing processes, ensuring strict adherence to our delivery date commitments.

Danny Inc 的優勢在高品質的產品、卓越的客戶服務、以及快速可靠的交貨時間。50 多年來，我們不只有設計、製造、安裝優質的訂製百葉窗，我們還建立未來。Danny Inc 擁有百葉窗專利的製造商和創新者。品質一直在我們所重視的。我們所有的產品都 100% 訂製，我們的百葉窗適合任何窗戶的外觀以及匹配您家室內的裝潢。Danny 的職員都接受專業的訓練。我們的目標是協助客戶快速順利完成的百葉窗安裝過程。為了控制生產設備的龐大工作流程，我們開發了有專利的百葉窗安裝軟體，使我們的工作人員能夠完全掌控生產過程的進度，嚴格遵守承諾的交貨日期。

1 範例

1-1. 自傳(1)

MMy name is Peter Chan. I have read in the local newspaper that Product promoter is recruiting candidate for the position of XYZ and I would like it very much to apply for this position.

I have had 2 years of working for ABC Computer System Company where I was responsible for sales and marketing activities. I have excellent presentation skills to demonstrate products to customers during trade shows and marketing activities through various presentation materials; communication skills to listen and talk to people; suggest and help customers purchase the suitable products by providing useful product information. For example, I was a key contact person between my former employer ABC Computer System Company and BBS, a USA shipping company. After talking to the purchase department from BBS, I found the cost of BBS's current inventory warehousing system were high and growing worse. At my suggestion, I helped BBS understand our system and develop custom software to meet BBS's needs. The result of custom-made software has been decrease 10% of BBS's expense.

Besides, I have excellent people skills. I get along with almost everyone and I have no trouble getting to know new people. I always received good performance reviews from my superiors and customers that I am persuasive but also have good listening skills.

I believe my abilities of developing new accounts and well-versed in the latest XXX trends and have knowledge of the market and a strong contact bases. My past accomplishments prove that my ability to initiate and foster partnership relationships. I am confident that those qualities shall contribute significantly to the success of your company.

我的名字是 Peter Chan。從本地的報紙得知貴公司 XYZ 招募產品解說員，我非常想要應徵這個職位

我曾在 ABC Computer System 公司工作 2 年，期間負責業務行銷活動。我具備傑出的展示技巧，在產品展示會或各種行銷活動的場合中，能夠利用各種的輔助展示產品的材料，向客戶示範操作公司產品；有效的溝通技巧，能夠聆聽客戶與客戶談話，從中了解客戶需求；藉由提供有用的產品資訊，建議及幫助客戶採購適合的產品。舉例來說，我曾經擔任 ABC computer Systerm 公司與美國客戶，BBS Shipping Company 之間的主要聯絡人。當時，與 BBS 的採購部門談話之後，了解 BBS 目前使用的一套存貨庫存系統，成本花費過高，而且愈來愈不好用。在我的提案下，我讓 BBS 了解 ABC 系統，並且研發一套符合 BBS 需求的一套軟體。最後這套量身訂做的軟體幫助 BBS 公司節省了 10% 成本費用。

除此之外，我的社交能力很好。我幾乎跟所有人都相處得很好，遇到初次見面的人，也沒有問題。我總是得到來自上司的良好評語；還有客戶認為我不僅是有說服力，也同時擁有傾聽的能力。

我相信我具備的相關能力，開發客戶能力、熟知最新趨勢與市場以及深厚人脈。從我過去的經歷，可以證明我具有促進和建立合作關係的能力。我有信心能夠提供貴公司所需的能力。

1-2. 自傳(2)

My name is Esther. I think myself an active and positive attitude person. My friends think I am enthusiastic, highly motivates, energetic, and adaptable. During the period of time in XZY University, I participated in all kinds of activities and I always played the roles of host; in addition, in order to be prepared for the employment market, I worked a part-time job at PP, which is a listed company on the NASDAQ to gain more experience. I serve as different positions, e.g. a product promoter during trade shows and a sales assistant. As a product promoter, my duties are answering customer's queries, convincing customers to buy our products or to otherwise change their minds or actions; dealing with customers in various situations. Enable to deliver the correct information of products; I was trained to be familiar with the products; because we, a product promoter ought to deliver customers correctly about products and demonstrate their use during the trade show.

Both my professor and my last sales executive said I am a very responsible and dependable person. They had a high opinion of me; especially my last sales executive was impressed by my good communication and interpersonal skills.

Through the experience, I learned the essentials of communication skills, product demonstration skills, customer service skills. And I believe my abilities will be an asset in a esteemed company like yours.

　　我的名字是 Esther，是一個積極與正面思考的人。我的朋友則認為我是個熱誠，非常有衝勁、精力旺盛、適應力很強。在就讀 XYZ 大學期間，我參加大大小小的活動，一直都是擔任主持人的角色。除此之外，為了提早適應就業市場，我曾在 NASDAQ 上市的 PP 公司得到打工機會，獲得很多寶貴經驗。 我的工作內容多樣，譬如產品展示會時的產品解說員，也是業務助理。作為一個產品解說員，我要負責解答客戶題問、說服客戶購買我們的產品，或者要改變他們的想法或者購買的行動；處理各種客戶情況；傳遞正確的產品資訊，身為一個產品解說員在展示會時，應該要能夠正確的告知與示範自家產品。

　　我的學校教授與前業務主管都說我是個負責任與可靠的人，對我有很高的評價，特別是前業務主管，對我的溝通與人際能力印象非常深刻。

　　從過去這些經驗，我學習到許多的基本能力，像是溝通技巧、產品展示技巧、與顧客服務技巧等等，我深信這些能夠協助到貴公司。

2 自傳寫作教室

2-1. 自傳(1) 寫作文法解析／小評語

　　針對有工作經驗的產品解說員來說，自傳的描述重點最好能強調過去的工作經驗，獲取哪些知識條件，尤其是產品解說員的職位屬於通才，工作內容可說是包羅萬象，最好是藉著舉例說明過去工作的表現，讓對方了解應徵者的能力與潛力，可以為未來的公司提供的幫助，爭取進一步面試的機會。

　　產品推廣員需要具備幾項知識，提供讀者參考：

- **Sales and Marketing**
  產品推廣員應該要有展示、推廣、以及銷售的概念；要能夠熟悉產品，正確地展示或示範給客戶；配合公司的行銷推廣活動，收集市場資訊；還需要知道銷售流程。

- **Customer and Personal Service**
  產品推廣員應該要有顧客服務的概念，譬如，要能夠理解客戶需要、顧客服務流程、以及顧客滿意度評估。

- **Language and Communications**
  產品推廣員應該要能夠運用各種溝通媒介與客戶溝通，特別是要掌握語言的能力，尤其面對國際性客戶要能夠運用國際通用語言作為溝通工具，英文已經是基本的溝通工具，如能掌握一種以上的語言能力，無疑是增加自身的競爭力。

2-2. 自傳(2) 寫作文法解析／小評語

　　產品解說員，不僅僅需要工作經驗的累積，涉及層面也很廣泛，尤其是參加國際型展覽，更需要具備語言的條件，才能與來自不同國家的採購做有效地溝通。如果是剛畢業沒有工作經驗的學生，則注重在在學期間的社團經驗，擔任的角色如有關應徵職位，更應該指出說明；在學校期間的學習表現，學校教授的評語或是得獎紀錄等等，這是可以好好發揮的部分;或是打工經驗，如果應徵職位相關的話，要特別指出說明。

　　在自傳中我們要描述過去一段時間中，做過的事件時可以用「During the period of time...」時間片語。用「to participate in...」告訴對方，參加過哪些活動，活動中擔任「serve as...」甚麼樣的職位。撰寫自傳時，文中多少會提及推薦人對求職者的正面評價時，可以用「...have a high/good opinion of me」，或者是用「...be impressed by...」舉例說明。

激勵小故事

The position of product promoter, as the name implies, has to demonstrate and promote products for sale at conventions, product trade shows, and international exhibitions, so interested buyers will purchase them. The product promoter may sell demonstrated merchandise. More than that, a qualified product promoter, especially being an international product promoter requires at least one language skills. Of course, English language is the basic.

When attending international exhibitions, we may travel to several countries. Getting to know other cultures and peoples is one of fascinating experiences. Familiar with products is the most important thing. This is the most attractive part of entire job; because I am able to use the fresh model prior to the market.

However, we also must stay a good adaptability to face different challenges. The most challengeing thing is that sometimes, you have to meet several buyers all at once. For examples, when you answer one of customers first may be accused of favouritism by others, such as " I am the first one to meet you, but you serve him ahead of me." At this kind of situation, I had to respond the situation as quick as I can. I tried to stop and divert their criticism; let all of them keep quiet and pay attention to my presentation; finally the dispute was settled successfully.

Another challenge a product promoter must have is a learning ability. You will never know what happens during the exhibition. Therefore, I have not only knowledge of the latest models, but also old ones few years ago, in case, customers inquire the old models. No matter how, a professional product promoter should express the correct product information and assist buyers select the suitable products.

產品解說員，顧名思義，就是在各種銷售會、產品展示會與國際性展覽中展示與推廣產品，引起購買者的興趣並購買產品。產品解說員可能還會銷售產品；

不只如此，合格的產品解說員，特別是擔任國際性的產品解說員，要能具備至少一種語言的聽說讀寫能力，當然英文能力是基本條件。

當參加國際性展覽時，我們會出差到不同國家，可以了解不同文化與民俗風情是一個令人雀躍的體驗。熟悉產品是非常重要的，這是整個工作中最迷人的部分，因為在投入市場之前，我能夠比其他人更早接觸新產品。

然而，我們在面對各種挑戰時，必須要有隨時應變的能力。在展覽會場，有時候會在一個時間點，同時需要接待幾位客戶，這是最艱難的地方；舉例來說，當你首先回答其中一位客戶時，會引起其他客戶不快，認為有不公平的情況，像是「我最先來的，你卻先招待他」；通常這樣的情況發生時，我必須要能夠快速的回應處理，我會試著安撫並轉移焦點，讓所有人安靜下來，專注在我的產品示範，最後成功的平復爭議。

產品解說員的另一種挑戰來自是學習能力。在展覽時你永遠不知道會發生甚麼，因此，除了要有最新展示產品的資訊，也必須要知道幾年前的產品，以防萬一，遇到客戶詢問。無論如何，一個專業的展品展示員應該要能正確傳達產品訊息，協助客戶選擇適合產品。

國外業務
工程師

A 口試篇

B 自傳篇

C 激勵小故事

1-1 常遇到的考題

Q 1

What type of experience do you have for the job?
你有何種經驗可以運用在這個工作上？

As you can see from my resume, I have a great understanding of all Engineering concepts, and have worked the past 6 years in various stages of the engineering process to include: research, development, production, and sales.

And the fact that have a Masters in Engineering, 3 years in Sales, and 6 years in Engineering. What's more, I am great with people, can multi-task, and communicate well the concepts of the products I sell.

What I know about the Sales Engineers primary role is to support the Sales department giving technical input and providing appropriate product solutions based on customer needs.

I am an experienced Sales Engineer, who wants to work for the best; and believe my experience, education, and skills make me your best choice.

如您在我履歷表上所看到的，我非常熟悉所有工程概念，而且過去六年前，我在各個工程相關職位待過，譬如研發、生產與銷售。

我了解電子產品與系統，特別是針對貴公司的產品，我相信我會成為貴公司最好的銷售員。 我本身是工程碩士，三年的業務經驗，與六年的工程師經驗。還有，個性上，我很容易與人相處，可以同時處理多項任務，並且我溝通好我要銷售產品的概念。

我認為業務工程師的主要角色，是給予業務部門技術支援，依客

戶需要提供合適產品的解決方案。

　　我是位有經驗的業務工程師，追求工作上的卓越，我相信我的實務經驗、教育背景以及技能會是貴公司最好的選擇。

Q2 What can you offer us?
你可以有甚麼貢獻？

　　I am looking for a better and challenging job position as a biomedical sales engineer in a well-established organization, where I utilize my exceptional qualities in boosting the sales of the company. Want to prove an important asset to the firm, and enhance the productivity of the institution.

　　I have 5 years of core experience in this particular sales profession; capable of handling the overseas sales assignment, and promoting the medical products of the company. I am skilled and well-experienced in dealing with different medical practitioners, and handling the sales team individually and efficiently.

　　This being a very professional job field, and as you can see from my resume, I have strong and complete knowledge regarding regional and local medical market. I am flexible, responsible, and active enough to handle overseas sales and marketing assignments. I believe you will benefit from my hands-on experience.

　　我希望可以找到一間卓越的公司，謀求一個能夠充分發揮所長並且富有挑戰性的生物醫學業務工程職位，在這裡可以利用我卓越的能力為公司提升銷售業績；證明我能成為公司資產，提升公司生產力。

　　在這特殊的產業，我有五年的核心經歷，能夠處理海外業務，推廣公司醫療產品；我有能力與經驗與不同的醫師打交道；且能夠獨立有效地處理業務團隊。

　　這是非常專業的工作領域，你可以從我的簡歷看，我有強勁和完整的知識，像是關於區域和地方醫療市場狀況。我很靈活、有責任心，並且積極足以應付海外銷售任務。我相信貴公司會從我的過去經驗中獲益良多。

Q 3 Please tell me the reasons that made you choose to apply to Sales Engineer?
請告訴我你選擇我公司業務工程師的原因？

I truly believe that your company produces better products than anyone else. Your company always leads the world in mobile phone market; also is known for its innovation. I am a lover of your products.

I am familiar with the duties of being a sales engineer, since I was one of several sales engineers with WYZ Manufacturing Company. I specialize in working with the production, engineering, or research and development departments to determine how products and services could be designed or modified to suit customers' needs and how best to use them.

My past experience fits me perfectly for sales engineer and I will bring my skills into full play.

我真誠地認為相較於其他公司，貴公司生產最好的產品。貴公司一直都是處於全球手機市場上的領先地位並且以創新聞名。我是貴公司產品的愛用者。

過去任職於 WYZ 製造廠，對於一個業務工程師的工作職責，我很了解。我專門在生產、工程或研發部門等合作，確認產品如何設計或修改才能符合客戶需求或者精進產品。

我經歷說明，我很適合貴公司需要的業務工程師職位、而且能夠將我的能力發揮極致。

Q 4 What are key tasks for a Sales Engineer? 國外業務工程師的工作是甚麼？

I know that a successful sales engineer combine technical knowledge of the products and services they are selling with excellent communication and people skills.

Selling, of course, is an important task of the job. A sales engineer used his or her technical skills to demonstrate to potential customers how and why the products or services they are selling would suit the customer better than competitors' products.

Using his or her engineering skills to help customers determine which products or services best fit their needs.

One of tasks as a sales engineer is providing technical support to clients who purchase manufacturer's products; helping solve any problems that may come up once a product has been installed.

Another task of sales engineer may be called to serve as a link between the customer and the company for which they work. Because of their experience in dealing with a wide range of client requests, sales engineers may also help other employees build ideas and develop new products.

一個成功的業務工程師結合了銷售的產品或服務有關的技術知識，以及卓越的溝通技巧與人際關係。

銷售，當然是這職位的一項重要任務。銷售業務利用他/她的技能展示給潛在客戶為什麼，他/她在銷售的產品或服務會比競爭者的產品更適合。

利用他/她的工程技能幫助客戶確定哪些產品或服務更能滿足需求。

業務工程師的其中一項工作內容，就是為採購公司產品的客戶提供技術支援，幫助解決產品安裝後產生的相關問題。

銷售工程師的另一項任務可能被要求擔任客戶和任職公司之間的聯繫。因為他們在處理無奇不有的客戶需求的經驗，銷售工程師也可以幫助其他員工激發創意和開發新產品。

Q 5

What are skills or knowledge that you used in your work as Sales Engineer? Please explain how to you use them?
甚麼是你在擔任業務工程師工作中，所使用的能力與知識？請解釋如何使用他們？

I think I have what you want. The position requires complete technological skills, interpersonal skills, problem-solving skills, and language skills.

I, being a sales engineer, have extensive knowledge of the technologically sophisticated products at this field, so that I know how to explain their advantages and answer questions. I have strong interpersonal skills for building relationships with clients and effectively communicating with other members of the sales team. I am able to listen to the customer's desires and concerns and then recommend solutions, possibly including customizing a product. I can speak excellent both English and German language to perform well when making sales presentations.

我相信我是貴公司要尋找的人才。這個職位需要完整的技術技能，人際交往能力，解決問題的能力，以及語言表達能力。

我，作為一個銷售工程師，擁有在這領域裡的尖端技術產品的豐富知識，使我知道如何介紹自己的優勢並回答問題。我有很好的人際關係技巧，建立與客戶的關係並有效地與銷售團隊的其他成員溝通。我能夠傾聽客戶的需求和關心事項然後提出解決方案，可能包括訂製的產品。當在銷售展式的場合，我可以講一口流利的英語和德語。

Q

6

Are you able to work on multiple assignments at once?

你可以同時進行多項工作嗎？

Definitely. Working on several tasks at once comes natural to me. Because of my position, most of time, I receive multiple assignments at the same time. The first step I do is to put them in the order of importance through a combination of deadline, difficulty, project length, team status and inherent importance. The second step, I will arrange my time accordingly. The last step is to update and keep track of its progress. The more I know about each task the better, because it will allow me to ensure that I am able to finish each task successfully. I have been told by my manager that works very efficiently.

是的。同時執行多項任務對我來說是很平常的一件事。因為我的職位，大多時候，我會同一時間接到多項任務。我首先是將它們依照截止日期、難度、專案長度、 團隊狀態、重要性等作順序排列。第二步，我會根據重要順序安排我的時間。最後，隨時更新和追蹤每個任務的進展。我愈能了解任務愈好，因為這樣一來，能確保我能成功地完成各項任務。我的經理告訴我，我的工作效率非常高。

7 Are you willing to relocate or travel?
你願意出差或調動工作地點嗎？

Yes, I do, because my previous role involved traveling at least twice a month. This opportunity is one of the key reasons I chose this career track, with its international scope. I like to come across different cultures, and it will help me to perfect my skills and knowledge. I know a key part of your company's growth strategy is USA. So, I am not only willing to travel or relocate, but I look forward to it. My family is also very supportive of my career.

是的，我願意。我的前份工作每個月至少需要出差二次。有出差或是調動工作地點，這也是會選擇這個職業的原因之一，可以擁有國際視野。我喜歡體驗不同文化，這樣會幫助我完善我的能力與知識。我知道貴公司發展策略的關鍵是美國，所以我不只願意出差或是調動工作地點，本身也非常期待能夠盡快去。我的家人也非常支持我的工作。

8 How do you feel about working overtime?
你如何看加班這件事？

As a sales engineer, to achieve sales goals and clients requirements, I may work long and irregular hours. When I am given a task, my focus is not only the time I spend at task, but the results I expected to produce. I am a result-oriented person. I am willing to invest whatever time it takes to produce the result. A sales engineer you must adapt yourself to working overtime. Furthermore, I think a sales engineer should have time management skills. Because, most of the sales engineers work over 48 hours a week to achieve sales goals and clients requirements. Sales engineers have time flexibility where we can set up our own schedules. Subsequently, we should be able to arrange the appointments ourselves because most of time, we travel to somewhere for meeting customers or attending any trade show.

身為一個業務工程師，為確保銷售目標達成與滿足客戶需求，我可以長時間工作，而且不定時。當我接到工作時，對我而言重要的不是工作所花費的時間，而是我所預期會產生的成果。我是非常重視結果的人。為了得到結果，我將不計投入多少時間。銷售工程師你必須適應加班。此外，我認為銷售工程師應具備時間管理技能。因為大多數的銷售工程師每周工作超過 48 小時，以實現銷售目標和客戶要求。銷售工程師要有時間的靈活性，可以安排自己的工作時間表。隨後，我們應該能夠安排自己的約會，因為，大部分時間，我們經常要出差到某個地方會見客戶或出席任何會展。

1-2 臨場反應篇

Q 1

What have you done to improve your knowledge in the last year?
去年你做了甚麼提升你的專業知識？

It is important for a sales engineer, like me to continue my engineering and sales education throughout my career. I was an engineer and then switched to sales engineer last year. I have strong technical background, but have little knowledge in sales and marketing. My previous company offered on-the-job sales training. My previous manager, who is a dedicated professional with profound industry knowledge and sales experience, was my mentor when I first entered sales engineer. I learned a lot about the company's business practices and procedures. He guides me how to work well with customers and be comfortable with speaking to small and large audiences. Because of him, I learned his methods and techniques, and try practicing about the sales and marketing skills. Besides, I also attend seminars and exhibitions to have newest knowledge of practical application of engineering science and technology.

對一個業務工程師來說，沒有甚麼比持續不斷的提升工程技術與業務技巧更重要的了。我之前是名工程師，然後去年剛轉換到銷售工程師。我有強大的技術背景，但是在業務行銷這方面的知識，幾乎沒甚麼經驗。前一家公司有提供銷售的在職培訓。當我剛進到銷售工程師職位，我以前的經理，具有深厚的業界知識和業務經驗，他是我的導師。我學到了很多有關公司業務實務和程序。他引導我如何與客戶接觸以及自在地面對大小群眾發表演說。因為他，我學習到有關銷售和行銷技能的方法和技術，並嘗試練習。此外，我還參加討論會和展覽會有實際應用的工程科學和技術的最新知識。

Q **2** **How long would you expect to work for us if hired?**
假如你被雇用了，你期望在本公司帶多久？

I look for challenges, opportunities to grow professionally and personally, and opportunities to make a difference for the company I work for and the customers it serves. I have no doubt that your company will be an good performer for years to come and will be providing me enough opportunity to grow and develop; and from my side I will make sure to provide my best services to the company in order to achieve its vision. I know that your company offers employees a sound, safe and stimulating work environment. You favor the promotion of your employees to vacant and newly created positions, when you feel that the individuals possess the training and abilities to take on new challenges. I hope I will be considered a valuable employee. As long as I continue to make contributions and grow professionally, there is no reason for me to make a move.

我在尋找富挑戰性、工作和個人方面都能成長，同時可以為公司和顧客帶來影響的機會。毫無疑問的，貴公司一直以來是業界的佼佼者，相信將會提供我足夠多的經驗學習成長；而我也將盡我所能貢獻給貴公司以期達到目標。我知道貴公司提供員工一個健全、安全和激勵的工作環境。當貴公司感受到員工擁有迎接新挑戰的能力時，貴公司很樂意提供升遷機會或設立新職位。我希望公司能認同我的價值，只要我還能有價值的貢獻，並且可以在這裡不斷學習與成長，我沒有理由離開。

Q 3　Aren't you overqualified for this position?
你不認為這個工作對你而言資歷過高嗎？

I believe that this could be very positive benefits for both of us in this match. Because of my unusually strong experience in biomedical industry, I could start to contribute right away, perhaps much faster than someone who'd have to be brought along more slowly.　Furthermore, I possess outstanding analytical and communication skills with the ability to assist with all sales activities. I can act as liaison between your company and the clients to relay special requests or information that can help to improve products.　Company will benefit from my additional experience. You would be getting all the values of that without having to pay an extra dime for it. What I have learned many techniques for improving the efficiency and productivity of this type of operation. I would welcome the opportunity to use my knowledge and experience to growth sales goals.

　　我認為這可以使我們雙方皆受益。由於我擁有生物醫療工程產業豐富厚實的資歷；相較於其他求職者剛進入公司需要一段適應期，我能立刻進入工作狀況；此外，我具備優秀的分析和溝通能力，能夠協助所有銷售活動。我可以成為貴公司和客戶間的橋梁，針對特別要求或資訊改善產品。公司也會從我豐富經驗中獲得利益。不需付任何成本，即可得到所有價值。我從過去資歷中所得的許多技巧，可以增進業務的效率與生產力。我非常希望活用我的知識與經驗，增長貴公司銷售目標。

Q 4 Could you have done better in your last job?
你可以表現得比上個工作好嗎？

I suppose with the benefit of hindsight you can always find things to do better, of course, but off the top of my head, I can't think of anything of major consequence. I was confident enough to say that I have given my best of what I can, to perform all my allotted tasks to their ultimate results and have been well appreciated by my peers and managers. However, there is always a good percentage of improvement and smart way in my same tasks, which may have lead to finish the work much better than my last job.

我認為事情過後總是可以找到將事情做得更好的利益。當然，我認為將不會影響到任何事。我可以很自豪的告訴您，我對我被指派的工作任務，總是百分百地投入執行完成，以得到最好的結果；並且得到我過去工作的同事與上司們的讚賞。然而，同樣的任務，總還是有改進的空間，或者是更聰明的方法執行，

1-3 我有疑問篇

Q

1

I learned that your three major competitors, AAA Company, BBB Company, and CCC Company. What do you think your advantages?
我知道貴公司的三家競爭者 AAA 公司，BBB 公司和 CCC 公司，您認為貴公司的優勢如何？

These three companies have larger market shares and enjoy greater name recognition, but our company is growing faster. These three have longer operating histories and are more established; yet our company is younger and more dynamic.

LA group is committed to developing solutions that help customers work faster, smarter and more efficiently, as proven by some of the groundbreaking ideas the company has brought to market in recent years. Through investment in research and development, manufacturing, distribution, human capital and training, LA group is well positioned to respond to the needs of a changing marketplace. LA group's heritage provides a strong foundation for meeting and exceeding market expectations by bringing continuous innovation to our industry. As long as our company continues to introduce more innovative products, it is only a matter of time before our company catches up and surpasses them.

雖然這三家公司，擁有比我們公司更大的市場佔有率，而且知名度高，但是，我們公司的成長速度快。雖然，這三家公司歷史悠久，地位也較高，但是我們公司年輕且充滿活力。 LA group 是致力於制定解決方案，協助客戶的運作能更快速、更聰明、以及更有效，這些都證明了我們公司近幾年帶給市場上一些的突破性想法。通過研究和發展、製造、配銷、人力資本和培訓的投資，適時回應不斷變化的市場需要。LA 的傳統提供了堅實的基礎，使到我們在業界不斷創新滿足並超出市場期待。只要我們公司持續推出更創新的產品，要超越他們只是時間的問題。

Q2 How will my performance be evaluated?
貴公司會如何衡量我的表現？

We will review your performance by three different sections: Customer Service Performance Dimensions, Sales Performance Dimensions, and Job Performance Dimensions. The ratio of three dimensions are 20% weighted value to Customer Service of evaluation; 30% weighted value to Sales Performance of evaluation; and 50% weighted value to Job Performance of evaluation, specific amounts agreed upon by manager and employee at beginning of review period. The key factors of Customer Service Performance Dimensions includes Listening Skills, Attitude, Dependability, Cooperation, Customer Service, Personal Appearance, Initiative, Adaptability, General Acceptance by Customers, and General Acceptance by Principles. The key factor of Sales Performance Dimensions are Product Knowledge, Customer Knowledge, Market Knowledge, Verbal & Written Communication, Planning & Organizing, Persistence with Priorities to Goals, Customer Engineering Interface, Customer Purchase Interface, Complementary Selling, Quality of Work, Quantity of Work, New Business, Practical Judgment, Delegation, and Productivity. The Job Performance Dimensions will review your key accountabilities, goals, and results.

我們會用顧客服務、業務績效、及工作績效等三個面向，評量你的表現。這三個評分比率分別為: 顧客服務占百分之二十、業務績效佔百分之三十、工作績效佔百分之五十，主要是主管與部屬共同制定出的工作績效指標。 客戶服務表現的關鍵因素包括聽力技能、態度、可靠性、合作、客戶服務、個人表現、自主性、適應性、客戶普遍接受度和原則普遍接受。銷售業績方面的關鍵因素是產品知識、客戶知識、市場知識，口頭與書面溝通，規劃與組織，目標持久與優先順序、 客戶工程面、 客戶購買面、互補銷售、工作品質、工作數量、 新業務、實務判斷、授權和生產力。作業表現將審查您的關鍵職責、目標和結果。

3　What is your strategy for the Asian markets?
貴公司最近亞洲市場的發展策略為何？

China ranks as the largest economic power of the Asia Pacific region with a projected GDP of Nine trillions US dollars in 2013. The Chinese government has launched a health reform program that aims to create a solid platform for universal healthcare access for all by 2020. The prospects for medical device spending is huge; the government has committed heavily to the construction of thousands of hospitals, healthcare centres, clinics and this will inevitably lead to spending on capital goods, most notably medical devices, equipment and furniture at an unprecedented rate in a relatively short space of time. As you know that we manufacture medical equipment and that XXX are our main product. Exports account for 30% of our company's sales. We recently entered the Asian markets, especially China market and that's why we need to recruit more sales engineers to develop the new markets.

中國，亞洲太平洋地區最強經濟實力，在 2013 年 GDP 約有 9 萬億美元。 中國政府已推出衛生改革方案，目的是希望 2020 年以前，為醫療保健普及建立一個堅實的平臺。醫療設備支出的前景是龐大的；政府，以前所未有的速度以及相對短時的時間，大量積極投入建設數以千計的醫院、 醫療中心、 診所等，將不可避免地大量採購重要物品，特別是醫療設備、設備和傢俱。

如你知道的，我們公司生產醫療器材，其中以 XXX 為主要產品。出口佔總營業額的百分之三十。我們最近已經進入亞洲市場，特別是中國，那也是為什麼我們需要招募更多的業務工程師，開發新市場。

Q4 Do I have any opportunity to travel?
我有機會出差嗎？

Yes. As an sales engineer you will have lots of opportunity to travel different cities or overseas. Because it is your responsible for developing business opportunities for our company in the standard products, optical metrology services and engineering service area. Such opportunities may be with new or existing with the government and commercial customers. Also, when a client needs help solving a problem with product installation, a sales engineer like you will help them figure it out. Your regions may cover several provinces in China. For this reason, sometimes, you may be away from home for long periods of time and are frequently travel by airplane. Sometimes, for customers in Taiwan, you may need to spend a few nights away from home and travel by car. Increasingly, you will have to travel internationally to settle deals or to attend international trade shows.

身為銷售工程師你將會有很多機會旅遊不同的城市或海外。因為你的責任是為公司標準產品、光學計量服務以及工程開發商業機會，可能是新的或現有的政府和商業客戶。此外，當客戶需要解決與產品安裝有關的問題，你將協助他們解決。您的地區可能涉及中國的幾個省份。所以，有時，你可能會很長一段時間不在家，要經常乘飛機出差；有時，為臺灣地區的客戶，您可能需要花幾個晚上不在家，乘搭車或開車出差。甚至於，你會有出差國外機會，確認交易或參加國際貿易展示會。

1 範例

1-1. 自傳(1)

I have a bachelor's degree in XXX Engineering and my classes centered on math, physics, chemistry and science. I am currently working in sales so I am very familiar with a variety of sales techniques and I have acquired excellent customer service skills.

My experience includes attending trade shows and seminars to promote products, or to learn about industry developments; responding to proposals for specific customer requirements; planning and modifying product configurations to meet customer needs; diagnosing problems with installed equipment; identifying resale opportunities and support them to achieve sales plans; developing sales plans to introduce products in new markets; and maintaining sales forecasting reports. With these experiences plus my excellent communication skills allow me to converse with buyers with positive results. I have the ability to introduce products and encourage sells. This is done by convincing them the products or services sold by the company are exactly what they're searching for.

I am familiar with mainframe computers and my experience includes working with Microsoft SQL Server and similar database software. I have excellent problem solving skills with the ability to troubleshoot and find solutions to complex problems that will improve product performance or make it more compatible. With these skills, I can assist with the design process and I have the skills to make upgrades or modify configurations in order to meet specific requirements requested by clients.

I possess outstanding analytical and communication skills with the ability to assist with all sales activities. I can act as liaison between your company and the clients to relay special request or information that can help to improve products.

I plan to continue my education to stay updated with the new technological advancements as they become available. I have the flexibility to travel as needed and to work nights and weekends to complete projects.

我有 XXX 工程學士學位，課程集中在數學、物理、化學和科學方面。我現在從事銷售工作，所以很熟悉各種銷售技巧，我已經習得卓越的客戶服務技巧。

我的經驗，包括參加商展和研討會，以促進產品或了解行業發展動態；針對客戶特殊需求提出應對，規劃和修改產品配置以滿足客戶的需求；已安裝設備的問題診斷；確認重複銷售機會並支持達成銷售計劃；制定銷售計劃在新市場推出產品；保持銷售預估。有了這些經驗，再加上我優秀的溝通能力讓我在與買家交談時得到積極成果;我有介紹產品並鼓勵客戶購買能力，藉由說服他們公司的產品或服務正是他們在尋找的。

我熟悉大型計算機。我的經驗包括與 Microsoft SQL 伺服器與類似的資料庫軟件。我有良好的解決問題能力，找到複雜問題的答案，提高產品的性能或使其更兼容的能力。有了這些技能，我可以協助設計過程，我有能力做升級或修改配置，以滿足客戶要求的特定要求。

我具備出色的分析及溝通能力與協助所有銷售活動的能力。我可以作為公司和客戶之間的聯繫，傳遞特別要求或資訊幫助改進產品。

我打算繼續我的學習，以保持更新與新技術的進步。因業務完成需要，可以配合出差或者是在晚上與週末加班。

1-2. 自傳(2)

I have a Master's degree in Engineering, four years of sales experience working directly with clients, and six years in engineering. I have remarkable understanding of all the engineering concepts, and have been working since ten years in different aspects of the engineering and sales process to include: sales, production, and R&D.

Being creative and highly motivated with the ability to reach out to new clients and draw in new business to help the company grow. My strong communication skills and technical knowledge combined with my very persuasive nature, gives me an edge when meeting with potential clients that helps to encourage new business deals in addition to keeping existing clients happy.

Besides, I am very familiar with your company and the products you sell, so I can represent your company and encourage sales by answering questions and addressing the concerns that potential customers may have. I also have excellent troubleshooting skills with the ability to solve complex problems and the communication skills needed to explain information in non-technical terms, so anyone can understand.

I am energetic, confident and resilient with a real desire to put my skills and experience to work for your company. I stay updated on all the latest information and always present myself in a professional, friendly manner. I have the ability to build strong relationships with customers and to close deals for your company.

我具有工程碩士學位，有 4 年直接面對客戶的業務經驗，以及 6 年的工程師經驗。我通曉工程概念，而且，這十年我在工程與業務等不同方面工作過，如業務、生產；研發。

我很有創意且積極接觸新客戶，開發業務協助公司成長。 優秀的溝通能力加之技術知識地配合，使我在面對潛在客戶時非常有說服力，很容易成交；而且也能使現有客戶滿意。

我對貴公司販售的產品很熟悉，所以在對潛在客戶推廣產品的回應上，很能得心應手。我能有效地排解疑難，也有能力對非技術團體解說產品，使其容易了解。

我精力充沛、有自信與彈性，真誠希望將我的經歷貢獻給貴公司。我不斷地充實最新的資訊，保持專業能力與友善態度，相信我與客戶建立關係的能力，可以為貴公司達成交易。

2 自傳寫作教室

2-1. 自傳(1) 寫作文法解析／小評語

　　其實業務與業務工程師的工作內容幾乎相同，只不過，科技產業的業務，在業務職稱後面加了工程師，通常具備工程等專業教育背景，專業技術門檻要求較高，因為，面對客戶時的談話內容不是規格、產品、就是產業趨勢。很多原本是研發工程人員，轉調成為業務工程師。由此可知業務工程師的技能除了要有業務的能力，還外加了技術能力。

　　在自傳中，要能凸顯出自己的價值，如自傳第一段，除了學位教育背景，還清楚地運用「my classes centered on...」交代了求職者集中選修哪幾項主要課程。而「I am familiar with...」是非常實用的片語，能很好的運用在自傳中，說明熟悉的專業。「possess」則是用來敘述，求職者所具備的能力「I possess outstanding analytical and communication skills...」。

2-2. 自傳(2) 寫作文法解析／小評語

在自傳中，我們將常會運用現在完成進行式的時態，如「I have been working since ten years....」敘述求職者過去到現在的工作經歷，在本篇自傳，求職者要表達的事本身跨部門的豐富經歷，讓雇主可以在自傳中瞭解對方的適應能力、求知力與積極性，進而看到求職者可以為新公司帶來的貢獻。

這裡列出幾項業務工程師所要具備的技能，提供讀者參考應用：

- Communication skill：
  溝通技巧
- Persuasion：
  有能力說服客戶接受或改變購買行為
- Demonstration：
  運用相關展示產品的技巧
- Active listening：
  積極傾聽，找出客戶的需求
- Troubleshooting skills：
  有能力找出問題，確認問題，並提供解決方案
- Critical thinking：
  能夠運用批判性思考能力，分析各種解決方案的優劣勢
- Customer relationship：
  維持顧客關係
- Coordination：
  具有整合協調公司內部與客戶的意見，提供客戶所需的產品
- Keep latest industry news and trends：
  保持產業最新的知識與趨勢
- Engineering and Technology：
  具備厚實的技術工程知識，才能提供

This chapter we are talking about the sales engineer's career. Since the sales engineer's role is a hybrid of selling and engineering, their day-to-day duties will vary. The primary role of sales engineers is to work together with the research, development, and manufacturing departments of a company to ensure that the products they offer meet the needs of the customers. Sales engineers also develop a strong awareness of the products to be able to sell them to customers more easily.

Today, I am going to share a story to you about I quitted engineer career and steered to sales engineer.

I graduated from Oregon State University with a four-year undergraduate degree in Electronic Engineering Technology. I had been employed for 3 years as an electronic engineer in the development of consumer electronics, specifically digital cameras, and video-recording equipment, for a well-known listed company.

Then, I realized that I didn't suit engineer position. Compared to others who like to immerse in engineers at lab, I prefer working with people. So, I talked to my director at R&D department about my decision about switching to Sales Department as a sales engineer.

To be honest, it was not easy. In the beginning, I faced many difficulties; especially, I had to reverse engineer's thinking into business thinking. At first, I got poor performance and couldn't find the right direction. But I tried very hard to improve further. Step by step, I found my own mode of conversation. I was able to understand and to meet customers' need increasingly, also able to obtain credit from customers. Finally, my performance advance by leaps and bounds.

I helped increase our sales to XYZ Company through

effective customer relationship management and successful incorporation of customer feedback into customer design. Moreover , I successfully introduced our new generation product to German market, where had a strong competitor at that time, but we took their market share away through effective cooperation between sales and R&D departments.

I love this job and find fun and sense of accomplishment as a sales engineer.

本章主題有關業務工程師的職業。由於銷售工程師的職責，混合銷售及工程，所以他們日常工作會隨著有所變化。銷售工程師的主要職責是與公司的研究，開發和製造部門通力合作，以確保他們提供的產品滿足客戶的需求。還有銷售工程師對產品的了解，使得他們更容易銷售產品給客戶

今天，我要與您分享一個故事，一個有關我放棄工程師工作轉戰業務工程師的故事。

我畢業於俄勒岡州立大學，獲得電子工程技術四年制本科學位。我在一家知名的上市公司，擔任了 3 年的電子工程師，主要在消費類電子產品，特別是數碼相機和攝錄設備的開發。

然後，我瞭解了我並不適合工程師的工作。相較於喜歡埋首於實驗室的工程師，我更喜歡與人接觸的工作。所以，我告訴了研發主管，我決定轉調到業務部門當業務工程師。

說實話，那並不容易。在開始的時候，我遇到了許多困難，特別是，我必須扭轉原本工程師的思維，轉換成業務的思考模式。 起初，我表現不佳，無法找到正確的方向。但我很努力改善。逐漸地，我找到自己與客戶談話的模式。我愈來愈能夠理解和滿足客戶的需求，也能夠從客戶獲得信賴。最後，我的績效突飛猛進。

我透過有效的顧客關係管理和將客戶的回饋活用在產品設計上，幫助公司擴大對 XYZ 公司的銷售額。此外，我成功地將公司新產品引進德國市場，在當時，我們有非常強的競爭對手，由於業務部與研發部門的有效配合，我們也贏得市場佔有率。

我喜愛這份工作，而且身為業務工程師的樂趣與成就感。

英文保全

1-1 常遇到的考題

Q 1 **Why are you interested in our company?**
你為什麼對本公司有興趣？

As everyone knows, HELMET Security is a leader in the security industry and is growing more than three times as fast as the security industry.

Recently, I learned that your company won two special glories, which are "Voted Consumer Choice Award winners for the 6th consecutive year", and "National PINNACLE Award for Customer Service Excellence". I believe that your outstanding people, ongoing training, state-of-the-art technology, advanced monitoring station and passion, enable you to provide the most responsive and effective customer service in the industry. Especially, the main driver of Helmet's success in the industry is due to their investment in their employees. Helmet Security commits to offering the best employment and clear development opportunities in the security industry and has been selected as the "Employer of Choice" the industry because of the way you treat your staff. I would love to become be part of such an admirable culture and practice.

眾所周知，HELMET Security 是保全業的領導者，成長速度是其他同行的三倍。

最近，我獲悉貴公司贏得了兩個特別的榮耀，分別是「連續 6 年被評為消費者選擇獎贏家」，和「國家卓越顧客服務頂尖獎」。我相信因為優秀的人才、持續的培訓、先進的技術、先進的監控站、以及

熱情，使貴公司能夠提供業界最積極有效的客戶服務。尤其是，HELMET 在該行業成功的主要驅動力是因為他們在對雇員的投資，HELMET Security 致力於提供最佳就業和明確的發展機會。貴公司對待員工的方式，已經在保全業裡被選為人人嚮往的「伯樂」公司。這樣令人稱讚的文化和行動力的公司，我也想要成為其中一員。

Q

2 What do you know about being a security guard at mall?
你對商場保全人員的職位了解多少？

I believe the most important requirement to work in a security guard position in a mall must be able to pass background and criminal record checks. Given the physical demands of the job, a mall security guard should be in good physical health and have quick reflexes, as well as be able to walk long distances; some mall security guards walk up to eight miles a day or more. Good observation and decision-making abilities, and excellent written and verbal communication skills are also important traits for a mall security guard. The job duties of a mall security are responsible for preventing criminal activities, like shoplifting, and maintaining order among the shoppers. A security guard may be needed to mediate disagreements or to escort people out of the mall. Security guards are present in malls during business hours and when the mall is closed. Security guards need to make sure that all doors and locks are secure.

我認為商場保全人員的職位最重要的要求是要能通過背景與犯罪紀律調查。鑑於這項工作的實際需求，商場保全人員要有健康的身體，反應能力要快，還要能夠長時間行走，有些商場保全人員甚至一天會行走超過八英哩或者更多，良好的觀察力與決策能力，優秀的書面與口頭溝通技巧的。商場保全人員的工作職責是要防止犯罪活動，像是行竊，與維持消費者秩序。可能會需要調解分歧，或者護送他人離開商場。保全人員在商場營業時間時必須巡邏，在營業結束時，需要確保所有門鎖都是安全的。

Q 3 **What are your skills related to this position?**
你有什麼關於此職位的技巧？

I have worked as a safety security with institutions like NK Institute and EH Institute. I have experience of working in both private and public sector, and I have the required knowledge about every existing and current safety regulations for both the kinds of institutes. I have been trained in setting up and monitoring surveillance equipment.

Besides, I have good verbal communication skills with articulate, firm, and self-confident when speaking to individuals. As security guards will likely deal with the general public as they enter and exit the premises being protected. I have observation skills and I am alert and aware of my surroundings, able to quickly recognize anything out of the ordinary. To well protect my client, I have good judgment skills and the ability to make fast decision when the event of break-in or any emergency happens. I strongly believe that you will benefit from the skills I have.

我曾作為一個安全保障與像通信 NK 機構以及 EH 協會。我在私營和公共部門工作的經驗，我熟悉這兩類機構現行的安全相關法規。我對知道如何設置與監控監視儀器。此外，我具良好口頭溝通技巧，能夠口齒清晰、堅定自信在與人說話。 由於，保全人員在監控出入口場所時，可能會與公眾打交道。我有觀察的能力，一旦我的周圍發生任何不尋常變化，能夠立刻警覺到。有任何闖入或緊急事件發生時，為保護我的客戶，我能很好的判斷與快速作出決定。

我堅信我擁有的技能，能夠對貴公司有所幫助。

4

What would you do if security guard job becomes monotonous at night shift?
如果警衛工作在夜班變得單調？你會怎麼做？

It is very important for a security guard be attentive, have complete focus on the job. When I feel tired or bored during my shift at night time, I will do something to help prevent monotony in my job. I will ask my supervisor about adding a few walks around the perimeter of the building. Because, one of the easiest ways to maintain focus is to get moving and keep the blood flowing. Since one of my duties is submit reports for each shift, another way to keep my mind sharp is to take notes after each patrol. I will ask permission to have a radio to help me focus on my duties and break up the monotony, but won't let it hinder my responsibilities. I might also consider taking few minutes to do some exercises while working to keep my blood flowing and prevent fatigue from setting in.

保全人員專心致力於工作是很重要的。在值夜班時，如果感到疲勞或是無趣，我會做些事情避免。我會請我的主管讓我多巡邏幾趟，因為保持注意力集中最簡單的方法就是不斷移動讓血液循環。由於我的工作之一是要在每次值班結束後遞交日報表，所以另一個保持清醒方式就是每次巡邏結束立刻註記。我會請求准許在值班時，聽廣播，但是不會影響我的工作職責。我也可能會考慮花幾分鐘時間，做點簡單地運動，讓血液循環防止疲勞入侵。

5 What trends do you see in this industry?
你覺得這個產業目前的趨勢是什麼？

When I first transitioned into the security industry, just over a year-and-a-half ago, employment of security guards was expected to grow by 19 percent within next following decade, about as fast as the average for all occupations.

Truly speaking, I was very motivated by that fact. Now, that growth has increased and the statistics support that position. I believe this is mainly due to the ongoing need for protection of property and people. Concern about crime, vandalism, and terrorism continue to increase the need for security. Demand should be strong in the private sector as private security firms take over some of the work police officers used to do. I foresee the working relationships between private security and government agencies becoming stronger, especially when it comes to information sharing that was not the norm a few decades ago. Due to ever-changing demands, the best managed security companies like BBC will be increasingly used in a supportive role alongside policing agencies, to respond to large-scale incidents and emergencies.

當我最初轉到保全業時，僅在過去的一年和半前，保安人員需求預期未來十年裡，約有平均 19% 的成長率，比所有的職業成長都快。說實話，我被這事實激勵到了。現在，產業趨勢也證明了。我相信這主要是由於要被保護的人與財產的需求增加。因為人們對犯罪、蓄意破壞和恐怖主義的擔心，增加對安全的渴望，也強烈地刺激私人經營保全公司的業務增加，這些私營的保全公司部分替代了傳統警務人員的工作。我預料私人保全和政府機構間的工作關係，會變得愈來愈密切，尤其是資訊共享部分，不像數十年前。由於不斷變化的需求，像 BBC 這樣優秀的保全公司，也將漸漸地與治安機構並肩合作，發揮支援作用，對大型事件與緊急情況做出反應。

6

What personalities are best to have as a security guard?
保全人員的個性最好具備甚麼條件？

A person's personality can affect the ability for a security guard to do their job correctly. To become a security guard is not for everybody. Only certain people can handle such responsibility and risk. He or she must be attentive and smart. A person who does not pay attention to what they are doing is not someone who would make an excellent security guard. A job in security requires someone to be smart, but most importantly have common sense. Many issues that a security guard has to deal with require common sense and critical thinking. Security guards must take job seriously. A security job holds a vast responsibility no matter what they are guarding. They are holding everyone's safety in the palm of their hands, so if they are not the right person to do the job they could be putting a lot of people at risk. It is vital that security guards do their jobs carefully and thorough.

保全人員的性格會影響他們正確的執行工作。不是每個人都可以成為保全人員，只有某些人才能承擔這樣地責任與風險。必須要專心與聰明，在值勤時無法專注，不適合成為一個保全人員；還有必須要機警，最重要的是要有常識，保全人員在處理很多事件時，都需要依賴常識與批判性思維解決。保全人員必須工作嚴謹，不管事做甚麼性質的保全工作地責人是非常重大的，眾人的安全掌握在保全人員手裡，所以如果不是嚴謹認真的保全人員，會讓眾人處於危險之中，所以保全人員仔細徹底做好本職工作是至關重要的。

Q

7 What are the duties and responsibilities of a security guard in your opinion? 你認為保全人員的職責是什麼？

I think that regardless of the place of business for which security guards work, there are some duties and responsibilities that all security guards are charged with. These include patrol business premises, monitor the entrance of visitors, write daily reports, and handle emergency situations. When carrying out regular patrols of the commercial or factory premises, security guards will check for signs of intrusion, ensure that doors are locked, and investigate the presence of any suspicious people.

In certain places of business, the security guard will be responsible for checking-in visitors' identification and recording this entry for later review if necessary. Security guards also are required to create daily reports about the activities that happened during their shifts, in order to help to keep other security guards and business owners aware of important events. Security guard must act as a first responder in the event of any problems. They must remain calm at all times and work with other security guards in order to prevent chaos during such times.

我認為無論保全人員在哪個工作地點，保全人員的職責包括巡邏營業處所、 監視訪客、 撰寫日報表、以及處理緊急情況。定時巡邏商業或工廠等場所時，保全人員要檢查有否入侵跡象、 確認大門處於鎖定狀態，並調查任何可疑的人的存在。在某些場所，保安人員要負責登記訪客身分和記錄，供以後有需要時可以查看。保全人員也需要填寫日報表，紀錄值班時的活動，讓其他保全人員和企業主知道重要事件。一旦出現任何問題時，保全人必須是第一時間有所反應的人。他們必須時刻保持冷靜，與其他保全人員通力合作，防止期間發生混亂。

8

Describe a typical day in your job?
請簡述你一天工作的行程。

A typical day as a museum security guard began with a staff meeting before the museum opened. The staff and the security guards went over the day's agenda including open exhibits, scheduled activities, contact people for special guests, and where each security guard would be posted. As a museum security guard, I am responsible for making sure the people and the art exhibits at the museum were protected. Closing time at the museum was always a challenge. I would start informing visitors of closing time well before 5pm and remind them that gift shop closed 4:55. As 5pm approached, we have to ensure people exiting the museum. I have to go through every exhibit and office in the building to make sure no one was accidentally locked in. There are after-hours responsibilities too, as a security guard will be called if an alarm goes off at night.

博物館的保全人員，在開館前會有一個晨間員工會議。所有員工與保全人員各自報告當天的議程，包括展覽開幕，預定的活動，特別嘉賓的聯繫人，保全人員的站崗表。我身為博物館的保全人員，我的責任是確保在展覽館的所有人與展覽藝術品受到保護。閉館時間在博物館一直是個挑戰。我會在閉館時間下午 5 點前提前通知參觀者，並且提醒他們禮品店結束時間為下午 4 點 55 分。到了 5 點，我們要確認所有人都離開博物館，我必須要巡邏整個博物館大樓與辦公室，以確保沒有人不小心被鎖在裡面。還會有下班後的職責，如果晚上博物館警鈴響起時，保全人員有責任處理。

1-2 臨場反應篇

Q

1

Tell me about how you deal with angry people?
你怎麼處理憤怒的人？

Being a security guard like me, must deal with angry people frequently. This can range from a person being denied entry to event, or fielding the wrath of those who have been waiting in long lines or crowded areas. When I find myself in this situation, I will use a basic knowledge of human psychology and communication skills to deal with them. Listening is very important. Such a simple acknowledgement of angry person's feeling can lessen the intensity of the situation. I will also show my understanding. Sometimes, all a person needs to hear to take his anger down is just saying something like "I can imagine how frustrated you must be, and I apologize for the inconvenience." Angry people often say things in the heat of the moment and don't mean much of what they're venting. And I will try to ignore insults and careless remarks as best as I can, despite my growing frustration. I will not react anything unprofessionally.

保全人員經常要處理發怒的人，像是被拒絕進入一些場合、排隊等很久、或者是過於壅擠的場所。當情況發生時，我會運用心理角度與溝通技巧解決。聆聽是很重要的，一個簡單地回應可以舒緩發怒的人的心情。我也會表達我的理解，有時候只需要向憤怒的人表達"我可以理解你現在的挫折，而且也很抱歉造成您的困擾"這類同理心的話語，即可減緩他們的心情。發怒中的人氣頭上說的話，並非有心，我會盡量地控制自己忽略這些侮辱的氣話，儘管我愈來愈失望，我也不會做出任何不專業的回應。

2 Tell me what cause the barrier of effective communication?
你覺得什麼會造成溝通上的阻礙？

Security guards must be able to speak with members of the public; therefore, effective communication is quite important; and understanding the barriers to effective interpersonal communication is also important. What I think several common barriers to effective communication includes:

Failure to listen. Most of us want to say something rather than listen to someone else. We sometimes even finish other people's sentences for them. Status differences. Rank and status make us listen to some people more closely than we normally would. It also can make us not listen to those of lower status than us. Language barriers. Everything said may not be clear to the receiver. Fear of criticism. Nobody likes to be thought of as not understanding. They claim that they understand when really they don't. Overloading of information. Sometimes there is simply too much information to process. Filtering information through our own life experiences can sometimes distort the information that the sender intended us to have.

保全人員要能夠與大眾交談，所以，有效的溝通技巧很重要，了解阻礙人際溝通的原因也同樣重要。我認為幾個常見阻礙有效溝通包括：

忽略傾聽，我們大部分人喜歡說話，卻很少聽別人說話，有時我們甚至會替別人完成要說出的話。地位差別會讓我們通常會聽到一些跟我們等級相近的，也會讓我們聽不到等級地位必我們低的。語言阻礙，說的人也許無法清楚傳到給聽的人。害怕批評，沒有人不喜歡被認為不懂，會不懂裝懂。過多的資訊，有時只是單純的訊息太多導致溝通阻礙。用我們自身的生活經驗過濾資訊，有時也會阻礙說話者想要傳遞給我們的資訊。

Q 3 **Do you have any legal power as a security guard?**
保全人員有執法的權利嗎？

Security guards are not police officers. The legal powers that we hold is quite different from that of a police officer. In fact, our legal powers might not be that much different than regular citizens. Because I am a security guard who is employed in-house by XXX company, property owner. My role is to watch property and to enforce rules and service standards set by my company. My company makes rules about the use of its property including rules about unwanted activities and behaviors, such as "no pets allowed", "no access allowed." I can ask a person to leave property and they can ban someone from property if rules are broken. When doing so, I should be professional and indicate which rule is being broken. If someone refuses to leave property when asked, he/she may be viewed as a trespasser. I can use reasonable force to remove trespassers and they can make a citizen's arrest if a trespasser actively resists lawful efforts to remove them.

保全人員並不是警務人員，具有的法定權力也跟警務人員不同。事實上，我們的法定權力跟普通公民擁有的法定權力並沒有兩樣。我受雇於 XXX 公司，產權所有人，我的角色是看管的所有物，與執行公司制定的規則服務標準。公司制定有關使用的規則，不必要的活動與行為，如「寵物勿進」、「禁止進入」。我可以要求不遵守這些規則的人離開業或者禁止行為，當這麼作時，我會專業且明確的指出違反的規則。如果有人拒絕離開時，有可能會被視為是侵入者，那麼，我可以合理使用武力將其帶離，而且如果入侵者抵抗保全人員合法的請離，我可以拘留他。

Q

4

How do you handle yourself as a security guard under pressure?
在壓力之下，你會怎樣做好你身為保全的工作？

Every security guard comes under pressure at some point in time. It might be pressure to do better at job to eliminate behaviors at the job site. When I find myself working under pressure I might be faced with emotions I didn't expect. I will try something to manage it so that it does not affect how well I do my job. First thing is keep control. I find the best way to avoid losing control is to feel comfortable dealing with emotions; and try to turn those emotions into energy that I will need to deal with whatever situation is at hand. Then, I will take a minute to evaluate the situation by asking questions, like who, what, where, when, why, and how, to figure out the condition and decide how critical it is. If I am familiar with the possible situations at my job and I know my environment I should be able to have a plan.

有時候保全人員會處於壓力環境下工作，壓力可能會使我在工作上更有效地處理工作現場的狀況。當我發現我處於工作壓力，並且產生情緒反應，我會調整我的心情讓它不會影響到我的工作。首先就是保持控制，我發現避免情緒失控的最好辦法，就是保持心情舒暢的處理情緒，然後將它們轉換成能量，讓我可以處理當下發生的事情。然後用一點時間評估狀況，問些像是人、事、時、地、物等問題釐清情況，與情況的重要性。如果我可以掌握當下情況與環境，那麼將有助我制定出行動計畫。

1-3 我有疑問篇

Q

1

What training do you provide?
貴公司提供甚麼樣的培訓？

Our training programs can be classified into the following categories: Pre-Employment Training, ABC Security Orientation, Pre-Assignment Training, and In-Service Training. Prior to being welcomed as a member of our company, all prospective Security Guards must successfully complete 40-hour of basic security guard training course. Once our security guards have successfully passed Pre-Employment Training, we provide them with a full orientation on all aspects of ABC Security. All security guards at ABC Security receive additional specialized training that is based on their site assignment and the industries we serve. As an example, Healthcare Security Guards receive between 40 to 120 hours of additional healthcare specific training. As part of our company's commitment to the ongoing training and education of our staff, we have created a safety and security based course curriculum that is unmatched anywhere else in the security industry. We encourage all of our staff to actively participate in all of the ongoing training courses that we offer.

我們的培訓計畫可以分為以下幾類：就業前培訓、ABC 安全方向、任務前培訓、以及在職期間培訓。在成為我們公司的正式職員前，所有準保全人員必須完成 40 小時的基本安全警衛訓練課程，涵蓋了成為 ABC 保全人員的基本技能。一旦我們的警衛已順利通過就業前培訓，我們會協助他們適應 ABC Security 各方面。在 ABC Security 的所有保全人員都收到額外專門的培訓，根據被指派的任務和我們所服務的行業。舉例來說，醫療保健安全警衛要接受 40 小時到 120 小時的額外醫療的具體培訓。由於 ABC Security 承諾職員持續的培訓與教育，我們設計了一套在業界無與倫比的安全防衛的相關課程。我們鼓勵職員積極參與我們提供的在職培訓。

2

How does your company motivate staff?
貴公司如何激勵員工？

We believe quality begins with our people, Top-A Company makes a very strong commitment to our employees, as they are ultimately responsible for our success. We seek to create and maintain an environment where every employee is rewarded according to their contribution to the success of our collective efforts. We will further reward our people with job satisfaction, recognition, advancement opportunities, leading-edge employee benefits, and bonus incentive programs. As a company, we do everything in our power to keep our people happy and satisfied throughout their careers with us, which in turn leads to happy clients - that really is the key to our business. As reflected in our Mission Statement, at Top-A Company we have developed extensive employee recognition and rewards programs that incentivize and motivate our people to provide superior client service. Just some of these programs include: Monthly Performance Awards, Daily & Weekly Performance Awards, and Peer Recognition.

我們相信品質始與我們的職員，Top-A 公司對我們的全體保全人員作出非常堅定的承諾，因為保全人員對公司的成功負有最終責任。我們追求建立與維持一個環境，按照每人在團體完成任務中的貢獻，每個職員都能得到獎勵。我們進一步用工作滿意度、表彰、晉升機會、領先同業的雇員福利和獎金激勵方案等等獎勵我們的職員。作為一家公司，我們盡我們的力量讓全體職員感到幸福和滿足，這樣，才會有快樂的客戶，這真的是對我們的業務的關鍵。為呼應我們的使命聲明，在 Top-A 公司我們開發了研發一套全面的員工表彰和獎勵程序，激勵職員以提供卓越的客戶服務。這套獎勵程序包括：每月績效獎、每日與每週業績獎勵和同儕認可。

3

What characters do you look for in your future employees?
貴公司在尋找甚麼特質的新血？

Here are what we are people we need. We expect all our employees to do their best in maintaining order at the locations they work and the best way to do so is to follow the instruction we are designated to do at each facility. We like our security guards to be able to tell when a problem is going to arise so to minimize the likelihood of an incident occurring. When on duty we expect our employees to quickly reply to any situation, not simply wait to see what happens. We all have heard the saying, "actions speak louder than words and by being on time," not calling off on important days, and performing tasks consistently we know that our employees are reliable. We look for employees who love what they do so much that they go above and beyond their duties to make sure they do an excellent job.

我們要找的人是：我們期望所有員工在他們的工作地點上能夠盡力維持秩序，最佳的辦法就是確實遵守我們給出的每一工作指令。我們的保全人員，能夠主動積極反應即將會發生的潛在問題，這樣可以儘量減少事故發生的可能性。當值班時，我們期望員工要迅速回復任何情況，不要只是等待，看看會發生什麼。聽過「坐而言不如起而行」，表現在工作上的意思是準時，重要的日子不罷工，確實貫徹執行任務，我們要的是可靠的員工。我們尋找的員工，熱愛他們的工作，並且表現總是超出預期，完美執行任務。

Q

4

Why did you get into the security industry and why this company?
為什麼要進入保全業？還有為什麼要進入這家公司？

I chose security guard because I wanted to gain experience for a career in policing, so that I could sharpen my skills. When I applied to PP Security in 2010, I thought it would be one of the better jobs to have and I believe that to be especially true now having joined the healthcare security team in a psychiatric healthcare facility.

During my time with PP Security, there have been countless scenarios where I have had to use my training from PP Security. Having to use these skills each day for situations that each have their own unique circumstances helps to keep the knowledge and skills I've learned fresh in my mind. Not only does my PP career use my current knowledge and skill sets, but each scenario I am put into teaches me something new. Everyone in this industry, no-matter how experienced, can always learn something new, and I believe that this ongoing learning will greatly aid in my success and advancement both in this industry and in my prospective career in the police service.

我選擇保全人員是因為我想得到警務工作的相關經驗，可以鍛鍊我的能力。當我在 2010 年應徵 PP 保全公司時，我認為是我警務職涯中較好的，事實也證明如此，我現在加入醫療保全小組，分配到一家精神病醫療機構駐點。在 PP 保全公司的這段時間，將受到的培訓，運用在無數的情境，每天，不僅僅是將所學靈活用到真實工作場合，我也從曾參與到每一事件中學到新知識。在保全業的每個人，無論多有經驗，總是可以學習到新知，我也相信，不間斷的學習，讓我的警衛職涯，大步朝向成功與晉升邁進。

unit B 自傳篇

1 範例

1-1. 自傳(1)

My name is William Lew and I have over 5 years' diverse experience in security and law enforcement positions. I have earned my TX Security Guard Training Certificate and passed Aid and CPR Certified.

Currently, I am working at SAFETY Inc. as a safety guard. I am in charge of patrolling the premises and adjacent area, direction traffic to and from the main building, performing safety inspections in order to flail off any negative activity, checking identity card of personnel before admitting into the building, investigate and report any nefarious activity, and taking necessary action on spot when needed. My diverse experiences as a security guard polished my protective, preventative and safety skills and provided me with a thorough understanding of potential threats. The proficiency which I developed to perform patrolling duties and handling emergency situations will be a definite asset for SEC Security.

My skills and training includes the ability to be observant and investigate unusual activity quickly and efficiently. I have a general knowledge of fire and security inspection procedures, the ability to maintain the security of facility and safety for anyone on the premises and a flexible work schedule so I'm available when needed.

Also, it is very importation to keep a good relationship with police offices and that you report to them whenever necessary. My excellent verbal and written communication skills and courteous nature makes this easy to accomplish. With my knowledge of all kinds of security procedures and protocols, I am able to handle undesired conduct and potential violations and maintain order in the assigned premises.

My extensive experience in monitoring and patrolling, and ability taking appropriate safety measures make me a great candidate for this position. I would like to contribute effectively to the SEC Security's mission.

我的名字是威廉·盧，我在保全和法律執法職位有超過 5 年豐富的經驗。我拿到 TX 安全警衛培訓證書，並且通過 Aid 和 CPR 認證。

目前，我在 SAFETY 公司當保全人員。我負責巡邏的辦公大樓和鄰近地區；指揮出入大樓的交通;進行安全檢查避免任何負面活動;獲准進入大樓前，檢察個人身分；調查報告任何犯罪和動；並當情況需要時採取必要行動。我的各種經驗磨練我的保護、防禦與安全技能，並且讓我嚴密判斷潛在威脅。我在執行巡邏以及處理緊急情況的專業能力表現，將會是 SEC 保全的資產。

我的技能和培訓包括，細心和快速有效率的地調查不尋常的活動。我消防和安全檢查程序的專業知識，所以我有能力維護整棟大樓的設施與人們的安全，以及彈性的工作時間表，配合調動。還有與警務人為維持良好關係是很重要的，必要時要向他們匯報。優秀的書面與口頭溝通技巧與禮貌，使事情容易達成。擁有這些專業的保全程規範，讓我能夠處理不當違規的行為，還有維持辦公大樓的秩序。

因為我在監控和巡邏的豐富經驗，與採去適當安全措施的能力，我認為我非常適合貴公司的職位，我希望能為 SEC Security 效力。

1-2. 自傳(2)

My name is Charlie Rick and I am currently working as a temporary security guard for the Security Agency that sends me out to a different job site almost every day. I am licensed in the State of New York and have my Certified Protection Professional(CPP) certification from ASIS International which I earned last year. I recently took some continuing education courses to renew my certification and also work towards the Level 2 Certificate. I have been working as a temporary security guard for just a year and six months now and have worked all shifts as well as numerous locations including warehouses, factories, office complexes, and retail establishments.

I have extensive experience with operating various kinds of alarm and computer systems as well as experience directing traffic, performing safety inspections and investigating suspicious events, demonstrating ability to handle and resolve conflicts in an effective manner, proven ability to work independently and cooperatively with others, in depth knowledge of law and order, outstanding communication skills, exceptionally dexterous skills with great physical ability, and ability to act with urgency in an emergency situation. I have knowledge of standard security procedures and am eager to go through the first rate training program to advance my knowledge.

I have experience holding suspects until police officers arrive to further investigate and possibly make an arrest. I also have experience testifying on behalf of clients in depositions and court cases. I am in excellent physical condition with no vision or hearing impairments. I have passed all the required background checks and drug tests to be licensed and certified in the State of New York. I am a diligent and competent security guard.

I am seeking a regular position as a security guard. After carefully reviewing all of the requirements and found that I meet all qualifications for a job as a security guard at your company.

我的名字是 Charlie Rick。我目前是在作為保全代理機構擔任臨時警衛，幾乎每天會調派到不同的工作地點。我在紐約有持牌，而且我去年有拿到 ASIA 機構頒發的 CPP 證書。我最近更持續的接受進一步課程的教育訓練，努力拿到二級保全證書。我一直擔任臨時保全只有短短一年和六個月，調任到很多不同的工作地點，譬如貨倉、工廠、辦公大樓以及零售場所。

我有豐富的經驗，像是操作各類報警和電腦系統，以及指揮交通，執行安全檢查和調查可疑事件，能以有效方式處理和解決衝突，獨立以及團隊合作的能力，熟悉法律與秩序，傑出的溝通技巧，異常靈巧的技能與絕佳的體能，並能夠在緊急情況下的迅速行動。我有標準安全程序方面的知識，並一直很渴望通過一流的培訓計劃，以提升我的知識。

我的經驗有，滯留犯罪嫌疑的人，直到警務人員抵達現場並進一步調查，或者逮捕嫌疑犯；還有代表客戶在法院案件中作證的經驗；我的體能狀況良好，並沒有視覺或聽覺障礙。我通過了紐約州指定授權機構的所有必要的背景調查和藥物測試。我是個勤勞能幹的保全人員。

我正在尋求一個正式的保全人員職位。在仔細審查貴公司於廣告中列出的要求後，我認為符合貴公司提出的所有條件。

2 自傳寫作教室

2-1. 自傳(1) 寫作文法解析／小評語

　　保全人員的種類有幾種 常見於商業大樓、醫院、工廠或是賣場的保全人員（Security guards、security officer）、運輸相關的保全人員（Transportation security screeners）、賭場保全人員（Gaming surveillance officers/guards）、以及保護個人安全的私人保鑣（private body guard）。不同種類的保全人員，需要的技能也各有差異。以本自傳來說，應徵的是有關商業辦公大樓這類的保全人員，整棟大樓的財產與人員安全，就交付在他們手裡，因此，就必須要有相對應的知識技能。

　　個人能力包括：Adaptable 適應能力、Teamwork 團隊合作、Execution Capabilities 執行能力、以及 Achievement Motivation 成就動機。

　　其他可用於自傳說明的職責：

Protect and enforce laws on an employer's property
保護和強制執行法律對雇主的財產
Monitor alarms and closed-circuit TV cameras
監控報警和閉路式監控系統
Control access for employees, visitors, and outside contractors
進出管控員工、訪客與外部承包商的
Conduct security checks over a specified area
指定區域的安全檢查
Write comprehensive reports outlining what they observed while on patrol
撰寫巡邏時的報表

2-2. 自傳(2) 寫作文法解析／小評語

這份自傳適合領有相關執照的保全人員，原本是在類似於保全短期代理公司，擔任保全人員，以接任務方式，接受保全短期代理公司的地點調派，之後想要謀求正式職位。

要成為專業的保全人員有幾個基本要件。首先要通過 background checks 背景調查，特別是針對 a criminal background check 犯罪紀錄調查；再來就是通過 drug test 藥物測試；最後，就是拿到政府 license 執照或者是相關培訓機構頒發的 certification 檢定證書。

保全業在歐美已經是逐漸成熟的學問，甚至發展一套專業的教育管理認證程序，這裡介紹給有興趣的讀者，國際知名的專業保全培訓認證機構，美國產業安全學會（ASIS International），全球皆有設立機構，對不同專業保全人員的需求，設立相關的訓練課程與認證，像是 CPP（Certified Protection Professional）是針對專業保全人員的證照。

I have been working as a security guard at TBC University for over three years, although I have been in the security industry now for 9 years. A typical day start with performing patrols of the site internally and externally, sorting and checking the post, interacting with colleagues, general reception duties and managing visitors and students. I have to deal with problems as they arise. Sometimes I may have to deal with a suspect package, fire alarms or intruder alerts. You never know what's going to happen from one day to the next.

The job can be fun and exciting, but most of all I enjoy meeting all sorts of different people. I get along well with my colleagues and we work well together as a team. Being a security officer is hard work and requires a lot of hours, but if you are hard-working, reliable and committed then you can progress in the industry easily. In terms of career progression, there are plenty of roles you can develop into, such as you could progress to a supervisory role or become manager, area manager or chief security officer (CSO).

To be a security guard you have to be trustworthy, honest, polite and non-judgmental. It is easy to specialize in a particular area of the job, and different roles require different skills. This might be something to bear in mind if you are thinking of pursuing a job in the security industry.

　　我現在在 TBC 大學當保全人員已經超過三年時間，雖然，我待在保全業至今已經有九年。 一天的工作的開始於，巡邏校園內外、分類檢查信件、與同事互動、一般接待職責、以及管理訪客與學生出入。當問題發生時，我必須要處理。有時候我要處理可疑包裹、火災警報或者是入侵警報。你永遠不會知道下一步會發生甚麼。

　　這份工作可以很有趣和令人興奮的，但最重要的是我喜歡與各種各樣的不同的人碰面。我與同事們相處融洽，分工合作。保全人員，工作辛苦且需要大量時間，但是如果你是勤勞、可靠、與忠誠的，那麼你在這行業很容易取得升遷。在職業發展方面，有很多角色可以發展，像是你可以朝向管理人員的角色，或者是成為經理、區域經理、或是安全總監。

　　要成為保全人員，你的人格特質必須要值得信賴、誠實、禮貌並且要客觀。保全人員是相當專業的領域，而且不同的角色要求不同的技能，如果你想要從事保全方面的工作，這可能是要記住的地方。

移民顧問

1-1 常遇到的考題

Q 1 Describe what an Immigration Consultant is.
請說明甚麼是移民顧問師。

When people migrate from one country to another, there may be certain laws in place that must be properly executed for them to be able to legally stay. Processing visas and permits badly may lead someone who wants to live in one country to be forced to go back to his native land. Immigration consultants are instrumental in giving those who want to become permanent residents the tools and guidance needed to confidently follow the legal proceedings for residency. So, what is an immigration consultant? What I think a immigration consultant provide assistance and guidance to individuals who are seeking to become permanent residents of an country. They aim to ensure that future residents are given the tools they need to confidently navigate the complex administrative and legal waters of the immigration process. An immigration consultant is often considered to be an expert in the field of immigration but without a law degree or any similar education.

當人們要從一個國家簽到另一個國家，可能有某些法律必須遵守執行，以便能夠合法停留。處理簽證和許可證的問題不好，會導致原本要移民的人，被迫遣回到他原來的國家。而移民顧問可以幫助那些想要成為永久居民的人，引領他們有信心地遵照法律程序可以永久在居留當地。所以，什麼是移民顧問師？我以為移民顧問對想要在一個國家成為永久居民的個人，提供協助和指導。他們的目標是確保這些未來的居民，在複雜的行政與法律程序中，提供導航功能。移民顧問師

往往被認為是移民領域的專家，但是沒有一個法律學位，或任何類似領域的教育。

Q

2   What does a Immigration Consultant do?
移民顧問師工作內容是甚麼？

The Immigration Consultant is responsible for helping individuals who are internationally relocating. Being immigration consultants, their job includes oversee all aspects of the immigration service to ensure that process runs smoothly; must interview all clients and deal with all applications face to face; must oversee the completion of all relevant visa and immigration documents and ensure that they are received within the time limit set by the government; must ensure that all of the information provided by the client is accurate and correct, preparing and checking all legal documents; must prepare all fee quotes and any information required by clients, colleagues or authorities; maintain strong working relationships with all clients and colleagues; they must be able to help the client to obtain Visas, Green cards and other documentation required. They must take full responsibility of all immigration issues and operations, remaining up to date with any changes to legislation.

移民顧問負責幫助要國際搬遷的人們。作為移民顧問，他們的工作包括指導有關移民方面的服務，以確保過程順利進行；親自面試申請者與處理申請文件；監督完成所有相關簽證和出入境證件，並確保政府規定時間之內遞交；確保客戶端提供所有的信息是精確的，準備和檢查所有法律文件，準備所有費用的報價和客戶，以及同事或主管機關規定的任何資料；維持與所有的客戶和同事牢固的工作關係，能夠幫助客戶獲得簽證、綠卡和要求的其他文件。他們必須承擔所有有關移民問題和業務的全部責任，與關注任何法例變動。

3 Can you tell the difference between Immigration Consultant v.s. Immigration Lawyer?
說明移民顧問師與移民律師的不同？

There are essentially two types of immigration representatives offering their services to clients: Consultants and Lawyers. Immigration Consultants are immigration representatives who are not lawyers. They are often referred to as paralegals, law officers and, immigration specialists. Some consultants are former immigration officers who have left the government to work in the private sector. Immigration consultants perform similar tasks as lawyers; however, immigration consultants cannot represent immigrants in any immigration proceedings nor can they offer any legal advice about immigration interviews or immigration benefits. They also cannot refer to themselves as legal experts on immigration procedure, and they must charge fees that are reasonable based upon their state of employment if they are working independently. And, Immigration lawyer is an attorney that specializes in handling immigration cases of foreign citizens. This person in authority needs to be licensed to practice immigration law in a legal manner.

移民顧問師是入境事務處代表，不是律師。他們往往被稱為律師助理、 法務人員和移民專家。一些移民顧問師是離開了政府在私營部門工作的前移民官員。移民顧問執行類似於律師的任務；然而，移民顧問師，在處理移民的任何法律程序中，不能代表移民者本身，也不能提供關於移民面談或移民福利的任何法律意見。他們不能自稱他們自己為移民程序的法律專家，他們必須收取合理的費用如果他們獨立地工作。而移民律師是專門從事處理外國公民入境案件的律師。這樣的權威人士需要被授權，以合法的方式執行移民法律。

4 What made you choose to become on Immigration consultant?
你選擇當移民顧問師的原因？

The main reason that I chose to become an immigration consultant was that it allowed me to help people who were truly deserving of help. There are millions of people who dream of moving to abroad, the process however is not easy to navigate. The laws that cover immigration are very complicated and these make it difficult for most immigrants. Being able to help those people is very satisfying. The other big reason that I chose to become an immigration consultant was that it is such a challenging and fascinating field. As already mentioned the laws are very complex and this means that there is a new challenge every day. Unlike other areas of the law I know that I will be handling something different every time I go to work. Some days it may be paperwork, others It may be a deportation hearing, no two days are ever the same which keeps things interesting.

我選擇移民顧問師最主要是我可以幫助需要幫助的人。有成千上萬的人想要移民到海外的夢想，然而整個辦理過程並不輕鬆。有關移民涵蓋的法律非常複雜，對大部分的移民者而言，相當困難。可以幫助這些人，令我感到滿足。我選擇成為移民顧問的另一大原因是，它是一個具有挑戰性和吸引人的領域。正如已經提到的，法律是很複雜的，這意味著每天有一個新的挑戰。不像其他法律領域，我知道，我每天去上班時，將會要處理不同事情。有些時候，它可能是文書工作，有些時候也可能是驅逐出境聽證會，沒有一天是一樣的，這使得事情變得相當有趣。

5 What is your greatest weakness?
你最大的缺點為何？

Being a fresh graduate, I have little work experience in being an immigration consultant. Probably that is my biggest weakness. However, in order to be prepared for the employment market and for an immigration consultant, I got a part-time job to gain some experience. In addition, during my school life, I selected some courses regarding to immigration law and policy. The more I understand knowledge of immigration law; the more I can help immigrant clients prepare immigrant matters.

Because one of the single most important parts of an immigration consultant's work is to serve as a translator, I also took French courses as my second foreign language besides English. Being an immigration consultant regularly encounters diversity and multiculturalism. As such, I also took a course in international studies or international relations. I believe that it is a part of a good program in immigration consulting. And I am pretty sure that I can be valuable member of your operations team.

作為一名應屆畢業生，並沒有多少處理有關移民諮詢業務的實際工作經驗。也許這是我最大的弱點。然而，為了提早適應就業市場，並為成為移民顧問師作準備，我找了一份兼職工作，獲得一些經驗。此外，在學校生活期間，我選擇關於向移民法律和政策的課程。我愈了解移民法律知識，我就愈能幫助準移民客戶準備移民事宜。因為移民顧問師的工作中最重要的服務之一是作為一個翻譯，除了英文，我也選修法語課程作為我的第二外國語言。作為一個移民顧問師，經常遇到的多樣多元的文化。因此，我修了國際研究或國際關係的課程。我認為，這在移民諮詢中很有幫助。我很肯定我能成為您的業務團隊中的重要一員。

Q 6 Do you have any plans for future education?
你有任何進修計畫嗎？

Eventually, I would like to become a full type of Licensed Immigration Consultant to provide advice on all immigration matters. I studied at the Bay of Plenty Polytechnic's Graduate Certificate in New Zealand Immigration Advice and successfully had completed assigned Courses A and B and got a provisional license. As a new entrant to this industry with little experience, I am only allowed of providing immigration advice in all immigration matters while working under the direct supervision of an immigration consultant with a full license. In order to upgrade to full license within two years. I plan to take advanced courses to complete my Diploma for required Continuing Professional Development Activities and collect more client files and gain more experiences. And I learned that your company is a well-know Immigration Consultant Company in this Industry and have a great program for a provisional license holder or limited license holder. I am interested in joining this program.

最終，我想成為持有頂級執照的移民顧問師，能夠提供諮詢所有的移民業務。我在紐西蘭政府唯一認可的專業移民資訊諮詢學校上課，完成指定 A 及 B 的課程，並且拿到臨時執照。因為我是剛進入這行業，沒有多少實務經驗，依規定，我只能在有頂級執照的移民顧問師的監督管理下，才能執行諮詢業務。為了能在兩年內拿到頂級顧問師執照，我計畫修一些進階課程，拿到學位，完成規定的持續專業發展活動以及實際移民業務處理案例，增加我的經歷。我得知貴公司在移民諮詢業務領域是非常知名的，而且針對拿臨時執照與有限執照的移民顧問師，提供一個很好的制度。我非常想參加這的制度。

Q
7 What are key skills and knowledge do you have as an Immigration Consultant?
作為移民顧問，你具備甚麼技能？

I am an OISC Level 1 regulated immigration consultant. I am permitted to provide basic applications and advice within the UK Immigration Rules. I have the ability to draft letters and complete application forms clearly and accurately in English; using the correct terminology and enclosing the appropriate evidence or a clear explanation as to why it has not been provided. Sufficient verbal communication and interpersonal skills to identify to whom an enquiry relates, establish their intentions and the relevant facts of the case; communicate advice clearly to clients, giving reasons and explaining all options; inform clients of what steps need to take, including urgent action. Have the ability to identify appropriate resources (e.g. textbooks, the internet) and use them effectively. Have the ability to act with an appropriate sense of urgency. Have the ability to maintain clear and structured records. I hope that you will consider me as a top candidate for this position.

我有 OISC-Level1 移民顧問執照，依照英國移民法規，允許我提供基本的移民申請與諮詢服務。我能用英文撰寫草案以及精準地完成申請表，使用正確的專業術語，還有隨申請表附上適當的佐證資料附件，或者是清楚解釋無法提供的原因。足夠的口頭溝通和人際關係技巧，釐清相關的詢問，確認申請案件的目的與有關的事實；能夠清楚的與客戶溝通意見，說明理由和提供所有的選擇；告知客戶申請步驟，保括緊急行動。有能力有效率地運用適當的資源（如教課書、網路）；有應對緊急事件的能力。有能力維持清楚系統的檔案記錄。我希望我會是貴公司的最佳人選。

Q

8 Tell me what the role of an Immigration Consultant is.
請說明移民顧問師的角色。

Generally speaking, the immigration consultant's role involves conveying and explaining information in an understandable form or manner, ensuring that prospective immigrants has a vivid picture of the immigration system. Immigration Consultants play an extremely important role in attracting qualified skilled immigrants, to fill specific labor market needs, moreover they perform an extremely crucial function by assisting prospective immigrants navigate the Immigration System. Foreign immigrants are not familiar with immigration rules nor are they capable of construing and comprehending such complicated terminology, this is when the immigration consultant's role is crucial in order to ensure that the public are provided with the best service and advice. Immigration matters can often be complex and difficult to comprehend. Many applications take several months or even years to complete. It is noteworthy mentioning that an immigration consultant performs similar tasks as lawyers and many might agree with the fact that some consultants have broader knowledge or expertise pertaining to immigration matters compared to lawyers.

一般來說，移民顧問的角色，主要是用理解的表單或方式，傳達與解釋資訊，讓準移民者可以清晰地了解移民制度。移民顧問師扮演一個很重要的角色，在吸引技術移民滿足勞動市場需求，甚至於，在協助準移民者指導移民系統方面，扮演一個極為重要的功能。外國移民者不甚熟悉移民規則，也不了解複雜的專業術語，這時專業移民顧問師就成了提供大眾最好的服務和諮詢意見的重要角色。關於移民常常是複雜和難以理解。許多申請者需要花幾個月甚至幾年才能完成。值得一提的是，移民顧問師執行類似律師的任務，很多人可能會同意，相較於移民律師，有些顧問在移民相關事情上，反而有更廣泛的知識或專業技能。

1-2 臨場反應篇

Q

1

How do you think an unauthorized Immigration Consultant?
您怎麼看待無照移民顧問師？

What I think an unauthorized providers of immigration services are operating illegally. Authorized Immigration consultants provide their services to individuals seeking help to navigate immigration issues. However, Immigration of XXX country will not accept files submitted by unauthorized immigration consultants. If an immigrant client use an unauthorized immigration consultant, his or her application will be refused and he or she will be barred from entering that country. Many immigrants find out that they will never get their permission or any immigration benefits because an "unqualified immigration consultant", unlawfully working as an immigration consultant, destroyed their dreams. Till today, CSIC investigators have tracked nearly 2,000 "ghost" consultants who are providing unethical advice. In order to provide protection for immigration and citizenship applicants, the Government examined ways to regulate these immigration consultants. ICCRC established self-regulation in immigration industry to control and discipline immigration consultants effectively.

我認為無照提供移民顧問服務是非法的。持照的移民顧問師提供服務，輔導個人處理移民問題。然而，入境事務處的 XXX 國家不會接受無照的移民顧問師提交的文件。如果準移民客戶，使用無照的顧問，那麼他們的申請將會被拒絕，也會被禁止進入該國家。許多移民者發現他們將永遠不會得到移民許可或是任何移民福利，因為「不合格的移民顧問師」摧毀了他們的移民夢。直到今天 CSIC 調查員已經追蹤到將近有二千名「幽靈」顧問提供不道德的諮詢意見。為了提供移民者申請人保護，政府用審查方式監管這些移民顧問師。ICCRC 建立了一套自我管理規範，有效地與紀律地監控移民顧問師。

Q

2

Assuming I am a potential immigrant client; how would you sell your company's service as my Immigrant Consultant?
假裝我是移民者，你如何向我推銷你公司作為我的移民顧問？

SimBest Immigration Consultant Company has been providing immigration advice and assistance for over 15 years. Every Immigration Consultant currently at SimBest has at least 6 years experience. Our services apply to both companies and individuals and we are here to advise and guide you through the maze that can sometimes be International Immigration Law. here are a wide range of different types of Visas and Permits designed to best accommodate your requirements. We closely examine these requirements and ensure that the route we take together is the most cost effective and efficient. The very important point is we are registered in the UK with the OISC and the JCWI. For non-UK immigration matters, such as US or Canada Immigration, our Immigration Consultants are either legally qualified in the relevant country and / or registered to provide advice and representation for that country. Please let us help you start the next exciting chapter of your life in Great British.

SimBest 移民顧問公司已經提供移民資訊諮詢服務超過 15 年。目前在 SimBest 每個移民顧問有至少 6 年的經驗。我們的服務適用於公司和個人，我們提供諮詢意見和指導您順利走出有時會讓人頭暈的國際移民法律迷宮。我們提供各類型的簽證和許可證，以最好的方式滿足您的要求。我們會仔細密切檢查您的所有要求，並共同找出最符合成本效益和效率的路線。最重要的一點，我們在英國的 OISC 與 JCWI 等有關移民協會都有獲得認證。處理英國移民以外的事宜，如美國或加拿大移民，我們的移民顧問師在這些國皆登記有案，也都能夠很好地提供諮詢意見或是協助申請相關事宜。請讓我們協助您在英國開啟令人興奮的新生活。

Q

3 **Regarding the new law about Immigration Consultants without a license, tell me what you think below case study?**
關於新法律針對無牌移民顧問師，說說你對以下案例的看法？

Case study: I am a recruiting and education agent and have a license from a government to recruit workers and students overseas. I have successfully handled and processed immigration applications in the past and there were no problem. Can I continue to process and handle immigration related papers?

The answer is No, you cannot continue to legally handle and process immigration related services unless you also obtain an immigration consulting license. A recruiting agent's or education agent's license is different from an immigration consulting license. The recruiting agent's license authorizes a person to recruit worker for local employers but it does not authorize you to handle and process immigration applications and other immigration related services. Before, there was no law that made it illegal for recruiting agents to handle and process applications, provide immigration advice for a fee, etc. However, now new law tells us who can legally handle and process immigration related services or provide immigration advice for a fee.

案例：我是招聘和教育代理，領有政府頒發的許可執照，允許從海外招聘員工與學生。過去，我已處理過許多這類的移民申請，並沒有問題。我現在還可以繼續處理移民相關的案件嗎？

答案當然是不、你不能繼續合法處理移民相關服務，除非您拿到移民顧問師執照。招聘代理或教育代理執照和移民顧問師執照是不同的。招聘代理執照僅僅是授權你代理本地雇主招聘員工，但它並未授權您可以處理移民申請和其他移民相關的服務。之前，法律並未明確說明招募代理處理移民事務，收費性質的移民諮詢是非法的。但是，現在新法告訴我們誰可以合法的處理移民業務與諮詢並且收取服務費用。

Q

4

Good practice means satisfied clients. Please tell how you provide good quality services?
好的執行力等於顧客滿意，請說明你要怎麼提供良好的服務？

First of all an immigration consultant candidate who wants to provide Canadian Immigration Services must be registered with the ICCRC. To register with the council, candidate first meet those conditions, which are: thorough knowledge of Canadian Immigration and Refugee law; full skills exam; good characters; language proficiency in English. After joining the council, the immigration consultant must act by the Canadian Immigration law and must obey the code of professional ethics, such as Serve Honorably, Privileged Role, Quality of Service, and Cheating Prohibited.The foundation of the business of immigration consultation is based on results and the service provided to the clients. I would make an extra effort to educate my clients and I am even thinking of putting up some seminars to make them understand the immigration process under which they have applied or will be applying. If I tell them clearly that a particular step will take say 8 months, I can reduce the call traffic significantly in contrast to the situation where I give a false processing time and make the client impatient.

我們都知道「有好的實行力等於顧客滿意」。首先，所有移民顧問候選人想要提供加拿大移民服務，必須在 ICCRC 進行註冊。註冊時，移民顧問候選人首先要滿足幾個條件，如全面瞭解加拿大移民法規和難民法、全技能考試、品行須良好、以及英語語言能力。加入認證協會後，移民顧問師的行為必須受到加拿大移民法律規範，必須遵守職業道德，如服務光榮、 特權角色，優質的服務，禁止舞弊等。移民諮詢業務的基礎，在於最終的申請結果，還有申請過程中提供客戶的服務。我會額外教育我的客戶，還有甚至考慮舉辦一些研討會，使他們瞭解移民程序，包括他們已申請或即將申請。如果我清楚地告訴他們，某個步驟會花到八個月時間，我可以大大減少不必要的溝通往返情況，相較於我提供度不正確的時間而讓客戶失去耐心。

1-3 我有疑問篇

Q 1

What are you looking for in this position?
你在找甚麼樣的人？

We are currently seeking a licensed immigration consultant to join our team located in our new overseas branch office. The position will report to the General Manager this position and will work closely with our current immigration consultant to increase services to our clients. The candidate must hold a full membership with ICCRC and with at least two years of experience in immigration consulting, preferable business, knowledge of non-immigrant and immigrant visas and work authorization processes, strong writing and communication and interpersonal skills. Must have foreign language fluency especially English. The candidate must be ability to work in a team-oriented environment and to be well organized, flexible, and adaptable in order to respond effectively and efficiently to various situations as they arise; he must have strong relationship-building ability, proactive, willingness to learn, results-oriented and resourceful. The candidate also has ability to meet deadlines without compromising accuracy, excellent product quality, and attention to detail; have high degree of critical thinking, analytical skills.

我們正在尋求持照的移民顧問師，加入我們位於新的海外分支機構的團隊。這個職位會向總經理彙報，並且會與我們的其他移民顧問師密切合作，以提高我們的客戶服務。求職者比需要是 ICCRC 正式會員完整的會員資格，而且至少有兩年移民諮詢的實際業務經驗是最好的。熟悉非移民與移民簽證和工作的授權過程。良好的文字表達技巧、溝通技巧與人際技巧。必須外國語言流暢尤其是英語。求職者人必須在以團隊為導向的環境中工作，且必須有好的組織、靈活和適應能力，以有效率地應對各種情況的發生；他必須要有很強的建立關係的能力，積極進取，願意學習，並以結果為導向、資源豐富。候選人

也有能力，在不影響精確度的情形下準時完成任務，完美的工作品質與注重細節；具有高度的批判性思維、分析能力。

2 What would you describe your company's culture?
請說明貴公司的文化？

ProCon has grown from a single office to a global network. With over 1,000 legal and immigration professionals worldwide, we have the experience, scale and flexibility to ensure that our clients receive the highest caliber of immigration services. People who work at ProCon are as intelligent and driven as they are passionate and caring. We have fostered a fast-paced, dynamic, and forward-thinking environment, and ProCon employs talented professionals who share collective pride and enthusiasm for what they do. Ethnic Diversity happens naturally at ProCon. Being specialists in immigration, we have sought to cultivate an employee population that is as rich in diversity as are our clients. It is through differences in culture, gender, race, sexual orientation, and life experiences that we are able to offer our employees a vibrant, creative work environment. The diversity of our employee population directly translates into providing our clients with a heightened understanding of their needs, and more effective solutions.

ProCon 從一個單一的辦公室發展成一個全球網路。1000 多位專業法律和移民專業人員遍步全世界，我們有經驗、規模和靈活性，可以確保我們的客戶獲得最頂級的移民服務。 在 ProCon 工作的人，聰明，充滿激情和關懷。我們孕育了一個快節奏、動態和前瞻性思維的環境，並且 ProCon 雇用的專業人員，分享團體榮耀與熱情。族群多樣化在 ProCon 是很理所當然的。作為移民顧問專家，我們力求員工盡可能多樣化，就如同我們服務的客戶。通過文化、 性別、 種族、 性別取向和生活經驗，我們能夠為我們的員工提供一個充滿活力和創造性的工作環境。專業人員的多樣性，可以讓我們更加地了解我們客戶的需求，和提供更有效的解決辦法

3

Q

What do you like the most about your job and this company?
你最喜歡工作及公司地哪個部分？

I love working at this company; because this company managed to develop a complex and thorough understanding of all areas or topics related to immigration, ensuring that we continue to provide the best available services to our clients. CoBest immigration Consultants always make every effort to maintain the highest standards of services and integrity. Certainly, I totally agree with this point. Traditionally speaking, a professional consultant puts its client's interest before its own. I have been working here for almost 6 years. Till today, I have worked hard to assist many new immigrants. A prospective immigrant planning to immigrate to abroad will require the guidance and assistance of an immigration consultant to guide him or her towards a successful new step in his/her life. I am satisfied with that moment when I successfully provide to my outstanding service to my clients by assisting them achieve their immigration goals. This is my favorite part. I always believe a satisfied client will bring me more business.

我喜歡在這裡工作，因為這家公司總是致力於拓展複雜的移民問題，與徹底了解有關這領域的所有議題，確保可以持續提供客戶最佳的服務。CoBest 移民顧問公司總是盡一切努力保持最高標準的服務和完整。當然，我完全認同這點。

傳統上講，專業移民顧問師是要將顧客的利益擺放在自己的利益之前。我已經在這裡工作了將近 6 年。直到今天我已協助許多的移民者。想要移民到海外的準移民者，非常需要移民顧問師的協助，成功地引導他/她走向新生活。當我得以完美協助客戶成功地實現他們的移民目標，那一刻我很滿足。這是我最喜歡的地方，我始終堅信一個滿意的客戶會給我帶來更多的業務。

Q

4

Could you please tell me how your career has developed at this company?
你可以告訴我您的職業生活如何在這家公司獲得發展嗎？

BellCon Group provides all staff with training and support to ensure ongoing development within the firm. This includes continuous professional development and technical training, both internal and external to ensure staff are equipped with the knowledge and skills required to provide migration advice and to consult with our clients. The firm also places strong emphasis on each staff member's more general training needs and offers staff the opportunity to attend training sessions to meet their development needs. BellCon Croup provides a great program for articled student and recent graduate. I have been working here for 6 years; and I started from a trainee and was trained for a legal immigration consultant with license. This firm offers me many opportunities for growth and learning. Working here, I am able to practice in an exciting, ever changing, and challenging environment with people who are passionate about immigration. Recently, I was assigned the opportunity to partner with a company of Big-Scale Multinational Corporations.

BellCon 集團提供所有工作人員培訓和支援，確保我們不斷成長。這包括持續的專業發展和技術培訓、 內部和外部，確保工作人員配備的知識和技能要求提供移民諮詢，並為客戶提供諮詢。公司還非常重視對每個工作人員更一般培訓需求和提供工作人員的機會參加培訓課程，以滿足其發展需要。BellCon Croup 為見習的學生和應屆畢業生提供了一個好的計畫。我在這裡已經工作六年了，從我開始當實習生和使用許可證的合法移民顧問進行了培訓。我從實習生開始，接受公司培訓，成為合法持照的移民顧問師。公司提供了很多成長和學習的機會。在這裡工作，我能和那些對移民事務處充滿熱情的顧問師們一同在令人興奮，不斷改變，和具有挑戰性的環境中工作。最近，我更是被分配到擔任一家跨國行企業的移民顧問師。

unit B 自傳篇

1 範例

1-1. 自傳(1)

I have a Bachelor's degree in Business Administration and have completed an accredited Immigration Consultant program that concentrated on immigration procedures, immigration laws, and ethical standards. University prepared me for a lot of things, mainly time management and problem-solving as well as working well in groups. I speak three languages fluently and have a great understanding of the laws and culture of all three.

I had worked with Mr. Joseph Hill who specializes in immigration consultant for last three years. He is my boss, who having a dedicated professional with profound knowledge and experience. From my previous job, I learned extensive experience of immigration procedures and consultancy services; profound knowledge of different categories of visas and immigration services; maintain all immigration cases related folders in computerized system in centralized manner. I have excellent reading, writing, and speaking skills, which are vital in this profession in order to provide immigrants with the information they need to make a smooth transition from one country to another. Also have the ability to translate documents and explain the information in a way the individual can understand. I have lots of patience to work with these individuals to help give them the information and confidence they need to follow the legal proceedings required to be a resident in a new country. I have outstanding research abilities and computer skills that play a major role in gathering information to help immigrants make the best choices when trying to establish residency in a new country. For example, it makes it easier to provide immigrants with information about visas, green cards and work permits so they know exactly what they need to do to comply with the immigration laws.

This is a very rewarding career and I hope that you will consider me as a top candidate for this position.

我擁有企管管理學士學位，已完成一個經移民顧問課程鑑定，主要在移民程序、移民法律和道德標準。大學生涯教會我很多東西，主要在時間管理和解決問題，以及工作井然有序。我會說三種流利語言而且非常了解它們的法律與文化。

過去 3 年，我曾在從事移民顧問的約瑟夫‧希爾先生之下工作。他是我的老闆，在這領域具有淵博的知識和經驗。之前的工作，我學到辦理移民程序和諮詢服務的廣泛經驗；不同類型簽證與移民服務的深刻知識；集中電腦化的方式保存所有移民相關案件資料夾。我有絕佳的閱讀、寫作和口語技巧，是這個行業的關鍵，主要是為移民提供他們需要的資訊，順利地從一個國家遷移到另一個國家。還有，有能力用可以瞭解的方式，翻譯檔案和解釋資訊。我有很大的耐心去幫助將要定居在新國家的人們，提供他們資訊與信心，遵守法律程序。我有傑出的研究和電腦技能，在我收集資訊的過程中扮演很重要的角色，因為可以幫助想要移民到海外的移民者做出最好的選擇。例如，簽證、綠卡與工作證的相關資訊，如此，他們可以瞭解要遵守的相關的移民法。

這是一個非常有意義的職業，我希望您會考慮我為這個職位的首選。

1-2. 自傳(2)

I earned my Bachelor of Arts in English from York University UK. After a year working as an administrative assistant at immigration department government organization, I decide to be an immigration consultant because I love working with people. I studied at XXX College's immigration consultant certificate program and got Level-2 OISC registered Immigration Consultation. Recently, I moved up my certificated level from level-2 to level-3 from The Office of the Immigration Services Commissioner (OISC).

I have more than 5 years experience in managing a diverse casework covering various asylum, immigration, and nationality issues. I have extensive experience in dealing with all levels of immigration casework from the very basic to complex entry clearance, and other visa applications. I maintain an approachable disposition to work and enjoy untying difficult cases for clients who have been disappointed in their previous experience of legal advice and representation.

Immigration consulting is a regulated profession in which we represent people while they're pursuing immigration status. The only difference between us and lawyers is that we cannot go to court. Working in immigration consultant industry, I meet people from all over the world, and their families. We get very close to them, because what you need for immigration purposes is their story, from their birth to their education to career and family. You know all the stuff those people are going through, and this is amazing because you get so much knowledge, inspiration and so many things to think about. I believe people who care make the best immigration consultants. Sometimes a consultant will take a case without telling people honestly what they can expect. It's a basic human quality, but caring goes a long way for an immigration consultant: it means fewer errors and fewer headaches.

I believe I am the person you are looking for. It would be my great honor to be associated with such an esteemed company.

我拿到英國約克大學的英語學士。在政府組織的移民處擔任行政助理一年後，我決定成為一名移民顧問師，因為我喜歡與人接觸的工作。我進入 XXX 大學開設的移民顧問認證機構就讀，並且拿到 OISC Level-2 移民顧問師證書。最近，我剛升級為 OISC Level-3 移民顧問師認證。

我有五年以上的工作經驗，處理過不同個案，涵蓋各類政治庇護、移民和國籍問題等。不同困難等級的豐富經驗，從處理最基本到最複雜的簽證，和其他簽證申請。工作上我平易近人，並且享受挑戰，譬如，當我成功地解決了客戶因為之前聘請的移民顧問無法順利解決的議題時。

移民顧問師是受規範的行業，我們代表準移民者。我們與律師最大的不同是，我們不能去法院。在移民顧問行業工作，我遇到來自世界各地的人們與他們的家庭，與他們近距離接觸；申請移民程序的關係，你會需要知道他們的故事，從他們的出生到教育到職業還有家庭。你知道所有的東西那些人正在經歷的，也是很令人驚奇的，因為你會得到許多知識、啟發以他們的想法。我相信會關懷照顧的人，會成為傑出的移民顧問師。有時候移民顧問不願誠實告訴準移民者他們可以期望。這是基本的人性，但是對移民顧問師來說，關懷可以讓你走地長遠，因為這代表少點錯誤少點頭疼。

我相信我是貴公司要尋找的人才，它將是我莫大的榮幸，成為貴公司的一員。

2　自傳寫作教室

2-1.　自傳(1)　寫作文法解析／小評語

　　Immigration Consultant 移民顧問師，涉及的領域知識其實很廣泛，所以，學歷上並沒有一定要是法律領域畢業，但是一定要經過專業機構的培訓，熟悉該國的相關移民法規與申請程序，拿到許可執照後，才能正式成為移民顧問師。Accredited、Registered、Licensed、與 Certificated 等，這些都是與認證相關的單字，經常會加在移民顧問師的前面。有關移民的法規、專業術語、以及申請流程，往往複雜難懂，而移民顧問師的角色主要就是導航功能，協助引導準移民者，準備移民相關文件與佐證資料，讓這些準移民者可以順利的申請獲准遷移到目的國家的移民許可。移民的種類很多種，一般常見的有以下，提供讀者參考。

　　Skilled worker immigration visa/permit 專業技術工作者移民

　　Work immigration visa/permit 普通工作者移民

　　Business immigration visa/permit 商業移民：investor 投資者、或 Entrepreneur 企業家

　　Study immigration visa/permit 學生移民

　　Family class immigration visa/permit 家人移民

　　Temporary Visitor immigration visa/permit 短期簽證

　　Permanent Resident immigration 永久居留

　　Refugee immigration 難民、避難者

2-2. 自傳(2) 寫作文法解析／小評語

　　不管之前從是甚麼職業，要成為移民顧問，只要經過專業機構的短期培訓，通過檢驗後，即可合法從事移民顧問諮詢工作，也是有原本就是在政府機構的移民單位工作的人員，轉職成為專業移民顧問師。各國家有各自的移民法規程序，所以，並非是「一照走天下」。為什麼要有證照呢？這是政府針對移民顧問服務品質標準上的嚴格管控，也是讓準備移民者在聘請專業移民顧問協助處理移民程序時，多一份保障，因為 unlicensed、unauthorized 無照的、未經授權的移民顧問的服務品質，令人堪慮。這些各國政府設立的申請頒發證照的移民顧問機構，設立不同等級的服務標準與項目，要申請移民顧問，可以依自身能力與需要，申請適合的等級或升與更新。

　　以本自傳為例，英國申請認證機構為 The Office of the Immigration Services Commissioner（簡稱 OISC），分成三個等級，明確規範各等級可以做（can do）與不可以做（can't do）的服務項目。

Level 1: Advice and Assistance（最基本，涉及範圍最小）

Level 2:Casework

Level 3: Advocacy and Representation
　　　　　（最高等級，涉及範圍最大）

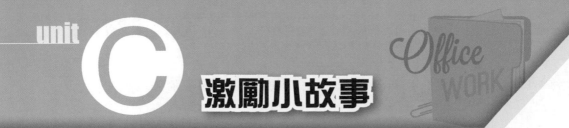
I have been working as an immigration consultant for several years. I have been asked by many people why I chose to work in immigration industry instead of one of the more interesting and exciting fields. Actually, there are quite a few reasons that I could share with you.

The main reason that I chose to become an immigration consultant was that it allowed me to help people who need help. There are millions of people who dream of moving to overseas, the process however is not easy to navigate. The laws that cover immigration are very complicated and this makes it difficult for most immigrants; and the result is that many immigrants who should be allowed moving from a country to another country are denied that chance. Being able to help those people is very satisfying.

The second reason, which is the big one, is that I chose to become an immigration consultant was because of such a challenging and fascinating field. Immigration consultant gives me such a wide scope of practice. As already mentioned the immigration laws are very complex and difficult; this means there is a new challenge every day. Unlike other areas, I know that I will be handling something different every time I go to work. It can be a question from one prospective immigrant about how to fill out paperwork; others can be advising one prospective immigrant on how to increase their chances of being approved. These keep things interesting. The last reason is that I chose to work in immigration consultant area is because of huge demand in this field. The career of an immigration consultant has turned out to be a great one for me. I thoroughly enjoy both helping people and the challenges that it presents. I would highly recommend this career to anybody who has similar interests and is not sure of what to do with their lives.

　　我從事移民顧問工作有好幾年了。有很多人問我為麼要在這領域工作，而不是其他更有趣、更令人興奮的領域。其實，有很多原因，我可以和你分享。

　　我選擇了成為一名移民顧問的主要原因是它允許我幫助需要幫助的人。有數以百萬計的人夢想遷移到海外，不過過程並不容易。移民法律非常複雜，這對大多數移民者來說是很困難，這導致應該可以從一個國家遷移到另一個國家的移民者機會被剝奪了，可以幫助這些人非常令人滿足。

　　第二個最大原因，選擇了移民顧問師職業是因為它是一個具有挑戰性和令人著迷的領域。正如已經提到的移民法是非常複雜難懂的，這意味著是每天都有新的挑戰。不同於其他領域，每次出去上班，我知道將會處理不同的事情；它可以是準移民者詢問如何填資料，也可以是提供諮詢關於如何提高準移民者被批准的機會。這些都令人感到新鮮有趣。最後一個我選擇移民顧問職位的原因，是因為在這領域的廣大需求。移民顧問的職業生涯，最終是我最好的選擇；我非常沉浸在幫助他人與挑戰的喜悅中，我極力推薦給跟我有類似興趣，且還不確定要從是甚麼職業的人。

11

英文導覽人員

1-1 常遇到的考題

Q

1 **What are the responsibilities of a Tour Guide?**
旅遊導覽員的職責是甚麼？

Role of tour guide is basically to provide the best tourist packages to the people who are interested to spend their holidays and wanted to go some different places. The most important part of being a tour guide is make the best possible arrangements of travelling for their customers; and makes their whole trip enjoyable. So, their responsibilities are: Look for an area that can generally be of great interest to a group or a particular group of people; during the tour, communicate with your tour group in a cheerful and engaging manner; lead the tour groups to points of interest and at the same time provide useful and interesting information in whatever medium — written, oral or through electronic presentations; make sure all the members of the tour group follow the schedules set; I have been travelling the world every since I was a child, and this is why I became a travel professional. I am qualified for your open tour guide position.

導遊的作用基本上是提供最好的旅遊套餐，給有意到一些不同地方度期的人們。當導遊的最重要部分是為他們的旅客，安排最好的行程，使整個旅行愉快。所以他們的職責是：尋找一個可以引起一個團體或特定族群最高興趣的地區；在參觀活動中，以開朗和動人的方式與你的旅遊團溝通；帶著旅遊團到各個不同的景點，並且利用媒介，如書面、口頭或是電子設備等，提供有用與有趣的資訊；請確保旅遊組的所有成員都遵守時程表。從小至今，我以旅行遍世界各處，這也是我成為旅遊專業的原因，我相信我有足夠的能力勝任導遊的職位。

2 Why do you want to change job?
為什麼你要換工作？

I worked for XXX Magazine as a travel writer since 2005. I travelled and saw places and using my writing skills to paint a picture for others, so they can get a real feeling of what it would be like visiting these places. I also have a lot of personal experience traveling to many of the most popular tourist destinations. After few years working as a writer, I find that I prefer leading tourists to visit and sharing the interesting story to tourists. Besides, I am very familiar with the travel industry, which encourages me to make this my career choice as a tour guide. My ex-colleagues said that I have an upbeat and friendly personality. They love getting along with me. I love meeting and talking with new people. So being a tour guide is the perfect career for me and I would like to share my enthusiasm and skills with your company.

自 2005 年開始,我擔任 XXX 雜誌的旅行作家。我將走過看過的景點，用我寫作技巧，在讀者心中，勾勒出彷彿實地造訪的畫面。我曾到過許多熱門旅遊地點旅行的經歷。幾年的旅行作家生涯，我發現我更喜歡帶領遊客參觀各景點和分享有趣的故事，娛樂遊客。而且我非常熟悉旅遊行業，這鼓勵我選擇成為旅遊導覽員。我以前的同事說我有一種樂觀和友好的個性。他們喜歡與我相處。我喜歡認識新朋友，喜歡和他們交談。所以旅遊導覽員非常適合我，我想與貴公司分享我的熱情和技能。

Q

3 Tell me about your job experience.
說明你的工作經驗。

   I am fascinated by art and history, so I took a museum guide as my job at the Pioneers Museum. The key role of my job is to ensure that the visitor experience at the Pioneers Museum is of the highest possible quality, including giving guided tours and leading workshops for a range of audiences. My duties at Pioneers Museum are conduct educational activities for school students. Research various topics to plan appropriate expeditions, instruction, and commentary about Pioneers Museum. Select routes to be visited based on knowledge of specific areas in the museum. Guide, teach and describe tour points of interest to group members, and respond to questions. Distribute brochures, show audiovisual presentations, and explain establishment processes and operations in the museum. Speak foreign languages to communicate with foreign visitors. Monitor visitors' activities to ensure compliance with museum regulations and safety practices. Provide directions and other pertinent information to visitors. I believe my qualifications meet the requirements in your posting.

   我著迷於藝術和歷史，所以我在 Pioneer 博物館擔任博物館導覽員工作。我主要是確保在 Pioneers 博物館的遊客有最高品質的體驗，包括提供特定團體的館內的導覽行程，以及研習。我在 Pioneers 博物館負責的工作有:為在校學生進行教育活動；研究並計畫館內各種適合的主題行程，譬如探索、教育和評論，選擇特定導覽路線；指導、教育解說趣事給團體或個人，回答的問題；分發摺頁冊、 展示視聽演示文稿和解釋建立過程和操作。講外語與外國遊客溝通。管控參觀活動，以確保遵守館內法規和安全操作。為訪客提供方向和其他相關資訊。我相信我的資歷符合您的需求。

4

Q

What is your greatest weakness?
你最大的缺點為何？

Being a tour guide, you will generally be speaking in front of a huge group of people on most of the tours you lead. Groups can have anywhere from 10 to 60 people, so you have to understand the basic principles of public speaking. My greatest weakness is probably that I got very nervous about public speaking. I remember that it was a challenge when I first had to do the commentary on tours. It is nerve-wracking and scary to stand up in front of all those people and speak. However, in order to overcome this by taking a public speaking course and preparing very well. I tried to imagine that I am just talking to a group of my friends, so that I can get more comfortable and confidence with addressing people in a relaxing and engaging way. And eventually, I even tried to improvise and add in a few of my own stories and extra bits of information I come across.

作為一名導遊，一般要在你帶領的一大群人面前演講，可以從 10 人到 60 人的團體，所以要了解大眾演講的基本原則。我最大的弱點可能是我在大眾面前演講會非常地緊張，我記得，當我第一次不得不在一個旅遊團面前作評論時，真是一個挑戰，站在所有人面前和發言，非常緊張和可怕。然而，為了克服這個問題，我去上了公眾演講課程，也會在事前做好完全準備。試著想像我是在對我的一群朋友說話，這樣一來，我感覺更舒適與信心，可以用輕鬆動人的方式與人們談話。最後，我甚至試圖即興添加我自己的故事，還有我遇到的一些軼事。

5

What skills do you have to be a good Tour Guide? Please name two.
要成為好的旅遊導覽員，你有甚麼技能，請舉出 2 個。

Communication skill is important as a tour guide for me. As a tour guide, I have to speak in public. When I guide a tour, I tell visitors some interesting events around the sight to entertain them and capture their attention. For example, instead of listing dates that certain structures were built, I would rather tie in the building of a monument with other things that happened in history such as the ending of a war perhaps. With more than 4 years for working experiences as a tour guide, I have excellent problem solving skills. Just like any jobs, problems tend to arise, but when you are on a tour with a group of people to look after, the problems can sometimes be quite big. I know how to deal with anything that comes my way quickly and effortlessly, situation like leaving the group stranded to one of the passengers getting ill and needing to get rushed to the hospital.

對擔任旅遊導覽員的我來說，溝通技巧是重要的技能，因為，我要在公眾場所講話。當我導覽參觀時，會告訴訪客關於景點一些有趣的事情，娛樂與吸引他們的注意力。例如，與其說明某個紀念碑被建立的日期，我寧可告訴他們與紀念碑有關的歷史，也許是場戰爭。我有超過 4 年的旅遊導覽員經驗，我有絕佳的解決問題能力。就像任何工作，問題總是會出現，但當你要照顧一群參觀的人時，有時可以有很大問題。我知道如何迅速輕鬆的處理任何事情，情況像是，因為其中一位生病的旅客需要緊急送醫，而耽誤行程的處理方式。

Q

6

What do you think you do best?
你認為你的專長是甚麼？

I held Master of Arts History and Religion at A&M University and specialized in the historical profession. I acted as a teaching assistant and my duty is substitute for absent teachers in middle and high schools. I applied this teaching experience to my following job, a museum tour guide. I had two-year experience as a museum tour guide at Michie Tavern in famous XXX historical town. I was responsible for leading tours of the museum and historic tavern in period dress; answering visitors' questions and providing additional information on the history of the tavern; collaborating with museum staff to create new exhibits and improving overall tour experience. I am organized and good at leadership skills. I have to be in control and completely organized at all times, I am organizing a group of people and sure of everything clear and in good order, chatting with them, informing them about various places, partying with them, and sometimes even counseling them.

我具有 A & M 大學歷史和宗教藝術碩士，主修專業歷史。我曾擔任過教學助理，我的職責是初中和高中學校教師缺席時的代課。我將這教學經驗應用到我後面的工作，也就是博物館導覽員。我在 XXX 歷史名鎮的一家 Michie 小酒館，擔任兩年的博物館導遊。我是負責帶領旅行團在博物館和歷史小酒館期間穿著；回答遊客的問題和提供有關歷史的酒館的資訊；與博物館工作人員合作，開發新產品提高整體的旅遊體驗。我有組織能力和好的領導能力。因為在導覽期間我必須要能完全掌控，確認團體能夠井然有序，與他們聊天、解說地方資訊，與他們玩在一塊，有時還要提供諮詢服務。

7 Describe the perfect tourist for a guided group tour.
形容你在導覽時的理想遊客。

I think the perfect tourist for me is a person with a positive attitude. He is relaxed, willing to learn and follow me. This tourist shows with his non-verbal communication that he is enjoying the tour. Tourist like that usually transfers their positive energy to the rest of the group. I will never forget that one guest from USA who shows his great passion while I was talking about historical area. With such this kinds of tourist's company would makes whole trip cheerful. Usually, I have some guests that I keep in touch with and a few of them are closer to my heart. Also, I still keep some messages written to me after excursions. Peter from Japan became a friend of mine. I can say the same for Blaga from Australia. Two weeks ago, Blaga came with four generations of females, who are her mother, Blaga, her daughter and granddaughter, to Taiwan since she wanted them all to see that beauty.

我認為理想的遊客是擁有積極正面態度的。他心態放鬆並請願意跟著我，不需要言語溝通，我就知道他很享受這趟旅程。像這樣的旅客通常會傳遞了正面能量給整個團體。我永遠不會忘記那位來自美國的旅客，表現出他極致的熱情，當我在導覽這具有歷史地區的時候。有這種遊客的陪伴會讓整個旅行愉快。通常情況下，我之後與一些遊客保持聯繫，這一小部分遊客都是跟我比較心靈相通的。所以，在行程結束後，我們仍會保持書信往來。從日本來的 Peter 就成為了我的朋友，同樣的從澳大利亞來的 Blaga 也成為我的朋友。兩個星期前，Blaga 帶著跨越四代的家族女性成員，她的母親、 Blaga、 她女兒和孫女一同來訪臺灣，因為她希望他們都能見到這裡的美景。

Q 8

Your last job is a museum docent ; describe what you usually do?
你前一份工作是博物館導覽員，說說你通常都做些甚麼？

As with any job, museum docents must be dependable, I always arrive at the museum prior to the scheduled tour time to ensure that they are ready to begin on time. Greet my tour group with a smile and cheerful, welcoming, "Good morning!" When on the tour, I would try to speak clearly, facing the group as you talk. While conducting my tour, if asked questions about the exhibit for which I do not know the answer, I will tell the asker that I will find the answer for them at the end of the tour. I would carry "Comment" cards with me, and hand each visitor a card after finishing tour. I would suggest that they make their comments on the card and drop it off in the reception area. Each day, Museum arranges various guide tours. Sense of the time is quite important. If another tour is scheduled to start behind mine, I will keep my group moving. Overall, we need to follow the docent guide book.

博物館導覽員跟其他工作一樣，必須是可靠的，我總是在博物館安排導覽的時間開始前，提早抵達定點，以確保導覽準時開始。我會帶著微笑，對著參觀團體，開朗的說聲「早安」，表示歡迎。在導覽時，我會試著講清楚，面對著團體談話。導覽中，有關當次展覽，如果我被問到我不知道答案的問題時，我會如實以告，並且告訴提問者，會後我會幫他們找到解答。我會隨身帶著「意見卡」，導覽結束後，每人發一張，建議他們寫下關於這次導覽的意見，之後放到接待處。

每一天，博物館安排各種導覽行程。時間觀念是很重要的，如果另一組導覽行程安排在我之後開始，我會留意每個點的停留時間，保持移動。整體來說，我們都應該遵循導覽指南書上規定的。

1-2 臨場反應篇

Q 1

What do you find the most attractive about the job, and least attractive?
你認為旅遊導覽這份工作最吸引人的與最不吸引人的地方是甚麼？

There are a lot of great things about being a tour guide. The best part of this job is that I am able to meet new people. As my references show, I have been very popular with many of the clients who specifically asked for me to be their tour guide on tours they went on. I am able to visit all the best locations around the world are the second best part of this job to becoming a tour guide. Besides, I am constantly learning and educating myself about all different destinations as I have to do plenty of research as part of my job. Well, the only least attractive I could think of, if I have to choose one, is probably when some situations happen, such as some members of the group arguing or tour buses breaking down on the road. Although, I am very good at dealing with these situations, but I still think it spoils the fun.

當旅遊導覽員，有很多棒的事情。這份工作最好的部分是我可以認識很多新朋友，正如我的推薦函顯示，我一直很受歡迎，許多客戶特別指定我當他們的旅遊導覽員。成為旅遊導覽員，第二個最好的部分是，我可以遊訪世界各地的最佳景點；除此之外，我工作的另一個部分是，我能夠不斷地學習和教育自己，大量研究各個景點。那麼，如果非要舉出不具吸引力的地方的話，我能想到的可能就是，某些意外情況發生，如團員爭吵，或是旅遊巴士在路上罷工了；雖然我很擅長處理這些情況，但我仍然認為那很煞風景。

Q 2 What motivate you?
甚麼事可以激勵你的工作？

I am a sightseeing tour guide. l generally work in a single area for an extended period of time. While I may get to see other areas, still the tours eventually become boring if you visit the same area over and over again. However, I lead the same route every day, but I can work with all kinds of new people from different places. I enjoy their company. This motivates me a lot because I am social person. This is exciting. I have enough passion to show them that I am just as interested as they are by the sights and attraction that I am showing them. It is satisfying to see that travel group leaving the sight with a great pleasure and looking forward to coming back again. The other thing that motivates me is that I am able to learn new skills, such as learning new language to serve more travel group from all over the world.

我是觀光導覽員，通常我會停留很長一段時間在一個地區工作，雖然我也會去其他地區導覽，但是每天待在同一個區域，一遍又一遍的導覽，會很容易索然無味。然而，雖然我走的路線每天都一樣，但我可以與從不同地方來的旅客一起探訪旅程，我喜歡他們的陪伴，這激勵我很多，因為我喜歡與人相處，這真是令人興奮。我有足夠的熱情呈現給他們，就好像我跟他們一樣對行程感到有趣，並且受到吸引一般。看到旅行團體高高興興地離開並且期待下次蒞臨，我感到心滿意足。另一激發我的事情是我能夠學習新的技能，像是學習新的語言，這樣一來我可以服務更多地來自世界各地的旅行團體。

Q
3 What was your customers opinions of you?
你的客戶對你的評價如何？

At the end of the tour, I would give tourists comment cards and let them write down their feedback about my service. I can give you two references.

Reference-1 from Japan tourist: Professional, knowledgeable and nice. Paul knows what he is talking about without overwhelming you, let's you set the pace and yet encourages you to see as much you are able to; the day we walked around for around the old city for over 6 hours! Highly recommend Paul and look forward to having him guide us our next time to historical city!

Reference-2 from USA tourist "Outstanding Tour in XXX historical city."

We booked Paul as a guide for our first full day in town. Paul was full of information on all fronts giving us an insight into life in here, modern and ancient history and politics. He also recommended restaurants frequented by locals that we may not have been drawn to left on our own. We would use his services again on another visit.

在參觀結束，我會給遊客意見卡，讓他們對我的服務寫下回饋意見。我可以提供給你兩個評論參考。

參考-1 從日本來的旅客：「專業、知識淵博、很好」

Paul 知道他在說什麼，沒有讓你頭昏眼花；他會配合你們的步調，還鼓勵你儘量地多看看，一天 6 個多小時下來，我們走訪了周圍的古老城市。極力推薦 Paul，並期待下回我們再回到這座歷史城市，再度請 Paul 擔任我們的導覽。

參考-2 從美國來的旅客：「XXX 傑出歷史城市之旅」

在這小鎮的第一天，我們預定 Paul 擔任的全天導覽員。Paul 擁有完整的資訊，洞察這裡的真實生活內情，現代的、古老的歷史以及政治。他還推薦當地人們經常光顧的餐廳，這些餐廳反而經常會被我們忽略了。我們下回還會在預定 Paul。

Q

4 **Can you share with me the memorable moments in your role as a museum docent?**
可以與我分享身為博物館導覽員的難忘時刻嗎？

I would like to tell you three memorable moments as a museum docent. The first memorable moment is when an editor of a certain newspaper told me, "I have joined eight guided tours on this special exhibition, and you are the one I have decided to do an interview with, though yours was the first I heard." The second memorable moment is in earlier days, we had to greet the Friends of the XXX Museum of Art at the basement and invited them to the gallery to view the exhibition. When I stepped into the room, I felt intensely uncomfortable and was so nervous that I had to calm down myself before speaking. Initially, there was little feedback from the visitors. However, the condition gradually changed. I was happy to see that they were listening with eagerness. Finally the tour came to an end, I was applauded and was asked by one of them if I were a curator. I was congratulated for having done a splendid job.

我想要告訴您兩個難忘時刻。一個難忘時刻是當某報紙的編輯告訴我，「我為這次特別的展覽，參加了八個導覽行程，你就是我決定要採訪的對象，雖然我是第一次聽說你」。第二個難忘時刻是，在早些時候的日子裡，我們要向位於地下室的 XXX 藝術博物館的朋友們問候，並且邀請他們到我們畫廊看展覽。當踏進了房間時，我覺得非常不舒服，很緊張，不得不讓自己在說話前冷靜下來。剛開始，訪客裡，只有得到一點點回饋，然而，情況逐漸改變了。我很高興看到他們有傾聽的興趣。等到最後導覽結束，我得到掌聲，其中一位訪客還問我是不是館長，讚賞我的出色工作。

1-3 我有疑問篇

Q 1

What are you looking for in this position?
你在找甚麼樣的人？

The Peter Automotive Museum is looking for tour guides for its tour program in the "Vault" collection storage area which has previously been off-limits to the public. Guides will lead small groups of specially-ticketed adults through the Vault where over 100 vehicles in the museum's collection from all areas of automotive history are stored. The Peter hosts visitors from around the world and guides act as professional ambassadors of the museum. Tour guides inform visitors about the historical, technical, and personal histories of the vehicles that make up the collection. Guides should be well-versed in automotive culture, history, and technology. The candidate's requirements are enthusiasm for automotive history, technology, car culture, and history; prior educational or tour guide experience, preferably in a museum setting; excellent customer service, interpersonal, and public speaking skills; experience working with diverse groups and personalities; professional appearance and demeanor; must be able to speak English fluently, bilingual candidates preferred; attention to detail, punctuality, flexibility, initiative, patience, and professionalism.

Peter 汽車博物館正在尋找導覽員，專門負責「Vault」收藏品專區，這區在之前是禁止民眾入內參觀的區域。導覽員將帶領拿有「特殊票券」的成人小團體，瀏覽 Vault 展覽區，超過 100 量在各地區蒐集到本博物館的所有地區的汽車歷史。

彼得招待來自世界各地的遊客，導遊將代表博物館的專業大使，告訴遊客歷史、技術和私有車輛蒐集的歷史。導覽員在汽車文化、歷史和技術指南應該要十分熟悉。對候選人的要求是具有對汽車歷史、技術、汽車文化和歷史的熱情；有導覽的培訓或相關經驗，最好是博

物館相關經歷;優秀的顧客服務、社交與公眾演講能力;與不同團體個性相處的經驗;專業的外型與舉止;必須能說流利英文,會雙語的候選人優先考慮;注意細節、守時、靈活性、主動、耐心和敬業精神。

Q 2 **When and why did you become a Tour Guide?**
甚麼時候以及為什麼你會成為一位旅遊導覽員?

Five years ago. It was the time when Russian tourists started to discover Taiwan and I decided to invest my efforts in that directions as a tour guide. Today I still work more with tourists from Russia than with tourists from English speaking areas, but maybe that will change in the future because I plan to work with different tourist from various countries. It's work still interests me and it has not become boring to me. The reason is that I still have things to learn, such as I do a lot of research and collect information about the sights where I am going to introduce people; I learn new language so that I am able to talk to people from another culture. I can still stay breathless; that's stimulating and it pushes me forward. This is a great thrill when you know people seeing something interesting after your presentation. It's enjoyable when you guide people to these beautiful areas with the history, literature, and mentality of a nation.

五年前。當俄羅斯遊客開始往臺灣觀光,我決定往這方向努力,成為旅遊導覽員。到今天為止,我接待的俄羅斯遊客比從英語系來的遊客還多,但也許之後會改變,因為我想多接觸不同國家的遊客。到現在,我依舊對這份工作感到興趣,一點都不會給我無聊的感覺。因為我還有很多東西要瞭解學習,譬如說我對於要參觀的景點,我會做很多的功課與蒐集資料,然後介紹給人們。我還學習了新的語言,以便我能與另一種文化的人群溝通;我持續保持著興奮的心情,就是這份刺激感推著我向前。這是多麼令人激動,當你知道別人在您的展示之後看到一些有趣的東西。當你帶著遊客造訪這些美麗的領域,了解歷史文學與一個民族的心態,那是令人愉快的。

3. Why did you join this company ? What does this job look like?
你為什麼加入這家公司？這份工作是什麼樣子？

As you know BusTour is a tourist bus company offers an extremely flexible "Hop-on, Hop-off" touring system. I joined BusTour in 2006 and was thinking the job of Onboard Guide was pretty cool, and something I felt I could do, too. I have to speak in public to complete strangers every day. I had some previous experience in radio so confidence was not a problem. The other requirements are to be organized, approachable, and capable of using computers. Full training is given before starting the job. BusTour has a thirty day training period which prepares guides to go straight onto the bus when the season begins in June. An internal radio system between staff enables us to keep updated with what is going on elsewhere on the network, and all the guides exchange information amongst themselves. Days off depend on how busy the season is; at peak times BusTour runs double buses to cope with the volume of passengers. We are always on call for any emergency.

如你所知 BusTour 旅遊巴士提供極其靈活的「定點上下」的旅遊系統。我在 2006 年加入 BusTour，當時我的想法是當個 Onboard 導覽員很不錯，我也能做。我每天必須要在一群完全陌生的人面前講話，因為我之前有過在電台工作經驗，所以我有信心。 另外，這工作要求必須有組織能力、平易近人和能夠使用電腦。開始正式工作之前，公司會提供充分的培訓。BusTour 有三十天的培訓期間，之後在六月旅遊季開始時，直接上崗。工作人員之間會用內部無線電系統維持最新訊息，還有各導覽員的資訊交流。休假取決於淡旺季節；旺季時我們一天可能要排好幾般以應付乘客量，必須隨時待命任何緊急狀況。

Q 4
When will the training begin? What training program do you offer?
培訓什麼時候開始？你們提供什麼培訓計畫？

Staff training usually begins around May 10th each year, with our first trip with guests starting shortly after this date. The season usually wraps up around Sept 20th. However due to the volatile nature of the rafting industry, these dates are somewhat flexible usually by a week or two at most. During staff training we will familiarize and train all of our tour guides / drivers with the respective hotel pickup locations, the route to the rivers we use and any emergency evacuations spots. We also hold one or two training days at the start of the season to refresh on emergency response, first aid scenarios and river rescue situations. Often the tour guides / supervisors / drivers will be involved in these days from an off river perspective. During a typical day at Chin Rafting we expect you to do anything and everything within your level of training to ensure your own safety, the safety of your fellow teammates and the safety of your guests.

工作人員的訓練通常約在每年的 5 月 10 日開始，在這日期之後不久，就開始我們與客戶的第一次泛舟行程，旅遊季約在 9 月 20 日左右結束，因為泛舟行業的不穩定性質，通常日期差距約在一周，最多不超過兩周。 在工作人員的培訓期間，我們會讓我們的導覽員 / 司機熟悉各酒店的接送點；我們使用的河流路線；緊急疏散點。在季節開始時，我們會舉行一到兩天的培訓，更新應急反應、急救方案和河流救援情況。通常，這幾天導覽員 / 督導 / 司機們都要參與，在岸邊觀看。

在 Chin 泛舟公司的工作期間，我們期待你能確實完成你份內的培訓，確保自身安全、同事們的安全，以及遊客們的安全。

1 範例

1-1. 自傳(1)

I have earned a bachelor's degree in Travel and Tourism and held the license. The first job of mine is worked as a tour operator at a Travel agent Company. Helping others plans a perfect holiday or vacation is quite enjoyable for me. I am self-motivated and have a real desire to help clients take the stress out of their travel plans and to help them have the best experience possible when traveling. To add to this, I have also spent most of my life travelling, and love the industry from a personal perspective.

I have excellent communication skills and the ability to pay close attention to detail. So, I have active listening skills and lots of patience, so I can listen to what the client is saying and make sure the travel plans meet their personal interests and budget. Many times, you can gather a lot of information just from listening closely and see the expressions clients have when talking about their plans. Once they make a decision, I have the training and skills to make all of the travel arrangements from reserving tickets for special events. Over years working as tour operator, I have gathered extensive knowledge includes information about each location such as the history, geography, customs, and weather. And I think it's time for me to guide people to those pretty places.

I have excellent communication skills with the ability to learn quickly. I have acquired the research skills to learn all of the important data concerning the tourist sites and I have a photographic memory with the ability to retain what I learn, so I can provide the tourists with accurate information. In addition to providing information, I have the skills to make the tour interesting and fun for the tourists, making it an event they will be talking about for a very long time. This encourages repeat business and it will help draw in new clients. I am confident I am a great match for this job.

我拿到旅遊業學士學位，以及旅行證照。我的第一份工作是在一家旅遊社，擔任旅遊規劃職位。協助他人計畫一個完美的假期或渡假，對我來說，是很享受的一件事。我可以自我激勵，渴望協助客戶無壓力的計畫旅行，並協助他們在去旅行時，可以有最好的體驗。除此之外，我大部分的時間也花在旅行上，從個人角度看，我很愛這各行業。

我有優秀的溝通技巧和能力，並且注意細節;我有積極的傾聽技巧和很大的耐心，所以我可以聽到客戶要說什麼，以確保旅行計畫符合他們的個人喜好和預算。很多時候，可以從仔細傾聽客戶談他們的旅行計畫中，收集大量的資訊以及想法。一旦他們做了決定，我的職責就是後續的安排，從訂購活動門票到特殊事件安排。擔任多年的旅遊規劃，我亦搜集了各景點的豐富知識，包括有關歷史、地理、風俗和天氣等。我覺得是時候，讓我來導覽人們到那些美麗的景點。

我有出色的溝通能力和快速學習的能力。我能研究關於旅遊景點的重要資料，並且過目不忘的記憶力，可以為遊客提供準確的資訊。除了提供資訊，我能使遊客對行程感到無窮趣味，使遊客之後很長一段時間，還津津有味的回憶旅程。這會使他們下回還想參加，並且有助於吸引遊客。我有自信能夠勝任這個職位。

1-2. 自傳(2)

I have a real interest in local tour guide position now available with BeTour Tourism Company. I believed that I fulfill all the necessary criteria and hope that you will consider my application.

I graduated from the University of TZX last year with my dual major of Tourism and History. I did very well on my history and geography at school and also I already have the tour guide license. Besides fluent English, I am able to speak some French and German and I am planning to take exams in both those languages within three months. My experience and education really prepared me for the role of local tour guide in many ways. First of all, I have lived in this city all my life and usually take a little trip around the city in my leisure time. I like to see different appearances of the city especially the countryside which makes me feel relax and energetic all the time. Further, I really enjoy being immersed in exploring the city no matter a museum, a coffee shop, a bookstore, or a little park because every place has always amazed me, has blown my mind, and I have learnt many local cultures or something I have not been known. During my school life, I was involved in extracurricular activities, like a volunteer work as a museum docent at XXX Historical Museum for especial exhibition. Recently, I have been working in an overseas summer camp for children. As a tour guide I need to take care of those children and tell our history and our cultures to them.

I am friendly, organized, and patient; able to work well under pressure; in addition, I have strong communication skills and confidence to speak freely with large groups of people. Therefore, I feel that I have a great passion to lead more visitors to this lovely historical city.

我對 BeTour 旅遊公司當地旅遊導覽的職位感興趣。我相信我符合所有必要的條件，希望您會考慮我的申請。

我去年畢業於 TZX 大學，主修旅遊和歷史雙重專業。我在校時的歷史與地理成績非常好，我也拿到了旅遊導覽員證照。除了流利的英語，我能說一些法語和德語，我打算在三個月內參加那兩種語言考試。不管是我的經驗還是教育背景，我各方面都已經準備好擔任這個角色。 首先，我這一生都住在這座城市，通常在我的休閒時間，會逛逛城市周圍。我喜歡看到這座城市的不同面貌，特別是鄉下，總是會令我感到放鬆與充滿活力。再來，我真的很喜歡正沉浸在探索博物館、 咖啡廳、 書店或是小公園，因為每個地方有總是帶給我驚訝，而且我學會了很多本地文化或至今仍未發現的東西。在我的學校生活，我參與了課外活動，像是在 XXX 歷史博物館舉辦的特別展覽時的導覽員義工。最近，我帶領一處海外夏令營的兒童，身為旅遊導覽員，我需要照顧那些孩子，告訴他們我們的歷史與文化。

我很友善、條理和耐心，能夠承擔工作壓力；此外，我有很強的溝通技能與信心面對一大群人侃侃而談。我覺得有極大的熱情介紹這座可愛的歷史城市給更多訪客。

2 自傳寫作教室

2-1. 自傳(1) 寫作文法解析／小評語

　　導覽員是甚麼？ 簡單來說導覽員的角色結合了專家 professor、演員 actor 以及顧客服務 customer service agent。要像專家一樣對熟悉導覽的領域，譬如歷史 history，地理 geography，民俗 customs 等，有收集資料 data collection 與研究資料的能力 research skills；之後，要有像演員一般的表演力，將這些資料用輕鬆有趣的方式傳遞給遊客；最後，畢竟遊客是顧客，除了有獲取知識 knowledgeable 以及輕鬆有趣 interesting 外，還需要有客服人員的精神，使遊客滿意。

　　大致上導覽依據導覽景點性質可分為歷史類型導覽 Historical Tour Guide 以及自然景觀類導覽 Nature Tour Guides。歷史類導覽員，會要求對歷史景點、或建築、或藝術品等有專業知識背景，如博物館導覽員 Museum Docent。而自然景觀類導覽，則必須要相當熟悉周圍的自然環境與生活形態等。以下幾個常見的導覽員，提供參考：

Sightseeing Tour Guide 觀光導覽員

Step-On Tour Guide 定點導覽員

Shore Excursion Guide 遊輪導覽員

Adventure, Sport and Eco Tour Guides 探險、運動及生態導覽員

2-2. 自傳(2) 寫作文法解析／小評語

導覽員的工作看似輕鬆愜意，其實也是有工作壓力的 a stressful job，也並不是人人都可以當導遊的，想要成為導覽員，我們先衡量看看有哪些優缺點 pros and cons，我們再看看甚麼特質 nature skills 的人，適合當導覽員：

優點 Pros of Tour Guide
- 公司付費請你到處旅行。
- 所有食宿交通費用，由公司幫你買單。
- 可以不停地説話，對有些人來説，大概是優點
- 可以學習新的知識
- 你的辦公室就是天然的戶外
- 時間自由彈性
- 認識新朋友

缺點 Cons of Tour Guide
- 要照顧一大群遊客，壓力也是挺大的呢！
- 在導覽之前，必須要做功課，先實際演練，記住每個要介紹景點的資料
- 時不時地會收到顧客抱怨或緊急事故，必須要立即處理
- 如果是海外導覽員，就要有時常不在國內的心理準備，你會要在各飯店穿梭
- 工作時間不固定

特質 Nature Skills
- Interaction skills 社交能力
- Excellent Public Speaking and Narration Skills 公眾演講與解說的能力
- Excellent Problem Solving Skills 極佳的解決問題能力
- Great Organizational and Leadership Skills 良好的組織能力與領導能力

Peter Thomas is an experienced mountain bike tour guide. I am now going to interview Peter about his unique career.

• What made you decide or choose to get into this sort of career?

I first started mountain biking 5 years ago when I was at university. It was a friend of mine who suggested that instead of taking out groups of friends for bike rides, I should think about leading people who lacked the time to organize their own rides. I was in a unique position to help these people to explore areas they hadn't visited before.

• Being a mountain bike tour guide, what is a typical day of this job?

Wake up early to make sure breakfast is ready for tourists, then a quick brief for a day trip, and then onto the bikes. The rest of the day follows a fairly typical pattern: ride until snack stop, ride again until lunch, ride up to mid afternoon stop, then on to the hotel. I need to then book clients into their rooms, organize dinner and eat, repair bikes as required from tourists, and then finally go to bed. In between all of this, there can be visits, mechanical problems, vehicle transfers, and skills tuitions. Of course, all the time you are riding in some of the most beautiful places.

• What do you like most about the job?

My bike is my office! Passing on my passion for mountain biking to others is a huge personal reward. The look on a client's face when you have taught them something new and I find this endlessly amazing.

> • What do you like least about the job?
>
> Being away from home often and often. That's probably the main issue, but then you do have opportunities to explore these incredible places.

Peter Thomas 是位有經驗的山地自行車旅遊導覽員，我們現在就來訪問 Peter 這份獨特的職業。

• 是什麼讓你決定或選擇這種職業？

我第一次開始山地自行車是在 5 年前大學的時候。當時我的一位朋友建議，與其和朋友團體自行車出遊，我應該可以帶領一群沒有時間自己計畫自行車之旅的人。因為這獨特的工作，我可以帶領他們去探索他們以前未曾造訪過的地區

• 山地自行車導覽員這份職業，平常一天都做甚麼？

早起為旅客安排早餐，然後很快的介紹一天行程，然後就準備騎自行車。其餘的一天大概就是一個相當典型的模式，騎自行車到小吃站，然後繼續上路直到午餐時間，之後就一直騎到下午的行程點，然後就回到酒店。我需要協助客戶登記入住，安排晚餐，修理自行車，之後就寢。我就在這些事情中打轉，如探訪、機械故障、交通轉乘與技術教練指導等。當然，所有的時間，你是騎在一些最美麗的地方。

• 你最喜歡這份工作的地方是什麼？

我的自行車就是我的辦公室。傳遞我對山地自行車的熱愛給他人，是一份很大的個人獎勵，當和你在一起時，教導他們一些新東西時，他們臉上的表情，我覺得這是非常令人驚喜的。

• 你最討厭這份工作的地方是什麼？

時常不在家，這可能是主要的問題，但那你更有機會去探索這些令人難以置信的地方。

英文採訪人員

口試篇

1-1 常遇到的考題

Q

1 **Why do you become a Journalist?**
你為甚麼會成為一名採訪員？

The journalism industry is highly competitive, but that's exactly the way I like it because I am a highly competitive person. I embrace all challenges thrown at me and I never back down. Being a journalist gives me an opportunity to talk to people whom everyone else won't get to talk to. The other reason is that I want to tell the truth. I want to go find the truths of the world and publish them. I ask questions, and then I find the answers to this question. When people open the newspaper, or click online to read my writing, I want them to feel like they are getting the best possible information out there. I want them to be informed and to want to continue coming back for more. In journalism, there will always be something new to write about. Becoming a journalist is my ultimate goal. I believe my experience and skills are ideal for this position.

新聞行業是極具競爭性的，但我就是喜歡，因為我是一個競爭心強的人。我熱愛所有挑戰，而且不會退縮。成為採訪員，讓我有機會跟平常人不會有機會說到話的人談話。另外一個原因是我想要說出真相。我想要去發現世界的真理，並予以公佈，我問個問題，然後找到這個問題的答案。當人們打開報紙，或點擊線上閱讀我的寫作，我想讓他們盡可能地得到最佳的訊息，我想要他們了解情況，並且想要繼續回來了解更多。在新聞行業，總是有新東西可以寫，成為一名新聞記者是我的最終目標。我相信我的經驗與技能非常適合這個職務的。

2 Can you tell me a little about yourself?
請稍微介紹你自己？

I have always been driven by a desire to bring quality story to people. My nose for news started during my days at the high school newspaper. I got to do an interview with Mr. Peter Russell, who was an alumnus of my school. I spent the day with him, touring around the school and talking with him. I had my first front-page story. I had applied for an internship at the XXX Newspaper during my junior year of ABC University. After I graduated and got Journalism Bachelor degree in 2000, The Top-Best Observer hired me as an assistant and journalist for one of the regional sections. That meant I did reporting as well tedious tasks, such putting together the crime blotter and MLS listings. Six months later, I was promoted to a full-time Community News Journalist position, and two years after that, I was promoted to the business desk as a business journalist, where I now cover the small business and entrepreneurship beat.

　　我一直被一股想帶給大家有質感的文章的渴望推動著。從我在高中校刊擔任採訪員開始，我就擅長發掘新聞，有一次我要採訪校友 Peter Russell 先生，我花了一天帶他逛逛校園，與他交談，之後，就完成了第一則頭版頭條新聞。在 ABC 大學三年級那年，我申請在 XXX 報社實習。在 2000 年，大學畢業並拿到新聞學士學位後，Top-Best Observer 雇用我作為助理和負責其中一個領域的採訪人員。這就意味著我要做採訪，以及繁瑣的任務，譬如犯罪紀錄整理與法拍屋等工作。六個月後，我被提升為全職的社會新聞採訪員；在那之後的兩年，我被提升到商業領域擔任一名商業採訪員，也就是我現在負責的小企業創業精神報導。

3 What do you like and dislike about the job?
這份職業，你喜歡和不喜歡的是甚麼？

I am work as a Journalist at XXX Weekly Report and I am in charge of community News beat. I am a naturally curious person and journalism gives me an excuse to ask questions and investigate those curious or interesting situations. I love getting out of the office and exploring story ideas. There are so many unique characters in this city where I want to show public people. Being a journalist is also a great way to learn new things, to stay informed, meet all kinds of different people and feel like you are contributing to the betterment of society. I like the sense of accomplishment I feel when I've finished a story I think it is important and I've done well. There is an adrenaline rush at deadline and the feeling that what you're doing matters and is important to people. The only downside I could think is that it is incredibly stressful trying to write well all the time.

我在 XXX Weekly report 擔任採訪員，我負責報導社區社會新聞。我是個好奇的人，而新聞給了我一個很好的理由，詢問調查那些令人好奇或有趣的情況。我愛走出辦公室，尋找新聞靈感。這城市有很多特別的地方，我想要介紹給大家，當採訪員最棒的地方是學習新事物，隨時瞭解事情，認識不同的人，而且感覺就像你正在為社會的福祉作出貢獻。每當我完成一篇重要報導，我會很有成就感。截稿時間壓力會讓你腎上腺素上升，讓你覺得你正在做一件對人們很重要的事。我唯一能想到為一個缺點就是隨時想要寫出好報導的壓力。

Q

4 **What type of experience do you have for a journalist?**
你有甚麼工作經驗？

For almost five years I had worked as a journalist at Eagle River Review. In my last job, as a full-time general assignment journalist for local dailies, I covered a range of areas, e.g., news, sports, business, education, healthcare, lifestyle, and travel. The main takes of mine are researched stories for publication in local, regional and national press; gathered information on a specific subject, event, occurrence or person; wrote information as a journalist for the press, radio, and television; attended press conferences, court sessions, council meetings and other scheduled public event; interviewed the people involved in new stories, in person or by telephone; wrote new stories from notes taken, often under tight deadlines; followed up news releases, called from public or tipped-offs from personal contacts. I believe not only my experience but also my strong communication skills and strong sense of urgency to meet deadlines are ideal for this position.

我在 Eagle River 評論擔任採訪人員將近五年。在我過去的工作中，我是當地日報的全職分派採訪員，涵蓋一系列領域，如新聞、體育、商務、教育、醫療保健、生活方式和旅行。主要都在負責為發表本地、區域和國家新聞研究的題材；收集特定主題、人事物的相關資料；為報刊、廣播和電視撰寫故事；出席相關新聞發佈會、開庭、議事會議和其他的公眾事件；親自面訪或電訪新故事題材；能夠在時間壓力下，撰寫故事；能夠對新聞作追蹤，民眾主動來電提供消息，或是私人情報。我相信我的經驗以及溝通技巧和應付截稿期限的急迫性，是非常適合這個職位的。

Q 5 How do you handle deadlines for multiple assignments?
你如何處理多項任務地截止期限？

Any job that does not involve multitasking is a job that is going to get really boring, really fast. Especially, the job as a journalist, I often have deadline after deadline. Working on multiple assignments at once comes natural to me. In order to reduce the stress of a deadline, I make sure that I have mapped out all of the tasks I need completed to finish the project before deadline. In general, through a combination of deadline, difficulty, project length, team status and importance, I look at these assignments and decide the easiest route to their completion. Sometimes it is easier to work on one project at a time, sometimes it is easier to switch back and forth depending on similarities in the type of tasks required. I also try to group time consuming projects together and get started early, so that when I brush up against the deadline I am not scrambling.

不涉及多項任務的職務，會很快的讓人感到無聊，作為一名採訪員的工作，我經常是一個截止期限接著一個截止期限之後。一次處理多項工作是我擅長的。為了減少截止期限的壓力，我會詳細列出所有必須要在截止日完成的任務。大致來說，透過組合截止日期、困難、專案長度、團隊狀態和重要性，我會規劃出一條最簡單的完成路線。有時在一個固定時間之處理一個任務，有時處理類似性質的任務時，我會在任務間跳來跳去。我也會將幾個比較困難且花時間的任務放在一起，提早開始進行，這樣一來，根據截止期限作更新，我就不會混亂。

Q 6 What qualities does a good Journalist possess?
一名好記者具備哪些素質？

In my mind, a good journalist not only has curiosity, passion for writing, communication skills, but also has knowledge. A good journalist needs an accurate awareness of current events. He must read a broad range of print and digital news sources in order to obtain the most updated information; Ethics, which means a great journalist knows how to balance a sense of ethics with a thirst for uncovering secrets; Professionalism, a good journalist means meeting deadlines, working irregular hours and accepting criticism from editors on articles. Confidence and dissatisfaction serve as two sides of the same coin. Journalists must maintain a sturdy sense of self-confidence in order to continually put their work out into the public eye. On the other hand, journalists must recognize their own limitations and always seek improvement. If an article receives criticism, the journalist must accept any constructive remarks and ignore any destructive comments.

在我心中，一名好記者不僅要有好奇心、寫作熱情、溝通技巧，也要有知識。一名好採訪員需要精準意識到目前發生的事件。他必須廣泛閱讀書面或數位新聞來源，掌握最新資訊。道德規範，這意味著好的採訪員知道如何平衡道德意識與揭露秘密渴望；要有專業精神，一名好採訪員指的是交稿準時、接受工作時間不固定和接受從編輯對文章的批評。信心和不滿如同一枚硬幣的兩面。為了把他們的工作持續地呈現在公眾視線下，採訪員必須保持強大的自信心。換句話說，採訪員必須體認自身的侷限性，並總是尋求改善。如果一篇文章受到批評，採訪員必須接受任何有建設性的意見，並忽略任何破壞性的評論。

Q
7
What do you know about our company?
你對本公司了解多少？

FB Press produces objective assessments of commercial opportunities in dynamic emerging markets through your numerous press agencies. These reports help key decision-makers keep their eyes on the latest global trends and influence the international business landscape. FB Press has contributed to producing special reports on subjects as far flung as OPEC, the wine industry in France and country reports on more than 180 countries around the globe. Your international scope and experience has given you in-depth knowledge and expertise in understanding different cultures and ways of doing business. I also know that as a member of one of FA Press business development units, I will be placed in any of your current 27 global destinations. I will need to spend an average of 3-6 months in each country to complete my project, responsible for gathering all the raw material necessary to publish both your online content and country reports, which are featured in leading newspapers around the world.

FA Press 通過遍布各地的新聞機構，客觀評估新興市場的商業機會。這些報導幫助主要決策者盯緊最新的全球趨勢與影響國際商業局勢。FB Press 針對像是石油輸出國組織 OPEC，法國葡萄酒產業，以及全球 180 個國家的國情等這類議題做了專門報導。貴公司的國際觀以及經驗，使貴公司徹底深入了解與理解各國文化和做生意的方式。我也知道作為一個 FA Press 業務發展部門的成員，我會被指派到 FA Press 全球 27 個駐點，我將會需要花平均 3-6 個的時間，在每個國家完成我的專案，負責收集所有要發佈在線上引領世界各地的內容與國家報告。

8 How do you write quality stories?
你怎麼寫出好的新聞？

Deadline pressures often mean journalists may not have the luxury of reviewing a story as thoughtfully as we would like. But there are several things I usually do to assure I am writing quality stories: I would start thinking what I want to say immediately after covering an event. I usually write down thoughts, possible angles, ideas for leads, or use tape recorder, so I will not forget ideas. Good stories begin with leads that grab a reader's attention. For me, a lead summarizes the story and it may come easier after all the facts have been laid out. Read stories aloud after they are completed. Slowly speaking the words of a story often will help me find mistakes I may miss. Review the story to determine if information is balanced. This means assuring an article is not slanted. I keep asking myself if both sides of an issue are represented in a story and if quotes correctly portray what was said.

截稿期限壓力往往意味著採訪員可能沒法如我們所願的思考周詳的審查故事。但我通常會做幾件事保證我寫出有品質的新聞：我會在了解事件後，立刻思考我想要說甚麼。我通常先寫下想法，可能的角度，文章標題或用錄音機等，我才不會忘記。會抓住讀者的注意力的標題表式好的文章。對我來說，標題是新聞的總結，隨著之後事實的展開，也會比較容易。完成後，我會大聲地朗讀文章。慢慢地逐字朗讀文章，往往會幫我找到可能的錯誤。重新審視文章來確定資訊是否平衡中立，確保文章不會有偏袒。我一直問自己，議題從雙方的角度都能在文章中被充分表達以及正確描繪雙方所說的。

1-2 臨場反應篇

Q 1

Do you handle stress well?
你能很好處理壓力嗎？

Journalist is a stressful profession. There's the stress of the deadline itself, there's the stress of the subject matter in the story, and there's whatever personal stress and professional stress we are carrying. The way I deal with stress is documenting my experiences. Last year, two journalists who were friends and colleagues were killed while working in the Middle East. I got several requests from media outlets to write something about them. Even though I initially wanted to be left alone to grieve privately, I wrote the requested articles. As I did, I understood that sometimes the best antidote to stress is to literally work through whatever is traumatizing or worrying you. I did not write journal entries about my friends, but the articles I wrote had the same impact on me emotionally. The ability to document is a major advantage for journalists because many psychologists recommend journaling as a self-therapy method.

採訪員是一個壓力大的行業。有本身的截稿期限的壓力，有身處在新聞事件當中的壓力，同時承擔來自個人和職業的壓力。 我處理壓力的方法是將我的經驗記錄下來。 去年，兩名採訪員，也是我的朋友兼同事，在中東地區執行任務時被殺害。我收到寄幾個媒體的邀請，寫些關於他們的文章，即使我剛開始是想要獨自私下哀悼他們，最後還是應他們要求寫了文章。 就如我做的，我能理解有時候壓力最好的解藥是通過書寫方是抒發令人傷神的事情。我並未寫下關於我朋友的文章，而是對我情感上的影響。對記者來說，文字記錄能力有很大的優勢，許多心理學家推薦寫日記也是種自我治療的方法。

Q

2

How do you make sure you have reliable information?
你如何確保你有可靠的資訊？

This is an interesting topic. Journalism is about finding facts, interpreting their importance, and then sharing that information with the audience. That's all journalists do: find, verify, enrich, and then disseminate information. A journalist must never accept what they are told without examining the information. Journalists must rely on a professional discipline for verifying information. We should always take a skeptical view of every piece of information shared with us. We should not blindly trust contacts, even if those contacts have proved reliable in the past. Caution is particularly needed if the topic is controversial. In such cases, too much haste to spread news without verifying truth can cause lasting damage to your news brand. In order to provide my quality and reliable news, I build my own network of trusted contacts. It is important for me to have my own sources. When having first-hand sources, I will double check the facts. To validate material submitted, I will confirm as least two reliable sources to prove any information.

這是有趣的議題。新聞是關於尋找事實，解釋其重要性，然後與觀眾分享訊息。這就是所有的採訪員都在做的事：發現、驗證、充實，然後傳播訊息。一名採訪員永遠不能接受沒有經過檢驗的訊息。採訪員必須運用專業訓練驗證資訊。對任何訊息，我們應該要抱持懷疑的態度。我們不能盲目相信連絡人，即使這些連絡人過去提供的資訊都是可靠的。如果是有爭議的主題，特別更需要謹慎。在這種情況下，過於倉促發表新聞而沒有驗證事實，會損害您的新聞招牌。為了提供品質可靠的新聞，我建立自己的連絡人網路。對我來說，有自己可靠消息來源是重要的。當拿到第一手資料時，我會仔細檢查事實。為了驗證拿到的資料，我會與至少兩名可靠消息來源作確認，檢驗資訊。

Q

3

About new social media, what are the challenges facing Journalists?
關於新社群媒體，採訪員面臨的挑戰是甚麼？

What I see as the most important effect of the new social media format is the democratization of information. Even if journalists do manage to get their stories published in an online paper, they could still be beaten to the scoop by millions of other people, or "citizen journalists." Social Network sites, like Facebook, mean that news spreads at amazing speeds so by the time stories are officially written by journalists, everyone already knows about them. Also, bloggers from around the world are always up to date on current affairs and because they operate on a global basis, while one hemisphere sleeps the other is updating, there's never a break in the reporting of news .We now live in a global village. The trends of blogging and online news sources are also taking potential jobs away from journalists because many people do not get their information from traditional sources like newspapers anymore.

我看新社群模式，最重要的影響是資訊的民主化。即使採訪員可以在網路上發佈新聞，仍舊抵擋不過數以萬計的人或者「平民採訪員」的獨家訊息。像 Facebook 這類社交網路網站，以驚人的速度傳播新聞，等到訊息正式發佈的時候，所有人早都已經知道了。此外，來自世界各地的博客隨時更新時事，所以，當地球一邊人們在沉睡時，他們已經更新訊息，永不中斷，因為我們現在是生活在一個地球村。博客和線上新聞來源的趨勢，使得人們不再從傳統的資訊來源，像是報紙取得資訊，這也間接影響採訪員的就業機會。

Q 4 What are the ethical standards for journalists?
採訪人員的道德標準是什麼？

Journalists are the gatekeepers and transmitters of news that take place in societies all over the world. The public expects the journalists' truthfulness as well as their willingness to write the truth. The public expects journalists to apply their professional code of ethics as they sit down to craft a fair and balanced news story.

Be Truthful. A journalist must make every reasonable effort to make sure the story reporting contains all of the relevant facts. Be Independent. The public depends on journalists to report the news in a fair and unbiased manner. A journalist should avoid obvious conflicts of interest. Minimize harm. Journalists must be cognizant of private individuals' right to privacy. All journalists must treat their subjects with respect. It is acceptable to show compassion and sensitivity when dealing with certain sources or topics, such as with children or victims of violence.

採訪人員是發生在世界各地的新聞的守門員與傳播者角色。大眾期望新聞採訪員寫事實的報導。大眾希望採訪員用專業道德守則，撰寫一則公平公正的新聞故事。要真實的，採訪員必須盡一切努力，以確保他報導的新聞涵蓋所有相關事實。是獨立的，公眾仰賴採訪人員報導的新聞是以公平中立的方式。採訪員應避免明顯的利益衝突。儘量減少損害，採訪員必須體認到私人的個人隱私。所有的記者必須尊重的對待他們的目標和來源。在處理某些來源或主題，如兒童或暴力的受害者，採訪員可以顯示其同情心。

1-3 我有疑問篇

Q

1

I want to know the key tasks of Trainee Broadcast Journalist.
我想知道實習廣播採訪人員的主要任務。

The purpose of trainee broadcast journalist who we are looking for is someone can find, research, write and broadcast news stories to the required standards and within agreed deadlines for any of the following media, TV, Radio, and Online. And the key tasks are: To find and research news stories and programme items; To interview and report, in both recorded and live situations, in the studio or on location; To prepare and present bulletins for local TV and radio; To prepare online and interactive stories; To produce live and recorded items for TV and radio; To suggest news story and programme ideas on a regular basis; To operate technical equipment for all media to the required standards; To develop and maintain contacts and to respond professionally to enguire from the public; At all times to carry out duties in line with ANC values and editorial guidelines; to write voice pieces, bulletins and programme items, exercising editorial judgement, maintaining professional standards and sticking to ANC editorial policies.

我們在找的實習廣播採訪人員，主要是能在規定的標準與期限內，為電視、廣播和網路等媒體，搜尋、研究、撰寫和播報新聞故事。主要的任務是：搜尋和研究新聞故事和方案專案；在錄製或實地現場，導播室或在某個位置上，做採訪報告；替本地電視和電台，編寫現場新聞快報；編寫線上互動式的新聞；替電視和電臺製作直播和錄製節目；定期提案新聞故事和方案的構想；依照標準，操作所有媒體的技術設備；與聯絡人保持聯繫，並專業地回覆公眾詢問；隨時履行職責，根據 ANC 公司價值和編輯準則；撰寫意見稿，公告和專案，練習編輯判斷、維持專業標準和 ANC 編輯準則。

2
What skills, knowledge and experience do you expect in this position?
你期望這職位要有什麼技能、 知識和經驗？

As a trainee journalist, ANC Company will train you to the level where you should be able to compete for broadcast journalist jobs within the ANC. We are looking for evidence of your skills and potential in the following areas: Excellent writing skills with the ability to tell a story in a clear and engaging way; the ability to find good stories and come up with ideas for programme items and explain them in a way which suits a variety of audiences, within agreed deadline. Ability to work co-operatively as part of a team. Ability to demonstrate resilience and flexibility with a willingness to learn new skills. A passion for news, current affairs and sport with an awareness of interest in what is happening; Accuracy and attention to detail. A keen interest, knowledge and awareness of local radio and local issues. Ability to exercise good judgement when selecting and writing stories, mindful of ANC editorial policies and legal issues.

作為實習記者，公司會培訓直到你可以勝任 ANC 播報採訪員的職位。我們在尋找具有以下技能與潛力的採訪員: 優秀寫作技巧與能力，清晰和引人入勝的方式，講述故事；在商定的期限內，有能力找到好的題材，提出企劃專案，用適合不同的觀眾的方式和詮釋題材。能夠團隊合作完成任務的能力；表現靈活彈性，願意學習新技能的能力；敏銳意識對正在發生的新聞、時事和體育，對其感興趣與熱情；準確性和注重細節；對地方廣播和本地的議題，有濃厚興趣與了解；當選擇和撰寫故事時能夠做出很好的判斷，對 ANC 編輯政策與法律問題警記在心。

3 What qualifications for a Journalist are you looking for?
你在尋找甚麼特質的採訪員？

We are looking for below qualifications of a journalist to join our team. He must show us his competencies, which refer to the skills, knowledge and behaviour required to do a job successfully. We are not looking for you to demonstrate all of these now; we are looking at your potential to develop your ability in these areas. The journalist must be able to write pieces which interest people. The candidate must have excellent grasp of English and is able to write creatively, clearly and concisely. Able to view from another's perspective, combined with editorial judgement, including keen interest in news and current affairs, sport and regional news. The journalist must able to work co-operatively with team and flexibility; able to build and maintain effective working relationships with a range of people which means team working. The candidate must have ability using computer based technology and stay up-to-date with technology, such as social media.

我們正在尋找以下資格的採訪員加入我們的團隊。他必須讓我們瞭解他的能力，包括技能、知識和完美做好這份工作所需的行為。我們不要求你證明所有這些能力，但是我們要看你是否有發展潛力。採訪員必須能夠寫公眾感興趣的文章。應徵者必須能掌握優秀的英文，有創意，清楚簡潔。能夠加上編輯的評論與從另一種是角度來看，新聞、時事、體育和區域新聞。 採訪員必須能夠與團隊合作且靈活；能夠與團隊建立和保持有效的工作關係。應徵者必須有能力使用電腦基本技術和最新技術，比如社交媒體。

4 What is the next step after interview today?
今天的面試後，下一步是什麼？

Our recruitment process is quite intensive and it is a lot to go through, but it is important that the fit is right for you as well as for us. The next step, successful candidates will then be contacted and asked to attend one of our assessment centres, or for candidates located overseas, a webcam interview. Here are our processes. Stage One: An invitation to attend one of our group assessment sessions usually held in London, Paris and Dublin, or an invitation to conduct an interactive webcam interview for candidates located outside of these destinations. Stage Two: An individual one-on-one interview conducted in our head office in Madrid or again for candidates located overseas via webcam. Stage Three: Selective Training. The Selective Training is a structured, five-day long group training event. The training is full time starting at 10.am everyday and represents the final stages in the selection process.

我們的招聘過程相當密集而且嚴謹，我們認為雙方的契合度是很重要的。 接下來，我們會聯繫適合的候選人，邀請到我們的評估中心，海外的候選人則是用 webcam 面談。我們的步驟分為 第一階段：邀請候選人到我們分布在倫敦、 巴黎和都柏林等地區的評估中心；不在這些評估中心的候選人，我們會用網路攝影機面談。第二階段：與我們馬德里總部進行個別一對一進行面談，或再次通過網路攝影機與海候選人面談。第三階段：選擇性培訓，培訓為期 5 天的集體培訓，每天上午 10 點開始的全日活動，這是篩選過程中的最後階段。

1 範例

1-1. 自傳(1)

I have a real passion for sports so pursuing a career in this field just made good sense. I have a bachelor's degree in Journalism and my courses centered on sports business, journalism fundamentals, technical writing and the function that multimedia plays in sports journalism. I also studied how sports fit into society and I acquired a good understanding of the legal issues and ethics used in journalism. During my school life, I have had some journalistic experience, because I had been editing my university magazine for nearly three years. I have also contributed a number of articles in such prominent Papers like "Sports World," "Sports News" etc. I have had two years of experience as an internship at World Sports Public Relations. I was in charge of social media, expending account from around 7,000 followers to 13,000 in six months by daily tweeting and live tweeting events. I can compile and sort through information to put together reports to share with the public. Since I am such a sports fan, I have the ability to know what information people want to hear and I possess the communication skills needed to pass this information along to the public. I can put together a report quickly to ensure your station is one of the first to have the details of the game. I am familiar with all audio and video equipment used to capture highlights of the game. I am a proficient writer and I have excellent editing skills. I also have the skills needed to post stories and update of the games on your website. I possess the ability to interview players and fans to talk about the game. I have excellent memory with the ability to compare statistics and special game plays to make the reports more interesting. I am energetic, self-motivated, and I know that I have the making of a great reporter.

　　我非常熱衷體育,所以希望能夠一直在這領域發展職業生涯,感覺很有意義。我有新聞學士學位,課程集中在體育商業、新聞學基礎知識、技術寫作和多媒體在體育新聞扮演的功能。我也學過體育如何融入社會,了解新聞行業的法律問題和道德。在校期間,我有過一些採訪工作的經驗,因為我已編輯大學雜誌將近三年。我也曾在傑出報刊,像是「Sports World」以及「Sports News」等投稿許多文章。在World Sports Public Relations,作為實習生,有兩年經驗。當時負責社群媒體,在六個月內,將在 daily tweeting 以及 live tweeting events 的追隨者,從大約 7,000 名增加到 13,000 名。我可以將蒐集分類資料,彙整成報導,與公眾分享。因為我是個體育迷,我能知道人們想聽的訊息,並且用溝通技巧將訊息傳遞給大眾。我可以很迅速地完成一篇報導,確保貴公司是第一個發佈賽事的頻道。我很熟悉所有的音訊和視頻設備,用於捕獲賽事最精采片段。我是個熟練的寫作者,有優秀的編輯技巧。我也有在網站上載故事和賽事更新所需的技能。我具備採訪球員和球迷們談談賽事的能力。還有優秀記憶力,能夠將統計資料和特別比賽作比較,使報導更有趣。我充滿活力,自我激勵,我知道我能成為優秀的採訪員。

1-2. 自傳(2)

I have always enjoyed writing, and my work presents the particular challenge of writing in an accessible, entertaining, and informative way about unusual and, sometimes, complicated events. After graduating, I completed a Master's Degree in Easton European Politics. I took Russian as my second language, and I use Russian on a daily basis. I speak French fluently as well. Many of the sources of information we use are not available in English, so my knowledge of Russian is crucial. It always helps enormously to have skills in addition to languages that I can offer a potential employer. Following, I took a range of ABC News training courses, including radio writing skills, radio feature skills, editorial judgment and writing for television news. The ABC News offers a huge range of courses to all journalistic staff to enhance and promote our abilities. I was a broadcast journalist working for the World Service that covers the Eurasia region. I wrote on political and social developments mainly in Russia and travel to the region three or four times a year. My work is used by World Service radio, ABC News Online and some other outlets. It is also re-published widely in the world media. My responsibilities are identifying news stories and long-term trends that reflect the changes in these evolving and often unstable societies. These may be major events, such as presidential or parliamentary elections, which have an impact on the wider region. They may equally be the stories about things affecting the lives of ordinary people, such as living standards, cultural events, health issues. The key is to make people far from the area take notice. I have been in this industry for over 5 years and bring a keen eye for newsworthy subjects. I am sure that my work profile and work experience perfectly suits to your needs.

　　我一直都喜歡寫作，對於不尋常複雜的事件，我的挑戰是用容易理解、娛樂的和內容豐富的寫作方式呈現給大眾。畢業後，我完成了在歐洲政治碩士學位。俄語是我的第二語言，而且運用俄語在平常基礎上。我還會說流利的法語。我們現在使用的許多訊息來源，不是英語，所以我對俄語的瞭解是關鍵。能多具備些語言能力對我在未來工作上，總是有極大的幫助。接著，我參加了 ABC News 系列培訓課程，包括廣播寫作技巧、廣電功能技能、編輯判斷和電視新聞的寫作。ABC News 針對內部的採訪人員們，提供廣泛的訓練課程，藉以增強我們的能力。我的工作是在 World Service 涵蓋歐亞區域的廣播採訪員。我寫關於政治和社會在俄羅斯發展和一年三到四次到俄羅斯出差。我的報導會用在廣播、ABC News 線上和一些其他媒體管道。它也會再次廣為發佈在世界媒體中。我的職責是發掘新聞故事，和反映不斷演變和經常不穩定的社會變化的長期趨勢。這些可能是重大事件，如總統或議會選舉，對更廣泛的區域產生的影響。他們也可能是普通人的影響生活，譬如，生活水準、 文化活動、健康問題等的故事。關鍵是能讓遠方的人們關注。我在這個行業已經有 5 年以上和對有新聞價值的主題，有敏銳的觀察力。 我相信，我的工作簡介和工作經驗完全適合貴公司的需求。

2 自傳寫作教室

2-1. 自傳(1) 寫作文法解析／小評語

對於喜愛體育的人來說，體育採訪員，這份職業可以說是「Best. Job. EVER.」夢寐以求的一份工作。我們來看看體育採訪員，大抵上都在做些甚麼：

Attending games and sporting events for firsthand information
出席各項賽事活動拿到第一手消息
Traveling to different sporting venue
穿梭於不同的體育場地
Writing entertaining and informative stories on multiple aspects of games and sports
用不同角度撰寫運動賽事娛樂消息
Keenly observe the details of the game
敏銳地觀察比賽，不放過任何細節
Interviewing sports stars and athletes
採訪體育明星和運動員
Establishing good contacts with sports persons
與體育相關人士建立良好的聯繫
Keeping in regular touch with athletes, coaches and managers
與運動員、教練員和經理保持經常聯繫
Working closely with publishers and editors
與出版商和編輯緊密合作

體育採訪員並沒有所謂「固定工作時間」fixed working hours，採訪員的工作時間遵循體育賽事活動時間，有時在晚上，有時在周末，賽事結束後，不管多晚，採訪員必須立刻為負責的媒體撰稿「contribute to」，以求第一時間發佈訊息。

2-2. 自傳⑵ 寫作文法解析／小評語

　　如果你有寫作熱情，但是非新聞本科系畢業，想要踏入採訪員工作，如「broadcast Journalist」的話，要怎麼辦? 如果你有某方面的專業，譬如本自傳擅長東歐政治與俄語能力，可以考慮到相關訓練機構，或是申請進入頗具規模的新聞媒體，以實習生身分接受一系列訓練計畫，結束後依照你的專業背景，指派報導路線，以本自傳來說，對東歐政治有所研究，所以專門負責觀察報導俄羅斯國家趨勢，成為業界的「Beat reporter」。「Beat」是甚麼意思? 在新聞界，所謂 Beat reporting 意思是採訪員專門研究、蒐集、撰寫發表或報導某一領域的新聞故事或是最新趨勢。所以 Beat reporting 也就是 specialized reporting，因為長期專研在某一個特定領域，在業界，也有一定的聲望，累積相當豐厚的訊息與人際關係，所以訊息來源 information sources 取得上也必較容易，也較能夠問出專業、有深度的問題。新聞產業，是相當複雜的，報導內容包羅萬象，從嚴肅的國際政治、軍事戰爭到輕鬆有趣的體育活動、娛樂時尚等。採訪訪員的角色是協助大眾了解發生在這個世界的大小事；有幾種 Beat 給讀者參考：Politic Beat, Sports beat, Business beat, Curt beat, Arts Beat, Science beat。

Is it your life-long dream to be a professional fashion journalist? You probably have a rough idea of what being a magazine journalist is like the film "The Devil Wears Prada." They show a good summary of job scopes in fashion. But many fictitious factors have been added to beef up the glamour. A career in fashion journalism, which may seem appealing to just about everyone interested in the world of fashion, is actually a competitive profession. A fashion journalist is someone who communicates fashion news, reviews and advice through magazines, newspapers, websites, TV or radio. They usually write about fashion trends, catwalk shows, street styles, and/or celebrity trends. Fashion journalists often interview and conduct extensive research before writing their articles. The job may involve writing, editing or even reporting. They must maintain cordial relationships with other people in the world of fashion, to have the most contacts and have access to the latest information in the industry. There are many benefits of being a fashion journalist. Firstly there is a lot of travel involved to cover all the fashion events happening all over the world. Secondly, there is the opportunity to work with established members of the fashion industry including models, editors, designers etc. Another perk of being a fashion journalist is the fame. With each article that is published, your name would be on top of it making the work that you do very glamorous. To be a successful fashion journalist, you need to have contacts of every influential person in the fashion world so that you can advance your own career and do the best job possible. As a fashion journalist you should also always have ideas on how to write your next piece. Another downside is that as there is a lot of travel involved, a lot of time is spent away from your friends and family.

　　成為專業時尚採訪員是你最終的夢想嗎？您大概以為雜誌採訪員就像「穿著 Prada 的惡魔」電影一樣。他們很好地展現這份工作的大致輪廓，但也添加些虛構因素。似乎人人對時尚界很感興趣，希望能從事時尚新聞職業，實際上，它是競爭性的行業。時尚採訪員是負責傳達時尚新聞、評論與通過雜誌、報紙、網站、電視或電臺提供諮詢意見的人。他們通常寫有關流行趨勢、時裝表演、街頭風格和名人的趨勢。時尚採訪員時常在寫文章之前進行採訪和廣泛研究。這份工作涵蓋寫作、編輯或報導。他們必須與在世界時尚的人們保持良好的關係，有最多的聯絡人才能訪問到這行的最新資訊。當時尚採訪員有很多好處。首先，有很多機會到各地旅行，踏足世界採訪有關時尚界的事件。第二，有機會與時尚界成員包括模特兒、編輯、設計師等一同工作。時尚採訪員的另一個好處就是聲譽。隨著每個發佈的文章，你的名字會放在上面，使你的工作變得非常迷人。要成為一名成功的時尚採訪員，你需要在時尚界中，接觸的每一個有影響力的人，這樣你才可以提升你的事業和將這份工作盡可能做到最好。身為時尚採訪員你隨時應該要想怎麼寫下一篇文章。另一個缺點是，因為有很多的出差，你和朋友和家人的相處時間變少。

好書報報－職場系列

結合流行英語，時下必學的行銷手法與品牌管理概念，讓你完全掌握行銷力！

全書分為6大章，共46組情境
★背景介紹＋實用對話
★練習題：中英對照，學習事半功倍
★相關詞彙：必備常用單字及片語＋文法加油站
★知識補給站：分析行銷策略＋重點訊息彙整
★10篇會議要點：對話急救包＋要點提示

題材充實新穎，增加語言學習和專業知識的深度！
行銷人要看，商管學院師生更不可錯過！

作者：胥淑嵐
定價：新台幣349元
規格：352頁／18K／雙色印刷

旅館的客戶為數不少來自不同國家，因而說出流利的旅館英語，是旅館人員不可或缺的利器，更是必備的工具！

特別規劃6大主題 30個情境 120組超實用會話
中英左右對照呈現對話內容，閱讀更舒適！
精選好學易懂的key word＋音標＋詞性，學習效率加倍！
隨書附有光碟小幫手，幫助你熟悉口語、訓練聽力！

從預約訂房、入住，到辦理退房，
設計各種工作時會面臨到的場景，
提供各種專業會話訓練，英語溝通零距離！

作者：Mark Venekamp & Claire Chang
定價：新台幣469元
規格：504頁／18K／雙色印刷／MP3

好書報報–職場系列

國際化餐飲時代不可不學！
擁有這一本，即刻通往世界各地！

基礎應對 訂位帶位、包場、活動安排、菜色介紹...
前後場管理 服務生Must Know、擺設學問、食物管理...
人事管理 徵聘與訓練、福利升遷、管理者的職責...
狀況處理 客人不滿意、難纏的顧客、部落客評論...

*120*個餐廳工作情境
*100%*英語人士的對話用語
循序漸進勤做練習，職場英語一日千里！

作者：Mark Venekamp & Claire Chang
定價：新台幣369元
規格：328頁 / 18K / 雙色印刷 / MP3

這是一本以**航空業**為背景，
從職員角度出發的航空英語會話工具書。
從職員VS同事 & 職員VS客戶，
兩大角度，呈現100% 原汁原味職場情境！

特別規劃→
以**Q&A**的方式，英語實習role play
提供更多航空界**專業知識**的職場補給站
免稅品服務該留意甚麼？ 旅客出境的SOP！
迎賓服務的步驟與重點！違禁品相關規定?！
飛機健檢大作戰有哪些...

作者：Mark Venekamp & Claire Chang
定價：新台幣369元
規格：352頁 / 18K / 雙色印刷 / MP3

求職英語一試双贏

作　　者／黃梅芳、吳悠嘉◎合著者
封面設計／陳小 King
內頁構成／菩薩蠻有限公司

發 行 人／周瑞德
企劃編輯／丁筠馨
執行編輯／徐瑞璞
校　　對／劉俞青
印　　製／世和印製企業有限公司
初　　版／2014 年 2 月
定　　價／新台幣 329 元

出　　版／倍斯特出版事業有限公司
電　　話／（02）2351-2007
傳　　真／（02）2351-0887
地　　址／100 台北市中正區福州街1號10 樓之 2
E m a i l／best.books.service@gmail.com

總 經 銷／商流文化事業有限公司
地　　址／新北市中和區中正路752號7樓
電　　話／（02）2228-8841
傳　　真／（02）2228-6939

國家圖書館出版品預行編目(CIP)資料

求職英語一試双贏 / 黃梅芳、吳悠嘉；
— 初版. — 臺北　市：倍斯特, 2014. 02
　　面；　公分
　　ISBN 978-986-90331-1-4(平裝)
　1. 英語 2. 會話

805. 18　　　　　　　　　　　103001018